I0584091

# The Road to Abilene

Karri L. Moser

Black Rose Writing | Texas

©2022 by Karri L. Moser
All rights reserved. No part of this book may be reproduced, stored in a retrieval system or transmitted in any form or by any means without the prior written permission of the publishers, except by a reviewer who may quote brief passages in a review to be printed in a newspaper, magazine or journal.

The author grants the final approval for this literary material.

First printing

This is a work of fiction. Names, characters, businesses, places, events, and incidents are either the products of the author's imagination or used in a fictitious manner. Any resemblance to actual persons, living or dead, or actual events is purely coincidental.

ISBN: 978-1-68513-079-4
PUBLISHED BY BLACK ROSE WRITING
www.blackrosewriting.com

Printed in the United States of America
Suggested Retail Price (SRP) $20.95

*The Road to Abilene* is printed in Garamond Premier Pro

*As a planet-friendly publisher, Black Rose Writing does its best to eliminate unnecessary waste to reduce paper usage and energy costs, while never compromising the reading experience. As a result, the final word count vs. page count may not meet common expectations.

"I ask you to pass through life at my side—to be my second self, and best earthly companion."
Charlotte Bronte
*Jane Eyre*

A story for everyone who has found their earthly companion... and for those who are still searching.

>

# The Road
# to Abilene

# CHAPTER 1

*Spring 1992*

Abilene Marigold Matterly always stood out like the first wildflower of spring to sprout from the dirt or a crack in the sidewalk. Being the new kid every other year didn't help her blend in either. She didn't mind standing out, though. Abilene knew there were worse things than being different, like being the same.

"Abilene Matterly? Could you please stand?" the teacher said from behind a lectern that jutted from the floor directly in front of Abilene's desk. Mrs. Saint-Claire slid her reading glasses down to the tip of her nose and peered out above them. Her eyes pierced through Abilene's heart as it pounded against her chest. She was certain the girls behind of her could hear it. Abilene swallowed and stood. She smoothed her plaid pleated skirt as she cleared her throat.

"Um, yeah, I'm Abilene Marigold Matterly," she said as she noticed a snicker from a girl sitting near the back of the class. That snicker slid off her back. She loved saying her name out loud. To her, it was like a poem or song title no one else knew yet.

Abilene could feel everyone look her up and down. She was used to being exposed like this on the first day at a new school, but she had to admit, it got harder now that she was a teenager, and the school year was winding down instead of beginning. Abilene noticed with each new grade, the girls were in a tighter group than the last year, making it harder to find a friend or two, any untethered soul drifting the halls just like her. She told herself before she walked into the class that friends didn't matter, but Abilene knew that was a lie.

"Marigold? Like the flower?" Mrs. Saint-Claire said. Her brown curls sprung from in front of her face as she pushed her reading glasses on top of her head.

"Yes, Ma'am. Exactly."

"You know we ain't got uniforms at this school, dontcha?" a boy said from Abilene's left. Abilene swallowed again.

"Yes, I know. But it's all I had. My old school had uniforms," Abilene said. She immediately regretted responding to him. Abilene knew better. He'd just keep prodding her now.

"Maybe get some new clothes then," he added as he turned around and rolled his eyes.

"Maybe mind your own business, jackass," Abilene said. She instantly wanted to grab the words back. She closed her eyes as gasps echoed around the room.

"Julien, be kind," Mrs. Saint-Claire said with an expected teacher inflection rising at the end. "And, Ms. Matterly, that's not how we respond to anyone in my classroom." She tilted her head down further as her eyes once again pierced through Abilene. Abilene nodded.

"I apologize, ma'am." Abilene drew in a deep breath. "May I sit now?" Her knees shook. The snickers and stares of the girls who all looked alike made her skin crawl.

"Not yet. So, where did you come from? And tell us a little something about yourself." Those requests always made Abilene cringe. She noticed a few girls on the side of the room eyeing up her red cowboy boots. They always eyed up the boots.

"Slidell. We moved here from Slidell, Louisiana, a few days ago. My mom manages hotels and got a new job here. We kinda move a lot," Abilene said as she sat down. She wasn't waiting to be asked more questions.

"You part of a traveling carnival or something?" Julien asked. The girls snickered again as they exchanged glances at each other. While each school and town might be different, those kinds of glances between fellow 16-year-olds were universal in their meaning. Abilene rolled her eyes. She reached in her bag for a notebook and thought this wasn't the worst first impression she'd made, but it wasn't the best either.

As the bell rang for the last time that afternoon, Abilene was grateful her mom had started her there on a Friday. She grabbed the packets she had gotten from each teacher and slid them into her messenger bag. It was a thrift store find, but she didn't mind. It was different from the backpacks everyone else slung over their shoulder. Between her bag, her old school uniform, her boots, and her hair that was most often compared to a wheat-colored tumbleweed blowing wildly, she already made a statement. She was done making statements for a while, at least until Monday.

Abilene walked up on the curb across from the school. She kept her eyes straight ahead. They had only been in Holden, South Carolina, a week, but she already felt she knew the streets. They rented a small house right next to the motel. It had three bedrooms and a large living room, which was more than the place they shared in Slidell. The Louisiana house was nothing more than a double-wide trailer that was falling apart at the seams. The gaps let tiny streams of water cascade down either side of the house where the living room ended and the kitchen began. Ashlynn, her mom, used to keep a balled-up towel on the floor to catch the little rivers of rain. Abilene's brother Dallas used to place a matchbox car as far up the wall as he could reach and release it to race the water down the wall. Her mom let him because it kept Dallas out of trouble. Anything was permissible if it entertained Dallas. He was 10 and had the most extreme case of ADHD any educator had ever seen. At least that's what teacher after teacher told Ashlynn. Being the oldest and the built-in babysitter for her four siblings meant it was usually up to Abilene to keep Dallas from destroying, disrupting, or upending the lives or property of anyone else. It was exhausting for Abilene.

Abilene's two next oldest siblings, Austin and Jackson, were of no help. They were a year apart—12 and 13 years old and had the same dad. That created a bond none of the other kids had. While they caused their own trouble, they saw no need to help if Dallas was putting up a fight against anyone or anything. They simply shrugged their shoulders and simultaneously ran their tanned hands through their towheaded shags and went about life. The youngest, Savannah, was only 3. Abilene was grateful for her, even if she required as much supervision as Dallas. Savannah oozed sweetness and had a desire to make everyone around her laugh.

While Abilene was in a hurry to get out of sight of the other students, she never wanted to rush home to fix snacks and corral the kids. She slowed a bit once the rest of the students dispersed. She was grateful no gang or individual student came beside her and tried to talk.

Just as the motel and house came into view, Abilene saw the boys make it to the front door.

"Jackson!" Abilene called out. Jackson slid a backpack off his shoulder and swung it low as he turned around. "I gotta go grab Savannah from mom and I'll be over. Keep Dallas inside, will ya?" Jackson nodded and turned around. Abilene walked into the office of the hotel. Ashlynn sat behind the desk, flipping through a magazine. Savannah was in a portable playpen behind their mom.

"Hey girl. How was the first day? Did they love your boots here? I bet they just loved 'em," her mom said in a slow southern drawl. She reached behind her to nudge Savannah. "Hey baby, wake up. Abi is here to take you home." Ashlynn shook the sweaty girl. Savannah had crumbs stuck to her chin and shirt. Ashlynn rose and held her protruding belly. "Abi, you're gonna have to pick her up. I don't think I can lift her anymore." Ashlynn stood up straight and tried to arch her back as she let out a deep exhale. Even six and a half months pregnant, her mom was a beauty. Flawless, at least in Abilene's eyes.

"I got her. It's okay, Mom. School was okay. Nothing too exciting happened," Abilene said as she stirred her sleeping sister.

"Make any new friends?" Ashlynn said. Abilene hated the way her mother's voice reached a high note at the end of questions. She knew her mom already knew the answer.

"No, Mom. I'm sure I will soon though," Abilene said. She reached down and pulled Savannah to a standing position. Savannah wiped her eyes and whimpered. "I gotta get back before the boys burn the house down. I'll make spaghetti tonight if that's okay?"

Ashlynn smiled. "Of course. I don't know what I'd do without you, my sweet Abilene." Ashlynn patted the top of Savannah's head as Abilene stood her up outside the playpen and squatted down to tie her little shoes. She knew damn well what her mom would do without her. She'd be without a babysitter, cook, housekeeper, homework helper, and friend to lean on after each breakup. Abilene was also the one to unpack most of the house as her mom started a new job at a new motel after they had to pick up and leave each town. For years, Abilene considered each new job as an opportunity, a promotion of sorts. She believed her mom was moving up in the world. However, over the last few years, it became painfully obvious her mom wasn't moving up in the world. The pay wasn't increasing, and the motels weren't more grand or beautiful. The houses or trailers they rented weren't getting more glamorous or spacious. Ashlynn was simply leaving one town, one motel, for more of the same, but usually with an additional kid in tow. At 16, Abilene realized it wasn't the job that led the family to pack up and head to another state. It was the men. The current baby possibly shared a dad with Savannah. His name was Tucker. Mitchell Tuckerson was a car salesman through and through. He was also a drinker, gambler, flirt, and downright creepy to Abilene whenever she laid on the couch trying to watch a movie or coming out of the bathroom in a towel after a shower.

Ashlynn first met Tucker when they lived in Savannah. They bought the El Camino from him. It was a yellow piece of shit car, but it fit everyone. Tucker wooed Ashlynn, and she was convinced he'd marry her. Once Ashlynn told him she was pregnant, he faded from their life little by little. He went from bringing pizzas on Fridays and staying all weekend, to driving up to talk to Ashlynn outside, rarely coming in. One night when Ashlynn was showing with Savannah, they argued in the driveway. Abilene knew he was drunk. He screamed about Ashlynn trapping him, wanting his money, and wanting him to be a dad to the others. Ashlynn cried on the front porch for hours while Abilene fed and bathed kids, got teeth brushed, and cleaned up toys while Ashlynn wailed, smoked, drank, and wailed some more. Abilene was only 12. It was only a few weeks later they traded in the El Camino for a station wagon and headed to Slidell.

Ashlynn gave birth to Savannah alone in the hospital, while Abilene skipped two weeks of school to watch the rest of the kids. Abilene couldn't help but be pissed that other girls got to go to the mall, the movies, and sleepovers while she was stuck mothering kids she had no say in having. Once Savannah was close to two, Tucker showed up again. He lurked, wooed, brought pizzas. He even took Savannah to his parents in Baton Rouge for a weekend. Then, he took Ashlynn to New Orleans for Mardi Gras. They were gone for a week. Another week of school missed by Abilene to watch everybody with the help of an elderly neighbor who dropped off groceries and checked on them. Abilene liked to pretend the neighbor was their grandmother. She even called her Nana Grace. Grace didn't seem to mind.

It wasn't long after their Mardi Gras trip Abilene realized her mom was pregnant again. After another driveway fight, bottles being thrown, and tires screeching, Ashlynn spent the next day on the phone looking for a new job. Before Abilene could make up missing school work and just weeks before the end of her sophomore year, they were packing and on the way to South Carolina. Ashlynn had a cousin there who guaranteed the house and motel job. Her husband was the landscaper who mowed the place and planted flowers each summer. The owner loved him and, just as Ashlynn's cousin, Susan promised, hired Ashlynn right over the phone.

As they made their way to South Carolina, Abilene wracked her brain trying to figure out how her mom was going to name a baby after Slidell. Maybe this one would just be called Louisiana or Louise. With a mom like Ashlynn, there was no way to predict. However, one thing Abilene could predict was that once they got settled in Holden, South Carolina, it would be no time before there'd be another Tucker, just like Monty before him. Monty was Dallas' dad, as far as Abilene could tell, although no one ever said it. Before Monty, there was Butchy. He was Austin and Jackson's dad. He lived with them in Texas and moved them to Mississippi. But to his credit, he still called and sent money for the boys. He also showed up each summer and took them for a week or so. As for her own father, that was a whole different story. He was a soldier, and she loved the moments she spent with him, rare as they were.

Once home, Abilene put Savannah on the couch with the blanket from the hotel. The boys ignored her as she went to the kitchen to start dinner. She first slid off her cowboy boots, a gift from a thrift store that Ashlynn stopped in on the way home from Mardi Gras. Abilene flexed her feet and aired out her cramped toes. She had been so excited to grow into those boots, and now they were getting tight. She wore those red cowboy boots almost every day, unless she went barefoot. They weren't the kind you would find in a high-end department store or in the flawlessly streak-free window of a funky downtown boutique. Those boots looked like they had traveled a thousand miles across deserts, cities, and swamps. Yet, they weren't like boots someone would be ashamed of or throw out when doing a yearly cleaning of the closet. They were just like Abilene—oddly alluring without trying to be. Abilene also noticed boots like hers made her legs look more muscular. She didn't feel too lanky when she wore them. She was able to glide along in the heels without looking like she was trying to be older than she was. Abilene hated that about other girls her age. She'd sneer at other 16-year-olds in heels too high and gaits too clumsy. They looked and smelled desperate to her, and she knew exactly how desperate women ended up. Their perfume and body sprays burned her nose. She preferred natural smells, florals. Even as Abilene cringed at the whiff of strong, cheap perfume, she couldn't help but wonder what it must feel like to own some, to open a bottle or spritz some on her neck any time she wanted to.

"Dammit, Dallas! What you break now? We ain't even unpacked everything yet," Abilene shouted from the kitchen after hearing a crash. Jackson was holding a football and Austin was holding a piece of a plate.

"It wasn't me, dammit. It was Jackson throwing the ball," Dallas shouted back at her. His thick red hair flopped from side to side as he sassed his sister.

"Imma start dinner. Y'all keep it in check for a bit, will ya?" Abilene said.

"You ain't mom," Dallas shouted. Abilene turned back around and glared at his freckled face.

"No shit, but I'm all you got for one right now and if you want me to make you dinner, you'll knock that shit off and keep an eye on Savannah." She glanced at the group that filled the tiny living room. Aside from them having a variety of dads, she looked different from the rest of them. Abilene was leggy. Not gangly like a clumsy giraffe, looking unnatural, off balance, mismatched with the rest of their bodies, or out of place. She was sleek, like a gazelle. Smooth. Hypnotic as she moved slowly across a room or street, even if she didn't intend to be. Her strides were graceful without effort. No one could take their eyes off Abilene when she was in motion, and she was always the last one to know it. That set her apart from her mother. Ashlynn was always keenly aware of the attention coming from any man, near or far. Ashlynn not only noticed the attention of men, young and old, she depended on it. She knew how to use it. As Abilene got older, she went from being amazed by the attention her mother got from men to being disgusted by it, especially once she was old enough to realize the type of men Ashlynn brought around. They weren't all bad, but they certainly weren't that great. They never lasted that long either. Abilene swore she never wanted the kind of men Ashlynn attracted to be attracted to her. And she certainly didn't want to be dumped time and time again by different men who left her with a baby on her hip.

After dinner, Abilene sprawled out on the twin bed that was inches from Savannah's toddler bed. She reached down for her bag and flipped through the packets given by the new teachers. She sat Savannah on the bed with her and handed her a few papers. Her dark springy curls bounced as reached for more. Savannah grabbed another sheet from the stack. Abilene snatched it back.

"Hey now, let go. I need that one." She said as the toddler scowled and pushed out her pink bottom lip. Savannah's big brown eyes narrowed. Abilene longed to not be the only adult in the house, wishing she wasn't responsible for each of her siblings. Knowing another one was coming in a few months filled her with dread and resentment. At least this one would be born at the end of the summer, so Abilene didn't have to think about skipping school. But it would still be one more kid to clean up after, more diapers to change, teeth to brush, and cries to soothe. One more kid to share blankets with. More space and privacy to give up. More everything to sacrifice, with no one ever asking her or caring what parts of her own childhood she was missing out on.

# CHAPTER 2

As the days unfolded in Holden, South Carolina, Ashlynn befriended a motel maid who wore the same size as Abilene. She gave Ashlynn some jeans and few t-shirts, so Abilene didn't have to wear old school uniforms to a school with no uniforms. There was even a sundress with little yellow flowers and bluebells on it. It had a few buttons on the top. It was above her knee and swished when she walked to school. With one week left of the school year, Abilene developed a routine of rushing from her locker to the sidewalk a block away from the school so she could cut across a field to get the motel to grab Savannah without running into other kids. Even though a few smiles and questions were thrown her way and two other girls told her to sit with them at lunch, she had no use for making any real friends or getting to know anyone more than she already did.

Just as her boots transitioned from sidewalk to wet grass, she heard someone come up behind. A shadow followed. Abilene turned around and gasped to see it was Julien, the boy who asked if she was part of a traveling carnival on her first day. Abilene rolled her eyes and faced forward as she kept on her usual track.

"Hey, wait up," he said. Julien switched his backpack to the other shoulder and ran his fingers through his floppy blonde hair. He matched her height.

"Why? What you want with me?" Abilene said. She thought of picking up the pace but didn't.

"Just wanna talk. You glad school's almost out? Whatcha gonna do all summer? I got a job at my uncle's shop. He fixes small engines and stuff. Mowers, generators, even cars some."

"I don't know. Who knows how long I'll be here. Like I said, we move a lot." Abilene swallowed a lump in her throat. Even though she couldn't care less about Holden, the thought of moving any time soon was exhausting. "Maybe I'll work somewhere if we stay. I could probably work at my mom's motel. I don't know. I gotta watch my siblings too all summer, every summer," Abilene said as she looked down.

"I hear your mom is preggers, right?" Julien said.

"Yeah, so?"

"Nothing. I don't mean no disrespect, just know people have said it. You got like what? Three brothers and a little sister already?"

"You stalking us or something? What's it your business?"

"It ain't. Just asking," Julien said.

"So, what about you? Do you got a gang of siblings and the whole town staring at y'all when you go to the Piggly Wiggly? Huh, do you?" Abilene drew in a deep breath and tried to slow her pace. She fought the urge to shove Julien to the ground.

"Well, yeah, kinda. My mom and dad got twins after me. I'm the oldest. They're 6. Sammy and Selena. It sucks," Julien said. Abilene slowed her pace and looked over at him. She never noticed how tan he was before, or how bright his eyes were.

"Sucks is right. I'm a babysitter all day, every day. I swear, I've changed more diapers than anyone and my mom's got another one coming by the end of summer. More diapers." Abilene looked up and realized they were almost at the motel. "Well, I gotta grab my little sister."

"Alright. We'll I guess I'll see ya tomorrow," Julien said as he nudged her arm, then sprinted back to the sidewalk. Abilene turned back to glance at him. He turned back toward her and shot a quick wave her way. He followed with a broad grin. His tan made his teeth look as if they were glowing. Abilene didn't want to, but she couldn't help but smile back.

For the next three days, Julien appeared at her side as soon as she crossed the street from the school. Abilene quickly found herself enjoying those few minutes of walking across the field with him. While a few conversations in school made her less apprehensive about suddenly being a new kid thrown into town right before the end of the year, a few minutes of talking with Julien her made feel like she almost had a friend.

On the last day of school, just as she slammed her locker shut and dreaded the thought of three months at home watching the boys and Savannah, and then a new baby, Julien slid next to her. He had given her nods in class and at lunch before, but they never spoke until away from school.

"Hey, you gonna go to the pool in town during the summer or no? Everyone goes. It's like all we've got except for running around chasing snakes in the woods," He said as he picked up a notebook she dropped.

"I ain't dragging Dallas, Austin, Jackson, Savannah, and a newborn to a town pool. Trust me. Dallas would get us thrown out before we even found chairs," she said as they walked out the double doors. A few kids ran past them, shouting about school being out. One jumped up and swept his hands along the top door frame and whooped loudly. Abilene sidestepped to avoid him. Julien took her arm. Abilene turned around and looked up at the school for a moment. She never knew at the end of the year if she'd be going back to that building or not. She always paused for a mental picture to store away.

"My parents get a real babysitter during the summer for the girls. I get to kinda run free for the summer when I ain't working. I only gotta work a few hours a day at my uncle's shop, then I'm free as a bird." Abilene nodded as they crossed the street. Horns from the senior parking lot filled the air. More whoops and tires screeching drowned out everything else. Abilene wondered where'd she be by senior year, if she'd have a car, friends to party with, anything other than the life she had now. She glanced at Julien and thought she wouldn't mind still being there and being friends with him. She could count her past friends on one hand. Sometimes that thought felt like a pit in her stomach, and other times she knew it was her choice to not bother trying to make friends.

"Well, maybe sometime during the summer I can get away or we can bring 'em. Whatever. And, by the way, I'd rather chase snakes than hang out by a crowded pool." Abilene said as she squinted from the sun.

"Cool, me too." Someone called out to Julien. He waved back. "How about weekends? Or after dinner? Your mom doesn't live in that motel office, right?"

"Yeah. I mean, once she comes back over home, I guess I can do whatever. Just never had much to do but take care of the boys and Savannah, especially Savannah. She's still so young," Abilene said.

"None of you got a dad to come around and help?" Julien said. He looked straight ahead as if instinct told him to not make eye contact after that kind of question.

"Sorta. Jackson and Austin got the same dad. He takes them some for the summer. Dallas, well, no one wants him, so he's where most of my time and energy is spent. Savannah and I think this new one got the same dad, but he hasn't been in the picture since he found out my mom was pregnant again. And yeah, I got a dad. I saw him a few years ago. He's in the Army. Moves a lot. Has a wife and two girls. From the way my mom talks, he was the only guy she snagged who was worth a damn." Abilene looked down as she made it across the field. "Guess he's a big shot in the Army now. Someday, I dunno, maybe he'll show up and take me with him. If he can find us, that is. Not sure when my mom last talked to him."

"Well, if it's any consolation, having both a mom and dad at home doesn't make life all that grand. Mine fight like cats and dogs. Friday and Saturday nights usually end in one kicking out the other after a drunken brawl and me keeping the girls in their room so they don't see them acting up like that." Julien stopped walking once they made it to the motel. "After seeing the way they fight, the way they treat each other, I know I ain't bothering to get married. Never. Ain't worth the fines from cops, broken shit all over the floor." He slid his hands in his pockets. "Well, I guess this is it?"

Abilene nodded and looked at the motel entrance. "Yep. I gotta get my sister and corral the boys. So, the pool you say? And catching snakes on the other days?"

"Yeah. Want me to stop sometime and see if you can go?"

"I guess. Don't have other plans while I'm here." Abilene glanced down at her boots. "Hey, thanks for walking me home. It's nice to talk to someone who isn't one of my brothers or one of them snotty bitches in school."

A smile slid across his face. "No problem. I'll see you soon." Julien turned to walk back across the field. He turned back to wave at her as he had done every day he walked with her. She furled her bottom lip and sent a small wave back at him. For the first time in a long time, she realized she was going to miss seeing someone regularly. Yells came from the house as the door slammed. She looked over across from the motel parking lot to see Dallas run out of the house like he was on fire.

"Dammit, Jack! I'm telling Mom!" He screamed as he ran to the motel office door. Abilene drew in a deep breath and picked up the pace to get to the motel door at the same time as Dallas. Whatever disaster or grievance he had with his brother, Abilene knew it would fall on her to fix.

# CHAPTER 3

*Summer 1992*

Every day of summer vacation felt like an eternity for Abilene. The heat in the small single-story brick house was unbearable. The noise of three boys made it worse. Sweat poured from Abilene from sunup to sundown. Savannah stuck to her with jelly slicked fingers and hot thighs. While Abilene had done a good job of potty training her, Savannah still had accidents when they played outside, chasing the boys around the house. As rambunctious and wild as Dallas was, he had a soft spot for Savannah. He was gentle with her and talked to her in a soft voice compared to his gravely snarls at his brothers or endless eye rolls when Ashlynn or Abilene tried to discipline him. He softened when he was close to Savannah. Abilene thought Dallas would probably make a good dad someday, even though he didn't have one or know anything about what a dad should do.

It was two weeks into summer when Julien finally knocked on her door as she was getting dinner dishes from the table. Her mom was nearly two months from delivering and came home exhausted each night, so she was never any help. Everything, housework, the kids, cooking, shopping, and general policing of the boys fell on Abilene's shoulders. A knock on the door that didn't involve cops, social services, an angry ex, or pissed off neighbor was a relief.

"Hey there." Abilene said as she slid Savannah to the floor. She had just wiped her face, and the toddler squirmed down Abilene's thigh. Abilene felt a mess, but didn't care once she saw Julien smile.

"You want to walk to town? Maybe stop in the one ice cream place we got? It sucks, but it's better than nothing in this shit town."

"My mom won't be back till like 6 tonight. About an hour or so. I can't leave till then." Abilene said.

"Well, I got paid by my uncle for helping fix a few mowers. We can bring them, and I'll spring for a few cones." Julien said. He leaned against the door frame and shrugged. "I ain't got a car or nothing, but it isn't far to walk." He glanced behind him, then back at her. Austin and Jackson heard ice cream and sprinted to the door.

"Hell yeah, we want ice cream," Jackson said as he ran into Abilene. "Hey guys, Abilene's boyfriend wants to buy us ice cream!" He yelled over his shoulder. Abilene's cheeks grew instantly red.

"He's not my boyfriend, Jackass," Abilene elbowed her brother.

"Yeah, man. I'm just another kid stuck in this shithole like you guys." Julien said.

"Whatever. I don't care what you are if you're gonna get us ice cream. Abilene doesn't get us shit," Jackson quipped back at him.

"That's because we're broke," Abilene said with an eye roll. She bent down to grab Savannah's sandals. "And you never deserve ice cream after I've been stuck watching you all day."

Jackson turned around to find his shoes. Austin and Dallas followed. Dallas walked through the doorway once he had shoes. He nodded up at Julien.

"Hey, thanks man," he said. Abilene and Julien both looked at each other wide-eyed and surprised at Dallas's show of appreciation.

Julien walked beside Abilene as she held Savannah's hand. The boys ran up ahead and tossed various sticks and rocks from the sidewalk into the woods, occasionally hitting each other. Shouts of "asshole" rang out every few seconds. It was the boys' favorite word to throw at each other when Ashlynn wasn't around. Abilene used to scold them, but realized as they got older, she should pick her battles like other 'moms' do.

"So, how's your summer been so far? I see you guys are still here, so that's a plus." Julien said as he slid his hands in his jean pockets.

"Alright, I guess. Just the same old same old. Watch the kids, keep them from killing each other, then go to bed exhausted after my mom gets home. The closer she gets to her due date, the more I wonder if the dad will magically show up." She looked down at Savannah.

"Do you worry about him showing up?"

"Nah, if he does, he'll just fight with my mom for a few weeks and take off again. They always do. But it would give me a break if he stuck around for at least a few weeks." Abilene said.

Abilene felt comfortable telling Julien the truth of her family. She had always worked to avoid answering questions by others. Something in her knew Julien could relate, or at least empathize.

"So, you haven't said much about your siblings." Abilene said.

"They're easy really. I can't complain. It's not bad watching them when my mom and dad are at work if the babysitter cancels. Dad is a diesel mechanic in town. His brother is the one who pays me to fix stuff." Julien said as he kicked a rock from the sidewalk. "My mom works the desk at the salon in town. She can take off when things are slow, which means I don't have to watch them too much. Most of the watching I do with them is when my parents are fighting or beating the shit out of each other. I kind of shield them from that."

"That sucks. At least that's one good thing about when my mom is single. No man around to fight with. But when she had a guy, she'd get us a babysitter when she would leave for days. But now, well, I'm the babysitter."

Julien nodded. She knew without looking over at him, he completely understood the feeling of raising siblings instead of being raised *with* siblings. It was hard to have fun with them. Abilene pictured movies where sisters and brothers were best friends, where they relied on each other, had secrets and secret languages. She watched Austin and Jackson couple up and be each other's best friend. She noticed them draw Dallas into their little circle, even though he didn't look like them at all. Maybe it was because they were boys, but she never felt on equal footing with them, like them. She felt above them, responsible for them even when her mom was right there. Abilene was always on guard, watching to be sure the boys didn't get hurt or hurt each other or anyone else. She never got to relax, sit down on the floor and play like they all did. There were always dishes, laundry, meals to plan out based on what was in the fridge. Abilene struggled to remember a time she wasn't taking care of her brothers. She watched them walk in front of her and listened to Julien talk about a real babysitter. Pangs of jealousy crept in.

"So," Julien asked as he sped up the pace, "the names? Y'all named after places. How come?"

"Mom always told me she wanted to name all of us after where we came from, kinda so we'd always have a place to be connected to," Abilene said. "I think it's cause she needed to keep track of where each kid came from. The last place we lived when she got pregnant this time was Slidell, Louisiana, so I don't know how she's gonna name this one. I sure as hell hope she doesn't go with 'Slidell Tuckerson' or whatever last name she gives this one." Julien nodded as he walked backward, facing her. Savannah asked to be picked up. Abilene assured her they were almost at the ice cream stand.

"What name does your mom go by?"

"Swenson," Abilene straightened her shoulders as pride bubbled up in her gut. "She grew up in a huge mansion in Abilene, Texas. My mom's family was super rich, but she ran off with my dad and they kinda looked down on her for that." Abilene said. She drew in a deep breath. "They pretty much cut her off, 'rich bitches and bastards,' she says all the time."

"So even after all these years after leaving your dad, they won't help y'all out?"

"Guess not. I dunno if she's ever asked. But someday I'ma go to Abilene Texas and walk right into that mansion, see it all for myself." She smiled. "Mom says it has a grand staircase, huge gardens for parties while she grew up, big old pillars, a balcony on the second floor. Said everyone in Abilene was so jealous she grew up there." Abilene reached down and lifted a whining Savannah on her hip. "Huh, Savannah? We'll go knock on that door and demand to be taken to the sitting room with Tiffany lights hanging overhead. We'll play that grand piano Mom used to sit at and tell 'em we're blood and we want ours." Julien let out a huff. "Mom says the sitting room alone is bigger than the house we got now. There are French doors, big fireplaces, crystal chandeliers, a huge lily pond on the grounds.

Maybe they'll throw us a party? A 'welcome home girls' party." Her smile grew.

"That would be cool. Kinda like royalty coming home. I ain't got nothing like that in my family." Julien said. "The ice cream shop is right there," he said as he pointed across the street.

"Hold up, boys. Wait for me to cross." Abilene yelled as they got closer to her brothers.

"I tell you what, if you head to Abilene to bust into your family home and claim what's yours, I'll be right there beside you. Sounds like a hell of a time." They both laughed.

"Deal," she said.

Eating ice cream while reining in the kids was the most free time she had since school got out. Even with one eye on the boys, especially Dallas, she could breathe, relax her shoulders, lick mint chocolate chip, and laugh at Julien's stories. His observations of the lameness of growing up in Holden gave her a feeling of pride in having lived elsewhere. No one had ever admired her past leaps from place to place until now.

Julien's entire family lived in Holden, always had. His mom, dad, their moms and dads, uncles, crazy aunts, cousins, grandparents. Julien had never heard any family member mention another town or state, much less visit anywhere else, except his uncle being in the Army during Vietnam. Julien had been to Myrtle Beach once, about two hours from Holden. His mom took him and the girls for a weekend once when she was so pissed at his dad that she swore they'd never go back. Of course, Julien said, they went back as soon as she sobered up. There was no tearing those two apart, he proclaimed. Abilene closed her eyes for a second and wondered if she'd ever feel that way about anyone, or if her mom had. She liked to believe Ashlynn was madly in love with her dad, the Sergeant, as she called him, but she was never sure if that was just Ashlynn's version of the story. As Abilene got a little older, she could see everything she knew was her mom's version.

As Julien walked them all home, dusk was creeping up behind them. They stopped at the field across from the motel parking lot next to the house they were renting. She paused as the boys ran wild and let go of Savannah's hand so she could follow.

"Hey, thanks for taking us. It was nice to go somewhere, talk to someone other than these asses." Abilene said with a smile. Julien put his hands in his pocket and shuffled his feet in the grass.

"No problem. I know you don't really know anyone else. Someone's gotta show you around." He laughed. "Hey, sometimes in the middle of the night, when it's crazy hot and sticky and I can't sleep, I sneak out and go to Mazzy's, the little convenience store on the other side of town. Late at night, when no one else is around, they start making the hot chicken for the next day. It's fresh outta the fryer at like 2 a.m." He looked up at the sky and drew in a deep breath. "I'm telling ya, the smell is heaven. I get it still dripping with oil and a large slushy, cherry, not grape. Grape is bullshit. Wanna come sometime?" He swallowed a lump that she could tell almost made him not ask her.

"In the middle of the night, huh?"

"Yep. If you wait till dawn, all the guys at the plastic factory grab up all the good pieces before work. Middle of the night is the only way it's worth the walk."

"Well, I guess there ain't no harm in sneaking out when my mom's home to watch the hellions." Abilene bit her bottom lip as she heard Ashlynn calling her from the front porch. "Yeah. Count me in. My room is the window right there on the side facing the motel. Just tap, I guess. But be quiet. I share with Savannah. She wakes easy." Abilene rolled her eyes. "I'm coming!" she said toward the house. "I gotta go." She ran across the grass. As she made it halfway, she turned around to see Julien still standing there, shuffling his feet. "Hey, thanks again for today."

As Abilene helped get the kids ready for bed and assured Ashlynn Julien was harmless, she felt lighter. She crawled into bed and knew some night soon she'd hear a tap on the tiny window covered by dusty venetian blinds that were lopsided. It would be her friend coming to get her for a stolen middle-of-the-night adventure. She smiled as she drifted off. It felt good to have a genuine friend, something to look forward to.

# CHAPTER 4

Julien slowed down as he got closer to home. He could see the kitchen and living room light on. His dad's truck was in the driveway, right next to the minivan that only ran half the time. He kicked a few chunks of gravel from the broken sidewalk and schlepped to the front stoop. There were two beer bottles on the ledge next to the large pot that held withering petunias. His mom loved her petunias but seemed to grow tired of taking care of them when the real heat of summer set in. As the screen door creaked when he walked in, he saw his dad's head turn toward him. Noah was standing in the hallway leading to the kitchen. His face was beet red, sweaty, and that telltale vein was bulging. Julien knew he walked in on another fight. Without looking, he knew his mom was standing at the tiny kitchen island with tears streaming down her face. He also knew Sheila, with all her tears and wounded deer expressions, had probably started it as soon as Noah walked in from work. He slinked past his dad and headed to his room, after stepping over the piles of papers blocking the hall. After the twins were born, the piles got deeper. The boxes in the corner, bags of hand-me-downs, and useless pieces of things 'to be repurposed' only got more all-consuming. Julien was sure the carpet underneath the stuff had to be a different color by now. His room was the only one that had any space to breathe, spread out, exhale the sense of the wall closing in. The girls shared a room. Julien knew they were hunkered down, if not asleep already.

"Where the hell you been?" Noah yelled out to him.

"I went for ice cream. Uncle Chris paid me today." He said without turning around. As he reached for his door knob, Julien felt his father's hand on his shoulder.

"Hey, go help your mom clean up. And stick around tomorrow. I don't need her paying no damn babysitter so she can run around and do whatever while we got you still living here." Julien froze and nodded like he always did. "And stop letting that money from Chris burn a hole in your pocket. Learn to save a little, kid." Julien took a deep breath as he ducked under his dad's arm.

"I will, Dad." He could smell the beer and sweat throughout the hall and into the kitchen. Sheila was bent down with the broom, broken plates at her feet. She already had a bag. She looked up at Julien with a mascara-stained face. He hated seeing her like but had to admit to himself it got easier over the years. It didn't sting as much as it did when he was little. Julien had become desensitized to the fights and aftermath. He forgot what it was like before the twins were born and the fights were much quieter, and certainly less violent. His main job during the fights was to occupy the little ones, keep their fear from consuming them. He did his best, but some nights, like this night with his father still in the house, there was no time to comfort them. There was only time to help Sheila clean up while Noah stood watch over them. It seemed no matter where or what Julien did, his dad was always standing watch. The smell of beer and sweat filled any room where he lingered. Julien hated his smell more with each passing year.

Julien stepped past the totes and stacks of papers and projects to cross the threshold of his bedroom. He sunk into his twin bed, still covered with a Star Wars comforter. It was a twin bed and smelled like the house, musty, dirty. He knew there was no sense in asking for a new one, even at Christmas. He rarely asked for anything. Even though he spent his money here and there, he saved some in an old box from his grandfather. Julien hoped to buy a car someday with the sole purpose of driving away from Holden, preferably right after graduation. He'd have to work at his Uncle Chris's more than just the summers to save anywhere near enough. All he knew was leaving Holden was a must, even if it meant leaving his sisters behind. Every time he envisioned them waking up and realizing he was gone, or standing at the end of the driveway watching him drive away in two years, he'd feel a slight twinge of regret, a momentary longing to take them with him. But Julien knew that wouldn't happen. There was no way it could. He didn't even have a plan to take care of or feed himself, much less his younger siblings. Plus, a small part of him felt he didn't owe them a way out. No one was coming to save him. No one declared any interests in guiding him through life with his parents and their never-ending roller coaster of madness, drunkenness, and lack of concern for their kids, not even his Uncle Chris.

As for his mom's family, they were all cut from the same cloth— gorgeous, passionate, quick to fall in love and just as quick to battle. He watched his grandmother and aunts treat the men in their lives the same, fall for abusive asses, fight with them till they ended up black and blue, then fall for them again. Julien had grown to realize his mom needed the conflict. She needed the aftermath of her only son looking at her with pity and worry, willing to fight his own father to protect her. She needed the chaos like she needed air. Julien's mom lived for nights that turned into screaming matches, pushing each other into walls, slaps across the face, and even the occasional punch or push to the floor. It was her release, her form of cardio, wearing herself out after a good fight and cleanup session depleted all the hate she kept bottled up, at least temporarily. The more Julien watched her spiral into a tornado, then collapse, get the broom and clean up the aftermath, the more he realized she wasn't even seeing his dad as she flailed, hit him, and cried hysterically after. She was unleashing anger and hate that had nothing to do with Noah. Julien also came to realize his dad knew, and instead of getting her help or trying to diffuse the powder keg, he fed the beast she had become every time she reared her vicious snarl at him. The fights gave him a level of release, too. Julien vowed to never fall into the only lifestyle they had shown him and his sisters.

As he passed the long June days working on whatever mower engine Chris didn't feel like bothering with, Julien thought more and more about Abilene. Their walks became the highlight of his summer. While Chris teased him about having a girlfriend, Julien would just smirk back at him. He knew there was no use in explaining to his narrow-minded uncle it wasn't like that. Julien didn't dream about her or fantasize about her like he did other girls in school. He didn't stare at pictures of her like he did Lita Ford on his wall in junior high, dressed in black lace with wild hair—even though Abilene's hair was just as much a wild train wreck most days. He just wondered how she was and wanted to be with her to talk, listen, feel like a normal person. She was fast becoming the only person he felt he could talk to, or who even saw him. While he hated the phrase and never gave it much thought, Julien was seeing Abilene as his best friend. He was sure he was her only real friend, too. He felt normal with her, whatever that meant.

Julien put his tools back in the toolbox his dad gave him when he started working on engines. It was the only thing his dad ever picked out for him.

"I'm a head out, Uncle Chris." He yelled as he wiped his hands on the rag he carried in his pocket. "You good with that?"

"Yeah, man. Go ahead. Hey, can I pay ya tomorrow? I ain't got the cash on me right now?" Chris yelled from the other side of the garage.

"Yeah, that's fine." Julien walked out into the sunshine. He stopped for a second and ran his greasy hands through his blonde hair, exhaled and slumped his shoulders. He asked Abilene to meet him at midnight to sneak out for some hot chicken and wanted to get home to shower and see his sisters first. Once home and clean, he pushed some papers out of the way on the counter to sit and gulp ice cold milk with the twins.

"Can you take us for ice cream after dinner?" Sammy asked, as she swiveled the stool across from Julien.

"Maybe. Wanna go get Abilene and her brothers and sister and all go? I didn't get paid today so you guys gotta bring your allowance if you want any, okay?" Julien said after his last gulp. He used the back of his freshly cleaned hands to wipe his mouth. The twins nodded.

Noah walked in as Julien washed his glass and took a frozen pizza out for the kids.

"Oh, Dad, I didn't know you'd be home early. I was just gonna give these guys a pizza and walk for ice cream. Thought you and mom would be late tonight." Julien swallowed a lump in his throat. He never liked his dad coming home early or unexpectedly. It was never for a good reason or to usher in a good mood throughout the house.

"I was laid off again. Your mom ain't here? Sheila!" he yelled as he peeled his boots off. Julien breathed a slight sigh of relief. Being laid off was much better than getting fired. When that was the case, there were usually a rough few days of beer-induced fights and lots of broken household goods. "Sheila!"

"She's not home yet. I think she works till 8." Julien pre-heated the oven.

"Bullshit." Noah muttered to himself. He squeezed between the twins and the wall to get into the kitchen. It momentarily surprised Julien when Noah ran his hands through Selena's long hair as he walked past. "What you up to, baby girl?" Selena smiled and looked up at him. His stubbled face was tan. His lines looked deeper in the summer. Julien always found it hard to believe he was only 20 years older than he was. His dad had the face and mannerisms of a much older man, a tired and beat down old man. "You girls eat that pizza and mind Jules here. He's the boss tonight." Noah winked at Julien. He grabbed a beer from the front of the fridge as Julien slid the pizza into the oven. Julien wanted to smile at the trust, the moment of normalcy, the past when his dad called him Jules all the time. It was his nickname for Julien when they were having fun, being light, doing guy things like fishing, mudding in his truck, or just stalking squirrels in the woods. Julien couldn't remember the last time his dad called him that. He took a minute to let his guard down and feel close to him, even though he knew it wouldn't last. His mom would come home soon, and Julien knew they'd fight either about her being late and not cooking dinner for the kids or his layoff.

"So, Jules, rumor in town you been hanging around with that girl whose mom works at the hotel. The pretty, leggy young thing always wearing them damn red boots, with all the little ones hot on your tails, am I right?" Noah popped open the beer and chugged. Julien could see his Adam's apple bob in and out as he swallowed nearly an entire bottle in one sip. Julien cringed hearing his dad call Abilene a leggy young thing.

"Yeah. She's my friend, that's all." Julien crossed his arms, just as tanned as his dad's.

"Well, if it goes any further, be careful, boy. You get what I'm saying?" Noah reached back to grab another beer. "I mean it. I saw her mom at the Piggly Wiggly and outside that motel. Those are the kind you gotta watch out for." Julien leaned back on the counter and glanced at the timer on the oven. His feelings of normalcy, comfort at hearing his dad call him Jules faded.

"I ain't doing nothing with no one. Don't worry about me."

"Those kind, the girls who look like that, they'll trap you quicker than shit. I'm telling you. Keep it in your pants cause you don't want to end up like me. Married and shit at 20. You finish school and figure out what you wanna do first. A girl like that, she'll fuck it up quicker than shit." Noah twisted the beer. Selena and Sammy looked down as they swung in the stools. "Sorry girls. Cover your damn ears, will ya?" He said with a snicker that made Julien cringe even more. He wanted to grab his dad, punch him in the mouth, and beg him to stand up and be a normal human being, not an asshole all day, every day.

"Like I said, she's just my friend. No one else in this town is worth hanging with. It's not like I got a lot of choices and I ain't standing around with all those jocks outside of Mazzy's bullshitting about winning the big game or getting a scholarship." Julien glanced at his sisters and wanted to apologize for swearing in front of them, too. He noticed them avert their eyes.

"Yeah, those guys are just like their dads were, assholes till the end. Only look my way when they need their foreign piece of shit cars or jacked up trucks worked on. Glad you ain't like them." He swigged and winked again. "What you gonna do after the next two years, anyway? You ain't said much and I know no colleges are gonna be calling. You ain't that smart." Noah said with a laugh. Julien drew in a deep breath.

"Not sure. I might just keep working for Uncle Chris or, I dunno, maybe talk to a recruiter about going in the service or something. I mean, he said it taught him some stuff." Julien shrugged.

"You really think that's a good idea? We just ended a damn war in Iraq all cause of that crazy shitbag Saddam. Now, I know ain't a lot of guys get killed there like when Chris was in 'nam, but shit, some did." Noah swigged and stared off past Julien and out the kitchen window. "Listen man, I know I ain't exactly a great inspiration. I didn't do shit like Chris did and was too young to go to Vietnam, but war, any war, can mess a man up. Joining up is noble and patriotic and all, but that don't mean it's for everyone."

"Well, there isn't too much else here, Dad. I mean, I love working with Uncle Chris, but I don't want to fix mowers forever. And you already said I shouldn't follow in your footsteps fixin' cars. And you're definitely right about no colleges calling." Julien let out a long exhale and tried to find his father's eyes. "What else can I do?" He rolled up his sleeves and slid the girls' plates to the edge of the counter by the sink. Julien filled the sink. Noah shrugged. That shrug always meant any meaningful conversation was over.

"What you doing wearing all my old flannel shirts now, anyway? Every day I see kids walking around with flannel tied around their waist like they going off to work as lumberjacks or something." Noah said with a laugh. Julien shrugged at his dad. Noah took the last sip of beer and tossed the bottle in the garbage. He patted Julien on the shoulder as the sink filled with soapy water. He tussled the girls' hair and leaned down to kiss Selena on the top of the head. "You kids listen to your brother. Be good if he takes you for ice cream."

Seconds later, he was slumped over in the recliner surrounded by old newspapers. Julien knew he would remain there except for trips to the fridge for more beer until his mom came home and a fight would erupt. He knew he'd need to make sure the twins were ready for bed before any pending argument unfolded. But first, he needed to clean up the kitchen, the only room that stayed somewhat usable besides his bedroom and the bathroom. Despite the sheer overwhelming clutter and dirt cloud that wafted from room to room, his mom cleaned the bathroom each week, and Julien cleaned the kitchen after dinner when he was around. But his room was his only real refuge. Julien tried for a while to help his siblings keep their rooms cleaned, or at least picked up some, but it was to no avail. They were content with their clothes scattered and balled up everywhere, even the clean ones, wrappers and cups all over the place, and a layer of dust on every surface. Julien made sure they brushed their hair, and they scrubbed away any visible dirt before they left for school. While he accepted they might have to live in a dirty house, he was hell-bent on making sure he and his sisters didn't look the part. They already had enough shit to deal with from the other kids in town. This was the one thing he could control.

Julien never had to worry about the outside world seeing in, getting a feel for their reality behind closed doors, because no one ever came over. His parents went to the bars and brought the bar drama home, no one else. Julien or the girls never thought to have friends over. Julien never had a friend until now. He would keep going to meet Abilene at her house or meet her outside of his, but she never expressed an interest in coming inside for anything and he certainly would not extend an invitation. Julien got the sense Abilene already knew why he never asked her to come inside. As they spent more and more days and nights walking around town together, with siblings in tow and without, Julien grew to love the feeling of being understood. It made being inside those walls a little easier. Someone on the outside, even if they got the chance to look in, would still be his friend.

# CHAPTER 5

Abilene heard a soft knock on the window. She gasped as she tossed the sheet off her legs. Her t-shirt clung to her stomach. Even with a fan blowing directly on her and Savannah, she sweated through her clothes every night for the last two weeks. Summers in South Carolina were notoriously humid, but the summer of 1992 was proving to be record-breaking. Abilene usually left the window open, but there was a band staying at the motel for the week. They had a gig at the bar across town. Each night, they came back and partied all night under the awning on the side of the motel, which was right across Abilene's bedroom window. The gruff voices and cigarette smoke had kept her up two nights in a row. Keeping the window shut was the only solution, even if it meant sweating through the night.

Abilene swooped her wild mane from her eyes and cautiously peeled back the curtain from the window. The drummer sitting outside his motel room door creeped her out, staring at her all day when she was trying to push mow the front yard earlier. The thought that he might be the one on the other side of the window gave her pause. She let out a deep breath when she saw Julien on the other side. She pushed the window open half way and rested her damp elbows on the sill. Slivers of white paint would stick to her skin anytime she touched that windowsill.

"Hey, I didn't expect you to come around tonight. What's up?" She whispered. Abilene glanced behind her in the dark to make sure Savanah hadn't moved.

"Just can't sleep. Wanna walk to Mazzy's and get something to eat? Maybe a slushy?" Julien tightened his flannel shirt around his waist. He always wore it with his black Nirvana shirt. Abilene glanced behind her, then back at Julien.

"Yeah, I guess. I can't sleep either. Too hot. Lemme get dressed. I'll meet you under the tree. Don't go under the motel light. I don't trust that night manager. He's getting a little too close to my mom. I don't need him telling her I'm slipping out at night, especially with a boy." She slid the window closed. Abilene fished around in the dark for her bra. She slid sweatpants on over her spandex shorts.

As she slipped out of the house and into the night, Abilene realized the night air was just as steamy as her bedroom.

"Jesus, does it ever cool down around here?" She said as she gathered her hair behind her head and put it up in a scrunchy.

"Nope, not this summer, I guess. Hey, I made you something." Julien reached in his back jean pocket and pulled out a cassette tape. He handed it to Abilene.

"Cool. What's on it?"

"Just some newer stuff you need to listen. None of that Mariah Carey and En Vogue shit."

"Hey, that's good stuff. Nothing wrong with a little TLC, either. I think you just hate girl groups."

"No, not at all. Just all sounds the same. Take a listen to that tomorrow if you get a chance. It's Nirvana, some Red Hot Chili Peppers, Jane's Addiction. Some stuff to get the blood pumping. Grunge is here to stay, mark my word."

Abilene laughed. "Yeah, I'm sure you said metal was here to stay when you bought that old Guns and Roses shirt you wore every other day to school, huh?"

Julien nudged her in the side with his elbow. "Fine, whatever. Just listen. You need to broaden your horizons. Maybe we can get to Lollapalooza this summer or something?" Julien said.

"Yeah, I wish. You know neither of us can afford that. Plus, we don't have access to a car."

"Well, maybe someday then." Julien said as they stepped off the curb and onto the dark, hot street. The trees stretched over the streetlights and cast shadows down in front of their path. Abilene glanced up at the stars and wondered if it was just as hot up there. As they rounded the corner that would put them on a straight shot to Mazzy's, Abilene noticed a group of girls sitting on the porch of the largest house in town. There were at least six of them, three sprawled across the porch swing and another three sitting with their elbows on bare knees on the grand steps leading to the covered porch. It was just after midnight, so Abilene figured they must be having a sleepover. She felt a twinge of jealously until she realized it was the group of girls who laughed at her name in school. She could hear whispers as they walked past. Suddenly, Abilene regretted slipping on old sneakers and sweatpants. At least when she wore her boots, she felt more confident, almost immune to their whispers and stares, even if she wasn't.

"Huh?" she said to Julien, as she realized she hadn't been listening to him.

"I asked if you had any cash? I think I left my wallet at the house." Julien said. "Shit."

"Yeah, I got two bucks, enough for slushies but not for chicken." Abilene answered. "It's too hot for chicken anyway," she said as she watched the girls out of the corner of her eye. Abilene picked up her pace as one girl stood. It was Charlene. She was the leader of their little group. She seemed to be the leader of every group in Holden. No one wanted to cross her, and everyone wanted to be her. As best Abilene could tell, Charlene's parents were both lawyers. They were obviously well off and as popular as Charlene. Her dad even had a commercial on tv advertising his help for anyone owing back taxes. The commercial always made Ashlynn livid. She'd yell out, "just pay your damn taxes like the rest of us!" every time it came on the tv in the motel office and the living room when she was watching tv as Abilene cleaned up after the kids.

"Hey, you two! Where you going this time of night?" Charlene yelled out to them. Her high-pitched voice pierced through the air. Abilene wanted to disappear, evaporate, and reemerge in her bed, stuck to her sheet. Julien nodded his head forward.

"Just keep walking. Don't pay attention to those snots." Julien said under his breath.

"Hey, freaks. Where you love birds going? Off to the riverbank to make out or what?" Charlene yelled out louder. The girls on the steps rose and crossed their arms. They looked like disappointed moms waiting for their kid to explain why they were late for curfew. Abilene heard Julien mumbling something. "What's that, Julien? You got something to say? Where you taking your girlfriend?" The other girls laughed.

"Leave him be, Char. His mom's crazy, you know. He might snap." The girl on the swing said. Julien stopped walking. Abilene reached for his arm.

"Hey, ignore them. That's what you said, right? They're just stuck-up bitches." Abilene said through gritted teeth. "Come on," she pleaded. Julien stood firm.

"You in love with her, Julien? Was it the boots that got ya?" Charlene said. The group laughed in unison. Abilene rolled her eyes. She never understood how anyone could see her boots as a joke. To her, they were the greatest shoes on earth.

"No, rich bitch. She ain't my girlfriend. We're just friends, if you must know." Julien shouted back.

"Then why you two always wandering around here late at night all alone? No one else ever with you? Seems pretty cozy, if you ask me." Charlene said as she waltzed down the steps and stood on the flower lined sidewalk in front of her house.

"We stick with each other because we fucking hate the rest of you and can't wait to get the hell out of here. Got any more questions?" Julien yelled back. Charlene stood silent for a moment. Her followers silently waited for her reaction, too. The air grew even thicker than it had been. Abilene had never heard Julien so angry before. He drew in another breath and took Abilene by the hand. "Come on, let's get out of here," His voiced cracked. Abilene swallowed and stepped forward with him.

"Yeah, well, your mom's still a nutcase. The whole town knows it!" Charlene shouted into the dark. Abilene squeezed Julien's hand. He lowered his head and squeezed hers back.

"Just keep walking," she whispered and swallowed another lump in her throat. They walked the rest of the way to Mazzy's in complete silence. As they got to the parking lot, Julien let go of her hand.

"Thanks," he said. "If I had been alone, I might've, I dunno, I might've hit her and I would never hit a girl, but dammit, Charlene would've deserved it." Julien pushed his hands into his pockets.

"Yeah, she would've deserved it." Abilene said as she fished in the pocket of her sweatpants. "A ha! Two bucks. We're golden, Ponyboy." Julien laughed. They had stayed up late watching The Outsiders on tv the other night when Ashlynn went to bed early and both swore they'd rather run off like Ponyboy and Johnny instead of being trapped in Holden forever. Ever since they watched it, Abilene thought Julien looked just like C. Thomas Howell in the movie.

Abilene wanted to rewind the last half hour, take another way to Mazzy's or race up Charlene's porch and kick her ass before she could say anything to hurt Julien. She wanted to tumble back in time and save Julien from any moment where anyone anywhere mocked his mother. She knew she couldn't. But he was her best friend, so she couldn't help it. It gave her a small sense of relief that referencing The Outsiders was enough to get a smirk out of him. Maybe it was enough to patch up one of the thousand little cuts he endured when confronted with the reality of having a mom the whole town talked about. The kind of mom who made every day harder and more chaotic than it needed to be for a kid. She squinted as Julien held open the door and the neon sign saying "HOT CHICKEN FRESH DAILY" flashed in her eyes.

They decided to take another way back home, an out of the way route to avoid Charlene and anyone else who might be out that night. Without saying a word, Abilene knew they'd take a different way to Mazzy's from that night on, which was fine with her. The fewer people they saw or had to talk to, the better.

After getting the largest slushies two dollars could buy, they went across the parking lot, across the railroad tracks to the river walk. It winded alongside the town without cutting through. The trail was a little rugged, but easy to follow, even in the dark. Abilene stepped over tree roots and winding sticker bush twigs that reached and snagged her sweatpants.

"Hey, don't drink it too quick. I got a surprise I stashed in the ditch across from my house." Julien said back over his shoulder.

"What are you talking about?" Abilene said mid-sip. The cold slush made the roof of her mouth numb. Her fingers froze around the massive paper cup as a thick layer of sweat covered the rest of her body. She loved the goosebumps she knew were on the verge of piercing that layer of sweat.

"You'll see."

He motioned for her to slow down more. She felt like a sleek, camouflaged gazelle, creeping along the wooded trail, running alongside the river with a cherry ice slushy in hand.

Once they reached the path to Julien's street, he slowed and turned around to face Abilene.

"Listen, be super quiet. Just wait under that pine over there. I'll be right back. Okay?" Julien said. Abilene nodded and ducked under stray branches that jutted out into the path. She watched as his shadow left the cover of trees and ventured back out into the world she was in no rush to return to. She liked the protection, the anonymity of the trail. Julien reappeared a minute later with a large bottle and a smile. Her eyes widened as she slurped another mouthful of red iciness.

"What the hell is that?" Abilene said as she cringed from brain freeze. Julien laughed.

"I stole it from my mom. It's peach schnapps. It's like drinking syrup, but man, I think you'll love it." He said as he reached his free hand to help Abilene step over a giant root and onto the sidewalk. "I just checked. Mom and dad are fighting in the back room and the van is in the carport. We can sit in there and listen to music. I got those other tapes I want you to hear." He darted across the street and behind a giant oak at the end of his parent's driveway. He motioned for Abilene to follow. She laughed at how he crouched down as he sneaked up the driveway. Abilene rolled her eyes at him and walked her normal long stride strut up his driveway like she did nearly every day lately.

After they slid into the van and gingerly closed the doors, Julien unscrewed the top. He took a long swig, filled his cheeks, and gulped. Abilene laughed as he cringed.

"Sweet?"

"Yep. Here." He said as he handed her the bottle. "You ever drink before?"

"Yeah, a few beers before we moved here, with some girls on the track team. I ran track for like a week. We got caught with beer on the bus after a meet. All five of us got kicked off. Mom wasn't too pissed because it meant I was around more for babysitting. That was right after she realized she was pregnant again." She took the big brown bottle with peaches on the label and tipped it back for a slow sip. Abilene let the sticky liquid slide down her throat easily compared to the forceful sip Julien took. The taste pleasantly surprised Abilene.

"Not bad, huh?" Julien said as he took back the bottle.

"Won't your mom know it's missing?"

"Hell no. My mom never keeps track of this shit. Dad neither. I could take half his beer every fucking day and he would have no clue."

They passed the bottle back and forth a few times as they both stared straight ahead. Abilene's shoulders relaxed in no time. She was thankful they were alone in the van, away from the outside world. Abilene wanted to bring up what happened when they passed Charlene's house and tell Julien not to listen to those assholes. She wanted to make sure their insults about his mom rolled off his back like he pretended they did, but she didn't. They sat in silence and darkness, and she never felt safer.

Julien reached over to the glove box in front of her legs. He popped it open and scooped up a few cassettes.

"You'll never guess what I picked up in town last week."

He slid in a tape and slowly turned up the volume. A wide smile crept across her face as music filled the van.

"You didn't?" She said with a chuckle. Abilene took another swig. "We gotta go see this if it's still playing."

"Damn straight we do. I'll see in the morning if it is. Maybe we can walk there Saturday after the pool, if your mom's off work?"

Abilene gave a nod as she took another swig.

"Here it comes," Julien said. Bohemian Rhapsody from the Wayne's World soundtrack filled the van. Just as the melodic rock-opera wound down, the song climaxed with Abilene and Julien both banging their heads and laughing with their best Wayne and Garth impersonations. She laughed so hard peach schnapps dripped down her chin and her side hurt. Julien couldn't catch his breath once the song ended. They both collapsed back into the seats and let out a collective sigh.

"So much better than En Vogue, huh," Julien said as he nudged her side.

"Shut up." She said as she looked up at the ceiling. "But, yeah. It is." Abilene let the feeling of the schnapps wash over her. Her mind slowed. Her worries faded. Time stood still. He ejected the tape and put in another. She tried to focus on the lights of the dashboard. The lights blurred. Julien slid his hand into hers. She drew in a deep breath and looked over at him. Nirvana roared from the speakers. Abilene rolled her eyes again as she let out a laugh.

"You can't even understand what he's saying," she muttered to Julien.

"Oh, come on. He's a genius. It's really deep if you listen." Julien smiled at her. She noticed how his perfectly white teeth glowed against the dash lights. He leaned in as she turned toward him with her hand still in his. Julien closed his eyes and kissed her. Abilene let his lips engulf hers as she began to spin. His lips were much softer than she would've guessed. Kurt Cobain wailed his raspy voice around them.

"Did he just say libido and mosquito in the same song?" Abilene said as his lips smothered hers and a giggle bubbled up from her gut. She tried to suppress a laugh as Julien reached for her face. Just as he dove in closer to kiss her harder, she erupted. He did too, as he fell back into his seat. Julien shook his head.

"What the fuck was that for?" Abilene said as she tried not to laugh again.

"I'm sorry. It just felt right in the moment, but now, not so much," Julien said as he nudged her. "Your taste in music sucks too much for me to make out with you seriously." She punched him in the side. He doubled over and rested his head on the steering wheel. "You forgive me? I don't wanna make things awkward between us. I think it was just the peach schnapps talking." He said with a laugh.

"Yeah, shut up. It's fine. Give me the bottle." They both swigged and passed the fast-dwindling bottle back and forth. Julien turned down the music as Abilene once again swooshed her wild hair from her eyes.

"Seriously, Abilene. I can't wait to get out of here and find someone. I swear I'm gonna marry a normal chick and have one of those stable families like we see on tv. Like the Walsh's on that show you watch, 90210 or whatever bullshit. Nothing like my mom and dad. You know?"

"Yeah, me too. I ain't having a bunch of kids, though. I think I'll just be happy if I find a guy that sticks around at all, not like the men my mom has always brought around. I don't wanna be a single mom hauling kids around the country, or making the older ones watch the little ones." She sipped and stared up at the ceiling. "I don't think I want any. I'm sick of raising kids and changing diapers already, and I'm only sixteen. God, I'm so tired." She exhaled. "Maybe I'll just travel around alone. I dunno." She slurred. Julien nodded.

"Well, let's make a pact. If you get out of here, travel around and I join the Army, and we run into each, we'll try to kiss again and see if goes anywhere." He said with a snicker.

"You just want any excuse to kiss me, Ponyboy." She laughed.

"Whatever, Conceited much? It ain't like there's anyone else in this town to make out with."

"Hey, what you mean joining the Army?"

Julien told her joining seemed like his only way out of Holden. She had the grades to take off for college if she wanted, and she certainly had the looks to hitch her wagon to any guy leaving if she wanted to take the easy way out of Holden, but guys like Julien didn't have those options. Abilene shrugged as she tried to steady her eyes and mind.

"Maybe you'll run across my dad out there somewhere? If you do, tell him his kid says hello." She laughed as tears filled her eyes. Abilene didn't want to cry, but there was no stopping it. "Honestly, though, from what I hear, he's a good soldier. I think you should join. You're the kind of guy who can be good at both, being a soldier and a husband, and a good dad too." She nodded. Julien shrugged his shoulders. He took the bottle and took an extra-long gulp. Abilene smiled at him and reached for his cheek. "Some girl will be lucky to have you, Ponyboy. I mean it." She swallowed a lump. "And when you meet her, you tell her you had the coolest best friend in Holden, and you miss me every day."

"I will, Abilene. I swear. But I mean it. If we meet up again and we're old and rickety, like 30, we'll give it a go together. Maybe you'll have some taste in music by then." She tapped his cheek and laughed.

"Asshole." She slurred as her eyes grew heavy.

"You're an asshole, too." He closed his eyes as Abilene leaned her head on his shoulders. They knew they needed to leave the van before they fell asleep right in the front seats. Abilene closed her eyes when Julien nudged her.

"Come on. We gotta walk you home."

"I can walk myself." She muttered as she tried to keep her eyes open.

"No, you can't. Come on, let's go."

Julien slid out of the van with the nearly empty bottle. He helped Abilene out and steadied her in the driveway. She laughed, which made him laugh. He 'shushed' her at least a dozen times before they made it down the street and to the motel parking lot. Julien stood her in front of him and held her shoulders.

"All you gotta do from here is get through the front door, down the hall, and into your bed. Don't fall over Savannah." Abilene laughed. He tapped her cheeks. "You hear me?" She nodded yes.

"I'm good. Hey, Ponyboy. Thanks for walking me home. You take good care of me, you know," Abilene said as she tried to keep her wandering, heavy eyes focused on him.

"That's what best friends do." He said.

Abilene made slow, deliberate steps through the lot and to the front door. She took a deep breath and straightened her body. She was still swaying. Before she turned the doorknob, she looked back at Julien. He stood tall under the streetlight with his hands in his pockets. His wavy blonde hair glowed under the lamppost as he flashed his toothy grin. He swayed a little, too. She smiled back at him before stepping into the house. She thought he looked like an angel, her own guardian angel.

# CHAPTER 6

August rolled in as a hot, sticky mess. The moss barely swayed from the lack of any breeze. The sun setting didn't bring relief. Sweat was the only scent in the air all day and all night. The motel office only had a window air conditioning unit meaning Ashlynn dripped sweat from her face, down her neck, between her swollen breasts, then it would trickle into a little river down and over her pregnant belly, seeping through her stretched-out tank tops. As much Abilene hated being the maid, mom, nurse, and co-worker to her mom and her siblings, she knew Ashlynn couldn't do it all alone. She could barely waddle from the office desk back to the house each night. When they first moved to Holden, Abilene would see her mom flit from door to door, dropping off towels when the maids were busy. She'd carry a stack on top of her expanding belly and deliver it all with a smile. Now, as summer wound down, the heat and increasing size of the baby had taken its toll. Abilene didn't remember seeing her mom slow down for a second when pregnant with Savannah. But this time, Ashlynn was living in slow motion.

Abilene had developed a system for getting the kids breakfast, keeping the boys from destroying the house and each other. Then she'd take a snack for Ashlynn and another large jug of water. Ashlynn drank more water than anyone Abilene had ever seen. After checking on her mom and cleaning up Savannah, Abilene usually tended to housework or waited for Julien to show up and walk with them somewhere. If the two of them could scramble enough cash, they'd walk all the little ones to the pool. The pool proved to be more relaxing than home because Jackson, Austin, and Dallas couldn't get into too much trouble. Sure, they got the whistle blown at them a few times for splashing girls or doing something stupid off the diving board, but no real harm. Abilene would just scream their names, threaten to take them home, and roll her eyes. She spent most of the pool time lounging in a chair next to Julien, talking about junior and senior year and how they would be out of Holden in less than two years year. Julien was certain the Army was his best bet and swore he was meeting up with the recruiter as soon as he turned 18 next January. Abilene was still unsure what path she'd take, or what path she could take, since a new baby was on the way in about a month. She hated that her life never seemed as if it would ever be her own.

"It ain't your kid, and neither are the rest. You gotta go live your life. Maybe join up with me?" Julien said as he smacked her leg.

"Yeah, right." She said as she rubbed oil on her thighs and forearms. Abilene slid her sunglasses down, an old pair from Ashlynn. "Do I look like I could go to Iraq and kick anyone's ass? Or better yet, do I look like I *want* to?" Abilene said as she reached to pull her hair up in a scrunchy she had around her wrist.

"Oh, come on, that war is over. You can stay stateside, march each day and get paid to get a tan, camp out, walk through the woods, all the stuff we do for free right now."

That war might be over, but Saddam is still out there, so you know we're gonna go back sometime again."

"Whatever. What else do you think you're gonna do?"

"I dunno. Maybe I'll go straight to Abilene and go right up to the front door of the Swenson mansion and ask for a room. Tell them who I am and it's about damn time they let us back in." Abilene leaned back and looked up at the cloudless sky. "Who knows, maybe they've been waiting for us to come back. I could convince my mom to come with me, make amends and live it up right."

"Sounds like a pipe dream." Julien stood up and peeled off his t-shirt.

"Yeah, well, it's my pipe dream. I know in my bones I got family, got roots there, and they'll take us in. I just know it."

"Oh hey, before I forget, I called and got us tickets for lollapalooza in two weeks. They're just lawn seats, but whatever. I'm gonna ask my mom about borrowing the van and we should be all set. You just gotta make sure you can go." Julien said. "It'll be awesome. I'm tellin ya, by the end of the day you'll love the Chili Peppers." He winked at her. She smirked. "I'm jumping in. You coming?"

"Nah, I'm gonna lay here and dream away. Picture myself walking down that long spiral staircase, waltzing along the lily pond in a gorgeous dress, eating the finest dinner under a gigantic crystal chandelier, dinner I didn't need to cook." She slid the sunglasses back down. "I'll tell my mom about the concert. She should be cool with it since I ain't done anything all summer, but hang out with you and all these kids."

"But what about a plan B?" Julien asked. "You gotta have a plan B. After we graduate, I mean, if you don't make it to Abilene?" He turned to run into the pool. Abilene sat up just in time to feel the cold water hit her face and legs. She screeched and curled up as she took off the dripping sunglasses.

"Asshole!" she yelled to her. Julien laughed and called her one back. He ducked under the clear chlorinated water. Abilene leaned back and once again stared up at the clear sky. She found the only cloud and followed it with her eyes as it slowly floated toward the sun. "Plan B," she muttered under her breath. She knew plan B was the same reality she was in now. Maybe get a job in town, one that still allowed her to be home to help her mom. Her gut seized as she thought about a new baby coming home, crying all night, then next year, crawling down the hall scooping up every piece of paper or trash the boys left behind. Savannah would be four. Maybe she'd be in preschool next year, meaning only one kid would be home full-time. One was still one too many for Abilene to think about. Ashlynn would no doubt have to go back to the motel full time once the baby was born, meaning next year would be school then picking up the baby from a portable crib in the office, taking it home to feed and change, and wild animals called brothers to keep alive. Maybe her mom would make manager and be able to afford a babysitter during the day by next summer. Maybe Tucker would come back, be a real dad so Abilene could worry less about a baby after school and weekends. Abilene drew in a deep breath and wondered what it was like for girls like Charlene and her friends to come home and be taken of instead of doing the caring.

"Abilene! Abilene! Wake up!" She heard in her sleep. Abilene felt her shoulders being shaken. She squinted as she opened her eyes to see Julien standing over her with Jackson, Austin, Dallas, and a dripping wet Savannah all around her chair. "The pool got a phone call. Your mom is in labor." Julien shouted at her. Abilene shook her head and sat up. She wondered how long she had slept.

"Wait, what?"

Julien explained the manager figured they were at the pool, and he called an ambulance. Ashlynn's water broke right there on the office floor.

"But she'd not due until the end of the month."

"Yeah, well, no one told the baby that." He pulled on her oil slicked arm.

"Hang on. We got time. She takes forever to pop one out. Give me a sec." Abilene said as she slowly sat up and pushed her sunglasses on top of her head.

Abilene was still groggy as she and Julien gathered the towels, pulled shorts and a shirt over Savannah's head, and made sure everyone had shoes. They scrambled from the wet, chlorine smelling cement through the locker rooms and out the main entrance. Abilene could tell her hair was already frizzing. Once the brood crossed the street, she told Julien to take his sisters home, and she'd be fine getting everyone to the motel. She'd call him later.

Abilene walked into the motel office as she fumbled for a comb to run through Savannah's hair.

"It's alright, kid. I got this. Natalie gets off in about a half hour and already said she'd watch all these youngens until you get back. Here," Amos, the motel owner, said. "Take my keys. You can drive my car to the hospital to be with her. Just call when you got news."

Abilene nodded. "Thank you so much, Mr. Gurka. You sure you got the boys? Dallas can be a handful."

"Hey! I'm right here, Abi. Dammit, why you always gotta make me sound like a wild animal?" Dallas said as he bounced on the office chair.

"Cause you are, idiot." Jackson said.

"Shut up," Dallas shot back with a scowl.

"Both y'all shut up. I gotta go check on mom. Keep your asses in line. You hear me?" Abilene pointed to her brothers and leaned down to kiss the top of Savannah's head. "I'll call and let you know whether you got a baby sister or baby brother, okay Savannah?" The little girl smiled wide and nodded. Mr. Gurka fished out a handful of lollipops from the front drawer. The boys scrambled for them before he said anything. Mr. Gurka's eyes widened.

"Maybe you should let Natalie off a little early tonight so you aren't overwhelmed."

"I got this, kid. I was a Marine. I can handle your brothers." He said with a scowl meant to drive the point home. "Go on, get to the hospital and be careful with my car. It's vintage, you know." Abilene laughed as tapped Savannah's head again.

Abilene started the lime green station wagon. It was a stick shift. While she learned to drive a stick earlier in the summer, thanks to Julien's uncle Chris wanting to be sure they both knew how, she was still a novice. The jerking and grinding scared her, but she kept trying. Once she was a few blocks from the hospital, it got easier to stop and start at stoplights. She rolled through the last two when they were yellow, just to avoid any mishaps. She knew Ashlynn couldn't afford for her to mess up her boss's car. Abilene lurched into a spot and exhaled once she turned off the limey, as she and Julien called it when they saw him driving around town.

Stepping into Ashlynn's room was a shock to the system. Just an hour earlier, Abilene had been lounging in the sun at the pool, rolling her eyes at Julien and his concert plans, and considering it a good day because none of her siblings were drowning or getting kicked out. Now, she was in an overly air-conditioned room, seeing her mother writhe in pain as a new sibling fought to enter the world. Abilene's shoulders dropped as she walked toward her mother. Ashlynn's face was dripping with sweat. Her cheeks were bright red. She contorted her face.

"Oh, thank God you're here, my sweet Abilene. It's too early. I keep telling them it's too early, but they ain't listening."

Abilene reached for her mother's hand. It was ice cold. "The doctor been in yet?"

Ashlynn shook her head no and twisted some more. "The nurses were gonna see about giving me an epidural, but needed to check that it isn't too early. I think they should try to stop the labor." Ashlynn was breathless. "I'm tired already, sweet girl. My head hurts. I think they should give me the drugs to pause everything. It's too early, right?"

"Well, not technically. So, I don't think they'll stop it."

"I'm only 36. Maybe 37, right?" Ashlynn's lip trembled. "Dammit. I know they're gonna bitch at me about not finding a doctor when we moved here. I was just a little busy working to feed all y'all, you know?"

"Yeah, well, I kept telling you to call someone and take a day off. Just because you already had five doesn't mean you don't need a doctor to check on you each month."

"Abi, I might not be too good at much and I sure ain't the smartest woman in South Carolina, but I know how to carry and birth a baby." Ashlynn tried to scoot up. "Can you go ask the nurses about the doc? I need ice chips or at least something for this headache. I feel like I'ma burst open from the skull on down."

Abilene wandered the halls until she found a nurse. She looked no older than Abilene, but promised to send someone in soon. She snagged a cup of ice chips and a spoon as her mom went from writhing in pain to rubbing her temples. Abilene had to watch the boys when Savannah was born, so she hadn't been privy to her mom bringing a child into the world. She wasn't sure she wanted to be now, but there was no one else.

After what seemed to be hours, a few more trips down the hall, and two calls to the motel to check on her sister and brothers, Abilene finally saw the doctor enter the room. She rushed in behind him as he checked her blood pressure and observed the fetal monitor. Abilene was already sick of hearing the constant beeping and wished the child would emerge where its heartbeat would be as silent as hers.

"Your blood pressure is a little high. I see we have no records from any other OBGYN? How's your pressure normally?" He asked without looking her in the eye. Ashlynn tried to scoot up and drew her knees up as far as her swollen abdomen would allow.

"I had a doctor in Texas, but no, I didn't bring any records with me. This is my sixth, so I kinda know my body. But I don't keep track of my blood pressure." She let out a deep sigh, then contorted her face as a contraction crept up again. Abilene figured they were steadily two minutes apart. "Listen, can I get an epidural or something like now?"

The doctor took his eyes off the fetal monitor print out and shuffled around to the end of the bed. He glanced over at Abilene. "I'm going to check her cervix now to see how far dilated and effaced she is to determine if she can have an epidural or not. You might want to leave or move to the side of her bed. Okay?" Abilene nodded and moved to her mother's side. Abilene grabbed her hand.

"Don't worry, Abi. This part doesn't hurt. God, please give me the epidural. I had one with my last two kids. I'm 35 now and too old and tired to do this without drugs." She squeezed Abilene's arm. "I swear, kid, this is my last one. I'm done with careless men." Ashlynn said as sweat dripped from her face. Her cheeks were bright red, yet her hands were still cold as ice. Abilene wanted to remind her she didn't end up pregnant solely because of careless men, but it seemed pointless and cruel, given the moment.

The doctor returned with the younger nurse, and Abilene cringed as she watched them lean Ashlynn up to prep her for the shot. Her mom looked relieved and more relaxed the second the needle entered her back. Within minutes, she was breathing easier and not contorting her face as much. She said she had an excruciating headache and begged for something to end it.

The day sauntered on between moments of Ashlynn looking bored to squinting her eyes and begging for the blinds closed and lights off. She told Abilene over and over she never had a migraine during birth. Ashlynn grew annoyed with nurses and doctor each time they took her blood pressure and checked her cervix. She just wanted it all over so she could sleep. The doctor kept asking Abilene if she knew anything about any prior health issues or blood pressure problems. As night fell, Abilene checked on her siblings again and got annoyed at how long the birth was taking. She kept reminding herself that even if her mom quit bitching and complaining, the baby wouldn't come quicker.

Abilene snuck away to get more ice chips and call Julien.

"Nah, she's still in labor. I'm beat from sitting in the sun all day. I feel rude, but I have to keep leaving her. She's miserable, all puffy and red. I just want it over with." She said into the phone. Julien entertained her with stories of what he heard about Charlene and a guy at the pool who was new in town. She smirked, thinking how she normally wouldn't care, but it was a pleasant distraction from her own life. Once she wandered back into the room, she saw her mom laying back in complete darkness. Only the beep of the monitor filled the quiet room.

"Mom? You okay?" she said as she shook her shoulders.

"Yeah, Abi. I think. Um, can you do me a favor?"

"Yeah, of course."

"In my purse. In the side flap of my wallet is Tucker's number. Can you call him?" Ashlynn said in a hushed voice.

"Tucker? I mean, I kinda suspected he was the dad, but wasn't sure. That loser? He hasn't done shit for Savannah. Why do you want him here for this one?" Abilene said. "Didn't you just say you were done with careless men? They don't get more careless than Tucker."

"I know, I know. Listen. I'm not saying I wanna marry the guy or anything. But he needs to know. He needs to be here, just in case."

"In case what?"

"Abilene, listen. I don't wanna scare you or anything, but this isn't going like the others. If something happens to me or this baby, Tucker needs to be here."

"Mom, stop. Nothing's gonna happen. You're doing fine. It's all gonna be fine." Abilene felt her lip tremble. She got goosebumps.

"Just do it, please. Just call him, please. Will you do that for me?" She kept squinting as she spoke. Abilene nodded and retrieved the paper from her mom's purse. It surprised her Tucker picked up on the first ring as if he had been waiting by a phone since the day they drove away from him. As soon as Abilene told him the town and hospital name, he said he's on the way and hung up. Abilene thought back to the pool and her wish that someone would show up and ease some of the responsibility of the kids. Then, picturing Tucker in whatever car he finagled from the dealership driving full speed toward them, she immediately thought, *be careful what you wish for.*

# CHAPTER 7

Abilene was both horrified and amazed at the sheer animalistic nature of the birthing process. She didn't know if she wanted to cry, puke, get her own tubes tied, or have a dozen babies of her own. The emotions rolling through her gut to her head and heart and back down to her knocking knees gave her vertigo. She held her mom's swollen and sweat-slicked hand as she bore down over and over again. Everyone in the room shouted 'push' as if the louder they yelled, the quicker the baby would slide out.

Ashlynn bore down, let out a grunt, and fell back again into the pillowy, drenched white linens. She looked up at Abilene as she forced a smile.

"I think I got one good push left in me," she muttered. Her cheeks were bright red. She seemed to fight for every breath. The feeling of wanting a dozen kids drained right out of Abilene as she saw her mother squint. "This damn headache needs to go."

"It will, momma. It will," Abilene said as she squeezed her mom's hand. "Come on, let's get this one out so you can relax, get some sleep." Last Abilene checked, it was just after 3 a.m.

With one more push and one final collapse into the bed, Abilene gave birth to a girl. The squirming, pinkish, wrinkled baby let out a yell that rivaled Ashlynn's hours earlier before the epidural kicked in. Just as a nurse swaddled the baby and Ashlynn wiped her own forehead, a tanned man in a mesh tank top and dirty jeans bolted through the doors. Tucker had arrived.

"Baby girl, why didn't you call me sooner?" He said as he rushed to Ashlynn's side. He leaned down to kiss her forehead just as the nurses placed the baby in Ashlynn's arms. They both stared at the new life and cried. Tucker covered both in kisses. Abilene realized she was rolling her eyes when her mother shot her a look.

"Come here, Abi, meet your sister." Ashlynn said. Abilene slouched and made her way to the other side of the bed. Ashlynn pulled the blanket down enough for Abilene to make out the baby's features. She looked exactly like Savannah. There was now no question she was Tucker's, too. They all three had the same skin tone, olive, tanned without trying, and springy brown hair that looked as smooth and fine as silk. Her big brown eyes searched until they landed on Ashlynn. For a moment, Abilene forgot Tucker hadn't been there all along, that he only showed up at the end and wasn't still part of their daily life, their family unit. She looked at the couple holding this brand new being and forgot they weren't always happy and content. Then she remembered Savannah and the last three years of taking care of her alone. If Tucker could connect, love, and pour so much of himself into Ashlynn and his baby in an instant, how could he just leave afterward? Abilene tried to remember how long he had stuck around after Savannah was born. Three weeks? Three months? It was a blur. Tucker reached down for Ashlynn's chin and pulled her mouth up to his as she held the swaddled baby close. He kissed her. Abilene could see her mother melt under his attention and affection. *So much for swearing off careless men,* Abilene thought.

As the three of them bonded, Abilene wandered to the pay phone down the hall. She fished for quarters and let Mr. Gurka and Julien know the baby arrived, a healthy girl, and she'd be back at the motel soon to get the kids for the day. A motel maid, Evie, stayed at the house with them so they could sleep in their own beds. Abilene felt a twinge of jealously that another young woman managed the brood and got them to sleep. She realized she was replaceable in every way.

Abilene made her way back down the hall and realized she hadn't showered or eaten since yesterday. The sun was coming up through the giant picture windows at the end of the hall. Despite the beautiful view, she felt grimy. Tucker dashed from the door and headed toward her.

"Hey kid, so glad you called last night. Boy, that baby is a looker, huh?" He said as he stood a little taller. He still looked as slimy and dirty as she remembered.

"Yeah, just like the last one. Savannah. Remember her?" Abilene said as her eyes strayed from his.

"Yeah, I remember her, smart ass. You always was a little smart ass." He snapped. He bobbed his head to force Abilene to look at his face. She cringed and just wanted him to disappear again. "Listen, it's complicated with me and your mom. Adult stuff you don't understand. And I don't care what she said, it ain't all my fault either. She can be a pistol, and she didn't want me around all the time." He looked around as he noticed his voice rising. "She left me. You got that? She packed you kids up and left in the middle of the night." He drew in a deep breath and looked up at the ceiling. "And you know what else, you little bitch? At least I'm here. Where's your dad been all this time? I've known your mom, what, 5 years, and I never met the sonofabitch once." Abilene darted her eyes away and fought back tears. She was determined not to cry in front of Tucker.

"My dad is a soldier, a damn good one, and that's why he isn't around. Probably won the war all on his own." She said in a low voice as she swallowed a lump. She hadn't realized it had been over 5 years until a moment ago. Tucker stepped closer to her. She could smell the cigarettes he chained smoked on the drive. The thick heat of his breath invaded her face. She swallowed again and closed her eyes.

"Yeah well, I bet he'd be real surprised to see how grown up you're gettin," Tucker lowered his eyes and bit his bottom lip. "You ain't a kid no more, Abilene. Are you?" He said in a whisper. The hair on the back of her neck stood straight up. She felt as if someone knocked the wind out of her. Her tongue went dry and stuck to the roof of her mouth. She felt Tucker place his dirty hand on her hip and slowly slide it up and over to her belly button. She shuddered. "What's wrong? You got nothing to say now, do ya?" He said as he leaned closer to her. He took his index finger and slid it inside the seam of her shorts, and pulled her a little closer. His breath stunk so badly she held hers. He encircled her belly button just above the waistband of her jean shorts. She felt goosebumps rise everywhere. Her stomach flipped. She thought she would puke in a matter of seconds. "I'm your daddy now." A smile crept across his face as he gave her a slight push backwards. "I'm getting breakfast. You want anything?" He said, as if the last twenty seconds hadn't happened. Abilene shook her head no. It was the only movement she could manage. He stepped past her, and Abilene exhaled.

Abilene was dizzy, scared, nauseated, and felt as dirty as Tucker was. His yellowed, crooked teeth had practically bitten her ear lobe when he leaned into her. She could almost feel him still in front of her. Her legs were heavy. Memories of feeling Tucker's eyes on her as she walked from the bathroom to her bedroom in a towel in their old trailer flooded her mind. The way he was watching her as she watched tv on the floor. The way he chewed a toothpick and swirled it around his tongue while grinning at her when he sat across from her at the table when she did homework. Abilene held her belly as the idea of Tucker coming home with them made her panic inside. She felt numb all over, yet the urge to run out of the hospital raced through her veins. Abilene took a deep breath and swore to herself that if Tucker ever touched her or let his steamy rancid breath fall on her again, she'd kick him in the balls no matter where they were. She glanced around, hoping a nurse, or anyone, had seen. But she was all alone, just doors from her mother's room. Abilene stepped forward and the idea of telling her mom, or never speaking a word of it, bounced from side to side in her head like a ping-pong ball. As she stood in the doorway and saw her mother cradle her newest sibling, words wouldn't come up from her gut. Ashlynn looked up at her and smiled. Abilene knew she wouldn't tell her at that moment, or any moment soon.

"Hey, come hold her. I gotta get some water. Tuck is getting me some food. Did ya check on everyone?" Ashlynn slid the baby into Abilene's waiting arms. Abilene took a deep breath and forced a smile for her mother.

"Yeah. Everyone is fine. I'll go home and shower, sleep a little hopefully, and make sure everyone gets fed. Unless you need me here?" Abilene prayed she said no. She needed as far from Tucker as she had been yesterday.

"I need to sleep too. My head is still killing me. The doc will be back in a few. They said my blood pressure is still too high for their liking."

"You sure everything is okay, though?"

"Yeah, baby. I'll be fine. Better with Tuck's help." His name made Abilene want to vomit. "Here, you can give her back." Ashlynn reached out for the baby. She drew her in close. The baby let out a tiny grunt. "It's alright, Paris." Ashlynn said in a hushed voice as she adjusted herself in the bed to breastfeed.

"What?" Abilene asked.

"Paris. I'm a name her Paris."

"What? Is there a Paris, Louisiana you guys stopped at or something when you made this one? A Paris bar or something at Mardis Gras? Where are you getting Paris from?" Abilene shook her head in disbelief.

"No, Paris, France. I always wanted to go. Maybe we all will someday. We'll sit on the grass near the Eiffel Tower on a blanket, drink French wine, eat French chocolate. Tucker says—"

"Bullshit. Tucker is filled with bullshit. This is all bullshit!" Abilene shouted. She felt her cheeks grow red and her temples throbbed as she approached the bed. "You named us all after where we came from, where we were conceived. You said... you said our namesake was so we'd have a place to call home, a place to be connected to." Abilene shook her head as her heart pounded inside her chest wall. "You ain't never been to no goddamn Paris, France! Paris? What the fuck is this bullshit? Paris?" Abilene realized her voice was booming across the room and probably down the hall.

"You watch your mouth, Abilene. You have no right to shout at me like that! My god, where's the doctor? My head is going to split open." Ashlynn rubbed her temples.

"No right to shout? Was I born in Abilene? Was Savannah conceived in Savannah? Dallas, Jackson, Austin? Any of them? Or are you just completely full of shit? Huh? Are you?" Abilene's voice rose again. Tears bubbled up and exploded from her face. "Is anything you told me true? You're gonna sit there in a hospital bed in Holden fucking South Carolina and name this baby Paris like nothing? Are you fucking stupid or crazy?" Abilene's voice cracked. "God, I really hate you sometimes. I hope I never end up like you!"

"Abilene Marigold Matterly! You shut your damn mouth right now! You have no right to talk to me like that. You have no right to judge me. Do you understand me? You have no right to judge me." Ashlynn squinted. She drew in a deep breath and looked up at the ceiling. Abilene felt a presence behind her and prayed it wasn't Tucker.

"Excuse me, young lady. I need to check your mom's blood pressure again." The doctor said as Abilene stepped aside. Beeping filled the room. She tried to settle the anger in her gut for a moment. Her mind raced as she tried to remember every zip code, every weekend getaway Ashlynn went on, every man and his story, every moment that led to this one as she stood there realizing her mother was a liar, or a fool. "Ashlynn, how you feeling? Is everything ok in here, ladies?" The doctor said as he made his way to her bed. Ashlynn's head bobbed a little as she looked up.

"Mom? Sit up. The doctor is here." Abilene stepped closer as Ashlynn steadied her gaze and looked at her. "Mom?" she said again. Ashlynn's mouth fell to the side. Sounds came out, but no words. The baby slid from her arm to her side.

"Abi. I'm thar." Drool slipped out, and both arms went limp. The doctor grabbed the baby and reached over Ashlynn's head to hit the red alarm. Before Abilene could reach for her mom's hand, a rush of nurses descended into the room and nudged Abilene out of the way. An alarm pierced through the air and hurt Abilene's ears.

"Mom!" Abilene screamed over the nurses' heads. One grabbed her arm and pulled her away with the force of ten men.

"Honey, wait outside." She said in a calm tone that seemed illogical for the situation. Abilene's head swirled, and she saw spots.

"What's happening?" she muttered as she tried to peer back into the room.

"I'm not sure, honey. I think her blood pressure was getting too high. They'll give her some meds and she should be fine. But you gotta wait out here. Okay?" The nurse kept nodding as if Abilene was supposed to imitate her. Abilene kept blinking. Her ears rang. Tucker sauntered down the hall holding a bag from the cafeteria. His face changed the moment he realized the alarms and excess activity was for Ashlynn's room. He stopped a foot from Abilene and grabbed her arm.

"The baby? Something wrong with the baby?" He shook his head as Abilene shook hers.

"No. The baby is okay. It's mom. She went... I don't know... she just went kinda blank. Her mouth wouldn't work right."

"What do you mean? What happened? Girl, look at me," he said. The panic in his voice was as palpable as the creepiness had been just minutes earlier. Abilene looked him dead in the eye.

"I don't know. They pushed me out of the room." She couldn't muster up the energy to say anything else. Abilene felt as if she had been unplugged. She glanced around for a seat and lowered herself. She wrung her sweaty hands as her knees and legs shook uncontrollably. Tucker sat next to her. He didn't say another word or try to console her. They both stared straight ahead. Abilene tried to remember every detail since last night. She tried to piece together what went wrong and when it went wrong. Abilene replayed their last few minutes over in her head. *My god, I think I told her I hated her.* She thought. Abilene closed her eyes. She heard her own voice calling her mom stupid, crazy, and full of shit. The last thing she said to her was that she never wanted to be anything like her. Tears rolled down her cheeks. Tucker took her hand. She didn't want to kick him in the balls. She wanted the comfort in that moment, anywhere she could get it.

After what seemed like hours, the doctor reemerged from the room. A nurse behind him held the baby. The noise from paddles, the rush of IVs being dragged in and out, and beeps had faded. His face was sweaty and deeply creased, pained. The nurse stepped forward and handed Paris to Tucker. He took her. His confused look morphed into tears and shoulders shaking violently.

"We did all we could. It looks like she had a stroke. A blood clot broke loose and the high blood pressure, well, that unfortunately can happen to some women after birth, women over 35 with blood pressure problems. It was preeclampsia that went undiagnosed since she wasn't seeing a doctor regularly." The doctor said slowly and deliberately. Abilene was still stuck on 'we did all we could.'

"Wait, what? She's gone? Blood pressure? What the fuck happened?" Tucker said as spit bubbles mixed with tears. "Pre what?"

"Preeclampsia. It's treatable if we had known about it, but it was just too late. The birth, the building high blood pressure, it all injured her brain. It can lead to stroke. Rarely. But in this case, it did." A long silence filled the hall, except for whimpering from Tucker. He rocked back and forth, squeezing the baby against his chest. He slobbered and slurped saliva as the baby squirmed. Abilene stared straight ahead, dumbfounded. She wrung her hands until they were dry again. She stood and almost fell right over. The dizziness and ringing in her ears made her wince.

"Sit, young lady. Get her some water." The doctor said to the nurse who had held Paris. "Can I call anyone?" He asked. Abilene looked around, unable to think of another adult in the world besides Ashlynn and Tucker. There was no one else. There was nowhere else besides that white, cold, echoing hall with a room at the end, a room where her mother was dead in the bed. Abilene stood again and shuffled to the doorway of the room. The ringing grew so loud she could no longer hear Tucker's cries and snorts. She felt a nurse's hand on her shoulder, light but there. Abilene looked at her mother splayed out on the bed. They draped a sheet over most of her body. Her face turned toward the door and arm stretched out to the edge of the bed with her hand open. Her hair laid out around her head like a halo, as if someone had gently placed her straight from the clouds. The nurse quickly went around Abilene to draw the sheet up to Ashlynn's neck and tuck her arm under as another nurse turned off equipment and picked up blankets from the floor. Despite the activity she saw out of the corner of her eye, the white streaks of nurses trying to repair the scene, cover up the chaos that had unfolded, all was quiet in Abilene's mind. She walked over and touched her mom's hand. It was already cold. How long had she been waiting in that hall? She wondered. Ashlynn's lips were purple and parted slightly. Her face was pale. Abilene could see the side of her mother's mouth turned down while the other wasn't, just as it had done when she tried to say something to Abilene, when her words weren't words. Abilene noticed a dried line of drool and one line from a tear that didn't make it past her mother's cheek. Time had stopped. Hours earlier, Abilene had been sick of hearing a heartbeat over the monitor. Now nothing filled the air. Abilene was hollow, gutted, sickened by the silence. Ashlynn Swenson, mom of six, was gone.

# CHAPTER 8

Abilene thought she might drown in the tears that ran down her face and dripped from her chin. The flurry of nurses and the social worker with a clipboard at her side faded into background noise. Abilene could see their lips moving, but couldn't process the words. She was sitting in a small, private waiting room all alone. They had escorted Tucker to a desk where he balanced a pen, a stack of papers, and the baby. The nurses and social worker kept tilting their heads and smiling at her through pursed lips. The "I'm so sorry for your loss" and "Everything's going to be okay" mantras finally pierced through the ringing in her ears. Abilene wanted to tell them to stop smiling at her.

"Your step-dad will be in here in a minute, okay?" the social worker said as she sat next to Abilene.

"He's not my step-dad." Abilene said without unclenching her jaw. She crossed her arms. She was colder than she had been since she made it to the hospital the afternoon before. Abilene glanced around for a clock. She didn't know what time it was. She hadn't eaten since she was at the pool, and Julien bought her an ice cream sandwich.

"Can I call my friend, please?"

"Sure, you can. But you might want to wait for your step-dad first."

"I said he's not my step-dad!" she yelled as loudly as she had yelled at Ashlynn right before she died. Abilene instantly regretted it as she noticed the social worker recoil and clutch the clip board.

"Sorry. Listen, I'm here to help you guys tell your siblings once you're ready and make sure your da—step-dad or whoever is prepared to take the baby himself." Abilene shook her head slightly. She didn't have the energy to explain that Tucker was a piece of shit who ran out on her mom twice. She suddenly realized she needed to tell her brothers and Savannah their mother was gone.

Once Tucker entered the room, the nurse and social worker turned their attention on him. Abilene couldn't focus on all their words and questions. She caught enough to know they were asking about all the kids.

"Yeah, this one and the next youngest are mine." He said. The social worker jotted notes.

"And the others? Abilene, right?" Abilene glanced up when she heard her name and nodded.

"My dad's in the Army. My brothers, Austin and Jackson, have a dad named Butch. His number is at our house. Butchy is a good guy. He'll want to know."

"And another, right?" the social worker asked as she glanced at the clipboard again. Abilene wondered if she had their entire twisted family tree scrawled on that board.

"Yeah, my brother Dallas is ten. He doesn't have a dad. At least no one who wants the job." Abilene suddenly pictured the wild animal that was Dallas standing alone in a field, in a storm, with no one to shelter or love him.

"Um, Mr. Tuckerson, would you consider taking temporary custody of," she glanced down at the clipboard.

"Dallas. His name is Dallas," Abilene snapped.

"Yes, um Dallas?" She cleared her throat. She looked as young as the nurse, and Abilene could tell she wasn't a mom.

Tucker let out a deep sigh and looked down at the baby. "Well, I'm not sure I can handle two little girls and a ten-year-old on top of that." He said. Abilene rolled her eyes.

"Mom was going to name her Paris, by the way."

"Oh. Okay. I think I like that." He used his index finger to brush a few wild strands of black hair from the baby's forehead, the same finger he used to paralyze Abilene hours earlier.

The adults laid out plans, appointments, expedited court hearing information, and support resources, all while Abilene sat there wondering why no one was saying Ashlynn's name.

Abilene wasn't sure how many hours passed or how she got to her house. She wasn't sure who told the boys and Savannah that their mom wouldn't be coming home. She wasn't sure why the social worker was in the house, still clutching the clipboard. Time wasn't registering. Tucker was in the kitchen making sandwiches as the boys cried silently, except for Dallas. He was in the backyard with a large stick beating the side of a tree. Savannah snuggled up in Abilene's lap like she always did. Tucker dished out hastily made peanut butter and jelly, then cradled the phone against his ear. Abilene heard him say Butch's name a few times. The world was reconfiguring around her. Just the day before, she had been in that living room getting towels, snacks, and making sure the boys actually put their swim trunks on. She was trying to have everyone and everything organized before Julien got there to go to the pool. She was worried about thawing meat for a meatloaf, making sure the dishes from breakfast were finished, and mindlessly tossing random toys into the giant toy basket next to the thrift store couch. Now, less than 24 hours later, she was watching as others made decisions, made lunch, made phone calls, and bustled from room to room looking for paperwork and phone numbers. She had been the head of that house most hours of the day while Ashlynn managed the motel a few feet away. Now, she was just one of the kids left to be handled by others.

She sat silently as Mr. Gurka circulated throughout the house asking Tucker and the social worker what all happened and what would happen next. The baby would stay at the hospital until they released her to Tucker the next day. He assured Mr. Gurka and the social worker he'd take the girls to Slidell and then to New Orleans with his mom. She'd be great at helping him raise them. Butch was traveling from Texas to get his boys. Abilene sat frozen as Mr. Gurka seemed to realize no one was coming for Dallas. He went out the back door. Abilene saw him place his large hand on Dallas's shoulder. Dallas brushed it off and took another swing at the tree.

"And you, Abilene? Mr. Tuckerson says your dad paid support and there's paperwork somewhere with his contact information. I can call him if you'd like, unless you know his number?"

"Abi, you can come with us. You can help me with the girls. I mean, if you'd like." Tucker said from the doorway to the kitchen. He crossed his arms and shrugged his shoulders as if he was suggesting what movie they watch, not whether she wanted him to take custody of her. The social worker nodded in blind agreement. Abilene cringed and thought she'd throw up as she remembered Tucker's hand on her. She shook her head no.

"I'll go through the closet where my mom kept other stuff and find my dad's number," she said to no one in particular.

"Suit yourself," Tucker said with another shrug.

Abilene slid Savannah off her lap and nudged Jackson to take her. He put his arm around his sister and wiped away more tears. Abilene wanted to comfort him, Austin, and Dallas, but she felt too numb herself. As she made her way down the narrow hallway to her mother's room, she stopped to take in a deep breath. Her mother's bed was unmade. Her socks were on the floor and a half-full water glass was on the nightstand. Abilene suddenly realized the calls, the plans, all meant they would divvy up her and her siblings between all the men Ashlynn had left behind, or who left her behind.

She remembered wishing for no more diapers to change or lunches to make, no more cleaning up wreckage left behind by Dallas, or no more mediating fights between Austin and Jackson. She had wished for silence and peace, alone time, or at the very least to be cared for like Charlene and other girls her age instead of being the care-giver. As she stood in the silence of her mother's room and with no control over who would end up where, she wanted it all back. The noise, the mess, the diapers, the exhausted mom who sprawled out on the couch and rubbed her pregnant belly as Abilene cleaned up dinner. There was a stabbing pain in her chest, as if her heart had realized everything had changed in an instant. She never pictured a day not living with Ashlynn and her siblings. Abilene couldn't wrap her mind around the idea that this wasn't some weird alternate reality or nightmare and she'd wake up hungover from peach schnapps with Julien the night before. She drew in a deep breath and went to the closet.

Abilene removed a small plastic tote and a file box from the top. She wasn't sure exactly what she was looking for. She didn't want to call her father or have a stranger call him and say, 'guess what? Your kid needs a new home!' She didn't want to ask and risk hearing him saying he can't take her in. She wasn't even sure what it would mean if he did. For all she knew, he was deployed somewhere. Then what? Go live with the step-mom she met twice? Go with Tucker? Change more diapers? God knows he wouldn't know how to handle a new baby. He knew nothing about Savannah's routine, her needs, her fears, her favorite blanket, or how she liked to pretend she was reading if you handed her paper. Should she to just go with Dallas wherever they placed kids that didn't have a dad? Or go with Butchy? Maybe convince Butchy to take them all. He was okay. He at least knew how to be a dad. She didn't remember anything horrifying about him.

Abilene opened the plastic tote. It was filled with pictures from the last few years. Then she saw bank papers and insurance paperwork. It listed Sgt. Matterly's address and phone number. The date was from a year ago. He signed up for automatic child support payments. It was strange to see his and her mom's signatures on the same paper. Abilene had never seen something that combined the two of them, other than herself. She traced her fingers over his address. Fort Patten, Georgia. He wasn't far. She faintly remembered her mom telling someone awhile back that Abilene's dad was getting stationed down south again. He had been up north somewhere for a few years and stationed in Hawaii the last time she visited him when she was ten. Abilene folded the paper and put it in her shorts pocket. She felt a rush of relief mixed with fear. At least she had means of contacting him or a number to give the social worker if she lost her nerve. Abilene felt a lump in her throat and tears well up with the thought of her or anyone telling him Ashlynn was dead. She knew her father had moved on, married and was living a normal life without them, but at one time he loved her mom, or so she always said. He rescued her from the stifling life of high society and wealth. He whisked her away from the confines of a family that demanded she be perfect. Sgt. Matterly carried Ashlynn Swenson away, and neither of them looked back.

Abilene stopped looking at the stack of papers when another option roared to the forefront of her mind. The Swenson family. Maybe she could take her shot at going to Abilene, Texas, and letting her mom's family know. Surely, they'd open the door, let Abilene collapse and sob in their arms. They'd probably want all the kids. With their money, power, and connections, the Swenson family could easily get custody from Tucker at least. Abilene even thought he'd probably be thankful for the out. They could take Dallas, too. Abilene opened the file box. She knew her mom carried it from home to home. It was the oldest thing she had. Paperwork lay on top. There were report cards from elementary school, a blue ribbon from a fair, a certificate from a science fair. Abilene smiled. She couldn't picture her mom entering a science fair. There was a hotel receipt from some town in Oklahoma Abilene had never heard of. It was dated June 1975 and signed by Thomas Matterly. Abilene thought about the math. It would've been around the time they married. Maybe the very week, as far as she knew. Abilene relaxed her shoulders and held the paper to her chest for a minute. For a moment in time, Thomas Matterly had checked into a hotel with Ashlynn and they were in love. Her mom had kept it all these years. Abilene put the paper on the stack of report cards and dug further.

Abilene pulled a stack of postcards out. She unleashed them from a rubber band. One was a grand staircase with dark wood banisters curved out toward a large oriental rug. Another was a giant, shiny black grand piano in front of paisley curtains framing a massive window. Another was of a white gazebo with a pond in the background. The flowers were so bright and perfect; they looked fake. Abilene felt her pulse quicken. Another was a picture of a mansion with a clay tile roof and large balcony jutting out from the top floor. Abilene knew the pictures were familiar looking. Had she visited this place? She flipped over the last postcard. A paragraph in small, faded print flanked one side. SWENSON HOUSE: Built in 1910 by William Gray Swenson, a well-connected Abilene, Texas businessman. Abilene's eyes blurred. Why were there postcards of her mother's childhood home like it was some tourist destination? She flipped over the rest. Written in cursive in faded pencil,

*August, 8th 1965*
*Dear Ashlynn,*
*Hope you are behaving for your grandmother. Dad and I are loving this trip across Texas! This is a mansion we toured. It's gorgeous. The flowers smell like heaven. See you in a few days.*
*Love Mom and Dad.*

Abilene flipped over the others and read them over and over again.

*August 10th, 1965*
*Ashlynn,*
*You wouldn't believe the size of this fireplace! Hope you're being good. We miss you!*
*Love Mom and Dad.*

Abilene quickly pulled out the other papers and flipped through them. Nothing made sense. She found a newspaper clipping. An accident just outside of Abilene, Texas. Two killed. August 15th, 1965. A couple traveling for business from Lawton, Oklahoma. Ruthanne and Jebediah Norwell, 30 and 32 years old. Mr. Norwell was a traveling salesman whose wife accompanied him on trips during the summer. Their car collided with a cattle truck on a dark back road during a rainstorm. They died on impact, leaving behind Ruthann's parents and the couple's only child, a daughter, Ashlynn Norwell, age 10. Abilene felt her chest tighten. She reread the postcards and dates again.

*August 12th, 1965*
*Ashlynn,*
*This is a picture of the dining room at Swenson House. Look at that wallpaper and chandelier! It's the most beautiful house on earth. We'll bring*

*you to see it next summer. We head to Dallas, then back home in a few days. We miss you so much. Be good for your grandmother!*

*Love forever, Mom and Dad XOXO*

Abilene was dizzy. Her hands shook, and she struggled to breathe as if something had sucked away all the air in the room. Her stomach churned and her mouth watered. She put her hand over her mouth and jumped from the bed to the hall and into the bathroom without a second to spare. Tears automatically escaped her eyes as she wretched. With nothing in her stomach to begin with, the heaving hurt worse than ever. She felt as if her very soul was lurching from her stomach, up her esophagus, and out of her mouth. She rested her head on the seat of the toilet and used the back of her hand to wipe her mouth. The social worker ran in.

"Dear God, honey. It's okay." She rubbed Abilene's back and pulled her hair back from her shoulders. "I know. I know. This is all a lot. But you're gonna be okay." Abilene heaved once again. Nothing more came out. Her throat hurt. Her teeth chattered. The social worker draped a fresh towel around her shoulders. She ran water over a washcloth in the sink. She gingerly placed it on Abilene's forehead. Abilene thanked her. Tucker appeared in the doorway.

"Jesus Christ. You okay, kid?" He asked. Abilene nodded. She had nearly forgotten they and her siblings were in the house. She heard the boys in the living room arguing over something and Savannah crying. The ringing in her ears got louder. She pressed the cloth against her forehead harder.

"I'm alright. I'll be okay." She muttered, even though she didn't believe it. "I just gotta, gotta get back in my mom's room."

"You find your father's number or anything helpful, honey?"

"Yeah. I got it. I'll be okay. Just let me go." Abilene fought tears as her lip trembled. She slowly stood and held onto the wall as she made her way past the social worker and Tucker. Abilene closed her mother's door behind her. She stared at the papers sprawled on the bed. The postcards of Swenson House sent to Ashlynn mere days before her parents died, the childhood papers and certificates from a school in Oklahoma. The name Ashlynn Norwell on everything. The name of a stranger. Nothing had been true about Ashlynn's childhood. Swenson House was a stop along the way, not a childhood home, not a legacy or heritage. A stop along the way for a weary couple trying to get home to Oklahoma to see their kid. Abilene stared at the dates on the postcards. Ashlynn was only ten years old when she lost her parents. She must've gotten the postcards in the mail after they died, after they were buried. Abilene felt like a kite that had suddenly become untethered from the string. There was no anchor to Swenson House, or even Abilene, Texas probably, just as there was no connection to Paris for a brand new baby who'd never know her mother. Abilene suddenly remembered her last words to her mother as she held her sixth child. She was a liar, a fucking liar. Abilene didn't want to end up like her. She hated her. Abilene glanced around. Nothing felt familiar anymore. There was no home to stay in or home to run to. There was nothing but a bed covered in papers that outlined the grand lie that was Ashlynn, who was nothing but a sad, broken orphan, pretending she was anything but.

Abilene swooped the stack of papers and postcards into one pile and ran with them to her room. She pulled her duffle bag out from under the bed and shoved the papers at the bottom. She opened her dresser and grabbed handfuls of clothes, underwear, socks, t-shirts, shorts, a few pairs of jeans. Abilene opened the closet and grabbed her jean jacket and the flannels Julien gave her. The hangers flipped and clanked as they hit the floor, knocking down some of Savannah's clothes too. Abilene grabbed her red cowboy boots from the corner and slipped them on. She checked her pocket for the paper with her dad's info. Abilene slung her messenger bag over her shoulder and then the duffle bag over both, so it hung on her back. She paused at the bedroom door. The social worker and Tucker wouldn't let her leave like this. The boys would beg for answers. She couldn't begin to picture Savannah's sad little face watching her leave. Abilene took a deep breath. She let the bags slide off her back and shoulder, then climbed across her bed to the window and flung it open. Abilene shoved out her duffle bag and messenger bag. She glanced back at the room, all pink and childish because she had to share it with her sister. She swallowed a lump, turned, and climbed out after her stuff. Abilene landed on the half-dead grass, threw her bags back over her shoulder, swooped her hair up in a scrunchie she had on her wrist, and ran down the road toward Julien's. She realized half-way there she was still crying. Abilene wasn't sure if she was crying over losing her mom, or losing her siblings and home, for her mother losing everything so young, or because she lost what her life had been until she opened that box. She didn't know who or what was true, where she was going, or even where she was from.

# CHAPTER 9

Once Abilene reached the tree next to Julien's driveway, she drew in the first deep breath of fresh air she had taken since she left the hospital. She slid her bags off her shoulder and back. Her shoulder ached. Abilene bent over and put her hands on her knees. Despite how much her mouth watered, nothing came up when she heaved again. She knew there was nothing left inside her. She was empty in every way. Abilene felt sweat and tears pouring from her body. Snot dripped from her nose onto the driveway. She swore every ounce of liquid in her body was forming a puddle that would rise and drown her.

"Abilene!" Julien said, as she looked up at the house. His arms were around her before she could even stand up straight. She wailed into his shoulder as he squeezed her tight into his chest. She wiped her face on his shirt.

"I heard about your mom. My God, what happened?" he said. "I was just leaving to run to your house and see if you were there." He said into her ear as he rocked her back and forth. She shook with each breath as she let out sounds she didn't recognize.

"I told her I hated her. I called her a fucking liar." Abilene said in a voice so low she wasn't sure she said it out loud. "I said I hated her. That was it. The last thing I said to her."

"It's ok. She knew you loved her. She knew."

Julien rubbed her shoulders and held her back so he could see her face. The second her eyes met his, she swallowed and drew in a few deep breaths.

She forced air into and out of her lungs slowly as she willed her heart to stop beating so hard. She wondered if that was how her mom felt as her blood pressure spiked. Did her heart feel like it would explode, too? The world stopped spinning for a second. Her stomach settled. She could see again. There weren't a million red spots and a sea of tears clouding her view or a million regrets fighting for space in her mind. She bowed her head and looked at the ground. She had forgotten it was even there.

"Let's get you back home." Julien said.

"No, I'm not going back home," she said. She glanced at her duffle bag. "I'm leaving."

"What do you mean? Where you gonna go? What about your brothers? Savannah? The baby?"

"That's the thing, Julien. We're all getting split up, no matter what I do. Austin and Jackson's dad is coming for them, like now." She swallowed and drew in another breath as reality set in. "Tucker is at the house. He's gonna take his girls. Dallas is... I dunno... gonna end up in state custody unless Butchy takes him with the others. And me, I'm going to find my dad. God, Paris will never even know her."

"Paris? Wait, wh—"

"She wasn't. She was never in goddamn Paris, just like she was never in Abilene either. It was all bullshit. That's why I called her a fucking liar." Abilene closed her eyes as she heard her voice screaming at her mother again. The words echoed and bounced around her mind over and over. She squinted and wanted to rewind time just as they would rewind songs in the minivan on hot nights, with stomachs filled with hot chicken and slushies mixed with whatever Julien could steal from his house. "Damn it, Julien. I can't believe she's really gone. I gotta get to my dad."

"Did you call him or anything? Is he coming for you? Maybe stay here? I don't want you to leave." He burrowed his head into her shoulder, just as she had done to him moments earlier. "Abilene, you're all I've got." His voice cracked. Abilene felt as if her heart would break in two.

"I got his info from her papers. I got his address right now. Last year, he was in Georgia. Fort Patten. I need to check out a map and see how far that is from here." Abilene said as she peeled herself from his grip. She wiped away fresh tears. Abilene broke her gaze from his when she saw the van. "Can you drive me to Fort Patten?"

Julien slid his hands into his pockets and shook his head.

"Just come in and call him. He'll come get you."

"No, I got my stuff and I'm ready to go right now. I'm not going back to that house with Tucker and waiting. I ain't listening to that social worker tell me how I should feel, tell me to say goodbye to the others, or try to talk me into staying with my brothers or take care of Savannah, or whatever. I can't look at that baby. I'm not going back. Not tonight. Not ever. I'm going to Fort Patten tonight, right now, one way or another." She stood straight and pulled her hair out of the ponytail.

"Okay. Let me get the keys. Stay here." He dashed from in front of her and into the house. She shook as she stood alone in the street. Before Abilene had time to panic or give much thought to what the social worker or Tucker would do once they realized she was gone, she was in the passenger side and Julien was driving full speed out of town. She knew he'd be in a ton of trouble once his parents realized he was gone, and she would be too, even though she wasn't sure who'd she be in trouble with. None of that mattered for the moment. She let her shoulders relax and settled her breathing as she stared straight ahead.

"How am I ever going to repay you?"

"You don't have to repay me. That's the cool part about having a best friend. Hell, we'll make an adventure out of it, Outsiders style. Maybe we'll see a burning orphanage along the way."

For the first time since her mother died, she snickered a little. She felt like her old self for just a few seconds.

"Now, pull that atlas out of the glove box and look up where we're going before it gets too dark, will ya? I got a few bucks in my wallet to grab some snacks when we get gas too." he said while glancing at her then the road again. Abilene knew what he was risking by stealing the van and taking her himself. She knew if she looked over at him, she'd cry. She flipped through the map and found their destination just as the last rays of light disappeared beside them. They veered onto the ramp for Route 20 toward Georgia. Julien gunned it as Abilene reached over to squeeze his hand.

The last few hours kept bubbling to the surface as they drove. She'd let the tears start up again, wipe them away, listen to Julien's reassurances that she'd, they'd be fine, then enjoy a quiet mind for a few minutes only to have the cycle start again. The sight of her mom's face in the hospital bed flashed before her eyes almost as if on a loop on tv. She shook her head to make it disappear. A few times, she'd let it linger in front of her as if she deserved to see that image forever. Then, she'd picture Ashlynn Norwell as a ten-year-old girl standing beside her grandparents on a porch in Oklahoma as a mailman slid postcards into the box. Abilene wondered if they came all at once or day by day, like some odd, beautiful torture seeing her mother's handwriting and well-wishes, promises to return spelled out before her little hands and eyes. Did Ashlynn cry as they handed each one to her, or did she feel relief, as if the cards were messages from beyond, messages of love and comfort? Did she sleep with them under her pillow each night, reread them to herself, her dolls? Did she pin them up on a board with tacks and picture her mom and dad touring Swenson Mansion? Abilene closed her eyes and saw her mom tracing the staircase in the picture, the dining room table, her tiny fingers making the pattern in the wallpaper, the outline of the lily pond and balcony from the second story. Maybe her mom reread them every night, or did she hide them away and try to forget her parents died days after visiting that grand home? Maybe it wasn't her mom's fault she told an entirely false narrative of her childhood and family. What if she stared at those postcards and her mother's handwriting so hard, so often, they become burned into her memory? Abilene took a few quick breaths and stifled the urge to jump from the passenger and run back to the hospital where her mother last breathed. What if, Abilene realized, Ashlynn came to believe that was her home, the place her parents sat each night having dinner, tea on the balcony, wine in the gazebo awaiting the return of their stubborn rebel of a daughter?

"Hey, you're gonna be okay. Okay?" Julien said as he reached for her hand again. Abilene nodded. Stars poked through the sky as it went from dark purple to black. Everything in sight was fading. She wanted to fade away, too. The sight of ten-year-old Ashlynn wouldn't fade, though. Every time she closed her eyes, it kept roaring back. Drizzle landed on the windshield and got heavier with every second. The sound of the minivan wipers did little to drown out the memory of her own cruel screams at her mother hours earlier. She leaned over the console to be closer to Julien.

"It's been five years, right? Since you saw him?" He said.

"Yeah." Abilene said. "What if he doesn't let me in?"

"He will. But if he doesn't, we keep going."

"You'd do that for me?"

"You know it."

She squeezed her eyes shut and tilted her head back. "I don't deserve you," she sniffed, and wiped her nose on her sleeve. "I was awful to her. I called her a fucking liar and told her I hated her. How could I do that? Please, please Julien, don't ever tell a soul those were my last words to her. Ever. Promise? She was holding a new baby, and I just lost it. I lost it over stupid lies she told because the truth... the truth about her, was too shitty."

"Maybe everyone's truth is too shitty. And you know you don't have to ask. I'll never tell anyone. Me and you, we know each other like no one else does, and I'd never let anyone know anything that could hurt you." He glanced at her. "Hey, your mom knew you loved her. Focus on that, not the last few minutes you had with her."

"How'd you get so wise?"

"MTV The Real World." He said. Abilene snorted, and he bent forward, hugging the steering wheel and laughing with her.

"Asshole," Abilene said as she shook her head.

Abilene smiled at him, and his bright toothy smile back gave her the biggest sense of relief, like a slushy hitting her stomach on the hottest summer night. She knew without him, she wouldn't have made it this far. If she didn't have Julien to run to, Abilene wasn't sure she could have survived the hours after her mom's death. Abilene swore to never forget what Julien was risking for her, for her future. She wondered if this was maybe what love was supposed to be, not a collision of sparks and flames that would burnout and leave her all alone like the loves Ashlynn had known or the push and pull of violence and anger that crashed into temporary passion like Julien's parents. Maybe it was a quiet knowing, two souls existing side by side just wanting to stabilize and protect the other. Like two stars co-existing in the sky, sharing the view of the moon, not burning out or burning brighter, leaving the other behind. Just together as partners, protectors, held together by a thousand little invisible strings that didn't strangle or stop the other from going free, but kept their souls quietly connected to each other because that's the way they were meant to be. That's the key to surviving the cruelty the universe could throw their way, that gentle connection. Maybe that's what genuine love is—your best friend sitting beside you when life is the shittiest.

# CHAPTER 10

"Are you sure you want to do this?" Julien said as the gate and guard shack come into view at the end of a dark rainy road.

"Yeah, I'll be okay," Abilene said as she reached for the door handle. "But, yeah, wait to be sure they let me in, please. I'll come back and grab my stuff in a minute, hopefully." She swooped a stray chunk of her wavy hair from her face, drew in a deep breath, and stepped out of the mini-van into the rain. Abilene flinched and blinked as the gate guards shined bright lights at the 16-year-old. She held up her hand to see around the blinding orbs on either side of the tiny building.

"Can we help you?" a soldier yelled out as he walked closer. "You got ID?" Abilene nodded. "Well, kid, you guys need to turn around if you don't have business on this post. This is a secure U.S. Army installation, not some make-out spot." He shined a flashlight at Julien. He squinted behind the wheel and held his hands in full view. Abilene swallowed a lump in her throat. The rain ran down her face as she stepped closer through the dark, so her whole body lit up. She shook.

"Sir, my name is Abilene Marigold Matterly. I'm the daughter of First Sergeant Thomas Matterly. I'm here to see my dad." She drew in a deep breath and tried to relax her shoulders, even though she was shivering. The guard motioned for her to come closer. She could see the rain bounce off his side arm.

"But you don't have an ID? Is he expecting you?" the guard motioned for the other two to lower the flashlights. Abilene took in a deep breath and moved her hand from over her eyes.

"Can you take me to him?" Her lower lip trembled from a mix of nerves and cold rain pummeling her exhausted body. He reached for her shoulder to guide her to the gate shack.

"Well, we ain't a valet service, kid, but we'll see if we can call him for you. You can't go beyond the gate though, without a service member. You know it's the middle of the night, right?" He said. In the light of the small guard shack, Abilene could see he was barely a few years older than her. They were all in uniform, had side arms, and two-way radios strapped to their belts. Inside the shack was a computer, two automatic weapons propped in the corner, and a control panel for the gate and alarms and lights. She caught a glimpse of a half-eaten sandwich and soda next to the control panel. They didn't let her enter, but they motioned for her to stand under a small awning. They looked her up and down. She suddenly wondered how she had ended up here without a plan or without thinking to call him first. The thought of these soldiers calling her father in the middle of the night, telling him to get dressed and pick up his long-lost daughter at the gate in the middle of a rainy night made her shiver even more. She was nauseous. What was he going to think? What would his wife think? Would he try to call Ashlynn first and ask what the hell Abilene was doing outside of Fort Patten, Georgia, in the middle of the night? For a split second, she considered running back to Julien, jumping in the van, locking the door, telling him to throw it in reverse, and drive like wildfire back to Holden, South Carolina, or anywhere else.

One soldier told the other to pull out the post directory and find contact info for Sgt. Matterly. He flipped through the pages and ran his finger down a list. Then he stopped and reached for the phone. Panic rose in her chest. She hadn't thought this far during the entire six-hour ride. He dialed the phone.

Abilene looked back at the mini-van. She squinted at the headlights and wondered what Julien would do on the way home. She closed her eyes to squeeze back tears as she realized how much trouble he'd be in for helping her. What had she done? It was too late to pretend none of the last 24 hours had happened. She couldn't go back to the hospital room and take back the words she flung at her mom. She couldn't go back and not stand at the foot of the bed, looking at her mom hold a newborn and scream, "What the fuck? You've never been to Paris!" as she pounded her fist in the air. It had all unraveled in less than a day and ended with her telling her mom she hated her just as she was dying right in front of Abilene. Her mom's face flashed before her eyes again.

The gate guard's voice sounded muffled, as if Abilene was underwater and drowning in regrets. "Yes sir. Yes. She says she's your daughter." He slid the phone from his chin. "What's your name again, kid?"

Her mouth was dry. Her tongue stuck to the roof. She peeled it off, and she tried to block out her mother yelling back at her. "Abilene. Abilene Marigold Matterly," she said. The guard slid the phone receiver back close to his mouth.

"You catch that, sir?" he said. Abilene heard a groggy "yes" Her stomach flipped. She hadn't heard his voice in years, not since Dallas was a toddler and Ashlynn had a new man to vacation with. She shipped all the kids to their respective dads for maybe two weeks. Abilene wasn't sure because they moved so much in those days, time was confusing. Maybe it was a month? Maybe an entire summer. All she remembered was it was sunny, her dad was stationed in Hawaii, and she loved the beach days with her step-mom Sandy. It was her only time on a plane. Sandy and Sgt. Matterly had just had a baby a year before that visit, and Ashlynn had told Abilene they had another after that. Abilene hadn't even stopped to wonder what her two half-sisters might be like now. She swallowed another lump in her throat as the guard nodded, said a few more yes sirs, and hung up the phone. She glanced back at Julien to be sure he hadn't left yet in case the Sgt. said no to picking her up.

"He'll be here in a few minutes," the guard said as he hung up the phone. Abilene relaxed her shoulders and unballed her fists. She didn't realize she had dug her nails into her palm.

"Okay, thank you. Can I say goodbye to my... my friend?"

"Be my guest," said the soldier who had met her outside first. "You want an umbrella? We got a few in here."

"No, thanks. I'm okay."

Abilene went back out into the rain and opened the sliding door of the minivan. Julien turned in the seat to look back at her. He was sweating.

"So? What's happening? He coming?" He said. Abilene nodded and slid the duffle bag across the seat and heaved it over her shoulder. It felt heavier than it did when she ran to Julien's house. Everything in her life did.

"Yeah. He's coming. You gonna be okay to get back home? Dammit. I don't know how to thank you. You're gonna be in a shit ton of trouble when you get back and it's all my fau—"

"Bullshit. I chose to go. I said I'd drive you and I'd do it again. My mom will get over it. I'll be back by lunch. So, I might get grounded the rest of the summer, that's fine," he said. "Ain't nothing to do in Holden anyway if you're gone." He let out a snort. "That pool is dirty as shit. I'm cool getting grounded." Julien flashed her the smile that made her heart jump months ago when he first came up next to her on her walk home from school. The dashboard lights made him almost glow.

"I don't know what I would've done without you, Ponyboy." Her shoulders slumped when she realized once he drove away, she didn't know when she'd see him again. "I'll call you." She glanced around the van once more. She wanted to run to the driver's side, open the door, and throw herself into his arms, but she couldn't.

"Go on. I'll be fine. I'll see ya soon. We're still best friends. Call me tomorrow and definitely call me if you need me to come get you outta here if things go south. Go on. Go be with your dad." He said followed by a nod. "I'll take care of everyone back home." Abilene bit her bottom lip and closed the door. As she turned to walk back under the awning in her red cowboy boots, the headlights of a car approaching the gate from inside the base caught her eye. She glanced back. Julien was backing up the minivan and turning onto the shoulder of the road. Their eyes met again through the rain. He winked. She smiled. He put the minivan in drive and taillights filled the blackness in a moment. She was alone for the first time in a long time. A car door slamming shut broke her trance as she watched the only person she trusted disappear.

"Abilene? Is that really you?" a deep, loud voice called to her from behind. She spun around. Her wet hair whipped across her face. One clump of blonde stuck to her cheek. Tears welled up and overflowed before she could stop them. He was everything she remembered him to be. Tall, lean, close-shaved blonde hair the same color as hers. It was easy for her to see why her mom had fallen head over heels in love. He gasped as she stepped from the guard shack awning. The soldiers on guard duty were silently standing in the rain, glancing back and forth at her and her father as if they were watching a tennis match. She nodded. He stepped close enough to grab her arm and pulled her into his chest. She cried into his black jacket. She didn't want to, but something opened in her and she couldn't close it.

"Oh my God, girl. How'd you get here? I got a call at midnight from some social services woman in South Carolina. They got the police and everyone looking for you." He said as he released her and held her back a few feet. He tilted his head and let out a sigh. "They told me about your mom, that Ashlynn died in childbirth. My God, I'm so sorry. I was gonna head there in the morning to help look for you. Thank God you're okay." He rubbed her shoulders and pulled her in again. "You are okay, aren't ya?" Abilene nodded into his chest and let the tears run rampant. "Let's get you out of this rain." His eyes darted from her head to her boots and back up before glancing around wildly as he rubbed her shoulders more as if he was looking for wounds.

He let go of her shoulders and walked to the guards, who instantly stood at attention. "Thanks, guys. I appreciate you getting a hold of me right quick. At ease," he said. They seemed to take a breath after holding it from the time he got out of the car. He led her to the passenger side and opened the door. Abilene slid into the passenger seat and instantly felt bad about getting the smooth leather interior wet. His car was cleaner than any she'd ever seen. She wiped her tears away and tried to steady her breathing. Abilene reached for her wrist for her hair tie to get the wet mop out of her eyes. It was gone. As she glanced around the floor for it, she noticed how different the Sergeant seemed to live compared to her mom, just based on the car alone. Any vehicle she kept for any length of time looked trashed daily. Food wrappers, containers of half-gone baby wipes, lip glosses rolling along the floor, glass bottles of juice or soda, various items of clothing that never made it from the car to whatever house or trailer they occupied for a few months. Abilene remembered their musty smelling station wagon. It was gross from the start. Abilene insisted it smelled of old vomit, as her mouth would water every time they got in it after it sat closed up in the sun too long. Her mom would laugh and call her a drama queen.

Sgt. Matterly stared straight ahead into the night rain as he drove. They drove past barracks, the motor pool parking filled with jeeps and large transport vehicles, all painted camouflage. Abilene realized camo paint really makes it hard to see them, especially at night. She remembered seeing convoys barreling down the highway from time to time during their moves. They looked and sounded like pure power, a force breaking through the masses. But at night, silent and still, the vehicles almost seemed like toys her brothers had lined up and forgot about. She wondered if her brothers and Savannah were sleeping okay or if they were too confused or worried to sleep. Abilene felt a pit in her stomach, thinking how hurt they must be to lose their mom then have her run off without an explanation. Jackson and Austin would be fine, but Dallas, he didn't have anyone else to love him and love his faults too. And Savannah was too young to know what was happening or why. Dammit, Abilene thought, Tucker didn't know what to read to her before bed or what animals she needed by her head and by her feet as she drifted off. Now Tucker would have to take care of Savanah and a new baby, which Abilene was sure he knew nothing about. She tried to remember if they ever met Tucker's mom and if she was capable of raising the girls. Abilene wondered if she could've taken them with her and if the Sergeant would've taken them all in.

The Sergeant turned down a street that revealed row houses on either side. There were four doors to a building with small porches jutting out to a little sidewalk that connected to a bigger sidewalk. Each was painted different shades of tan, gray, and yellow to give each unit an independent feel. Abilene noticed flower boxes and hanging pots of petunias swinging in the rainy breeze. There were streetlights brightly perched on every corner. It all looked quaint. Clean. Orderly. It was the exact opposite of any street or town Ashlynn ever rolled them into. He pulled into a short driveway at the end of one of the row houses and put the car in park.

"Now listen, I've got blankets in a hall closet and extra pillows I'll get out. The girls are asleep, so we want to be quiet. You can have the couch tonight and tomorrow we'll start on a room for you." He said as he jangled the keys and raised his eyebrows. Abilene could tell he was used to talking slower and softer to his much younger daughters. She nodded. "I'm gonna call that social worker, too. Let her know you're safe. Okay?"

"Wait, will I be in trouble? And what about Julien? Is he in trouble for driving me? Will they make you bring me back?" Her voice got higher, and she felt her heart pound again. "If you send me back, I ain't going to live with Tucker even if he takes my sisters. I don—"

"Hey, hey, relax, Abilene. No one is in trouble. I'm not sending you back. I promise." He said as he leaned in and pulled her over for a hug. "Listen, I know I haven't been around the last few years. We moved a few more times and then had Kayla. But you're my kid. Even before you showed up tonight, as soon as that woman said Ashlynn died, I knew I was coming to get you, bring you here with us. No question about it. Sandy said so, too." He released her. "Now, let's get some sleep and talk about all this in the morning. You've had an awful day and I can tell you're exhausted. In the morning, everything will be clearer." He got out and walked to her side, opened the door, and put out his hand. She had never seen someone do that in real life before. Abilene took it and followed him into the house. It was dark, but smelled like jasmine. He slipped off his shoes and peeled his wet coat off his shoulders. He flung it on a coat rack by the door. Abilene slid her boots off and followed her father down a darkened hall. Even though she could barely see, she could tell family portraits filled the entire hall. She couldn't remember if she had ever been in a picture with him and Sandy. She thought she had one from the beach in Hawaii. The hall opened to a living room. A sliver of moonlight shone through French doors leading to what Abilene assumed was a backyard. There was a matching couch and loveseat facing each other and an entertainment center with a television on top against the wall. A coffee table with a glass top and curved legs was in between the couch and loveseat.

"Here. Have a seat. I'll grab the blankets and pillow." He said as he pointed at the couch and walked on through what Abilene figured was the kitchen. She got goosebumps as the air conditioning blew on her wet arms as she put her duffle bag on the floor. Abilene felt behind her neck to see if her hair was dry. She wondered how far away Julien was now. Part of her still wanted to turn and run toward the minivan and stay inside with him forever. She heard voices at the stairs. They were hushed. It had to be Sandy. Abilene swallowed a lump and glanced around, wondering where'd she actually go if Sandy walked right in and told her to leave.

Sgt. Matterly returned with an arm-load of blankets and two pillows squished between the pile and his chin. He forced a smile. A figure followed him into the room.

"Hey there, Abilene. I'm so sorry about your mom," Sandy said. Abilene rose and was taken aback when she realized she was now taller than her long-lost step-mother. Sandy not only looked smaller, she sounded smaller, too. She sounded as if she didn't want her voice or presence to fill up the room. Abilene wrung her hands together as Sandy stepped out of the shadow of the Sergeant.

"Thank you. I'm so sorry I came in the middle of the night. I just—"

"Honey, it's fine. You're fine." Sandy held up her hand, peeking out from under her terrycloth robe. Abilene noticed it had tiny flowers on the edges of the neckline and pockets. It reminded her of something she'd see an old woman schlep around in while carrying a cup of hot tea. Abilene stifled a snicker, thinking her mother would never drape herself in something so dowdy. "Do you need anything? Water? Tea? Food? When did you last eat, honey?" Sandy asked as the Sergeant fluffed the pillows and placed them at one end of the couch. He went to the other room and Abilene heard him take a phone off the hook and dial.

"I'm okay. Really. You don't have to go to any trouble. I'm sorry to get you guys up." Abilene lowered herself to the couch. It was firm. It didn't feel like any Abilene had sat on before. Sandy gathered up the bottom of her robe that graced the carpet and sat beside her. As comforted as Abilene was that they had taken her in, she cringed at the thought that Sandy might try to hug her. Abilene was all hugged and teared out. She heard the Sergeant talking and knew he must've gotten a hold of the social worker. Abilene wondered if she should run in and ask about her brothers and now two sisters. She let out a deep breath, realizing she was no longer in control of what happened in that house.

"We're just glad you're safe. If you need anything before morning, feel free to ransack the kitchen or come to the top of the steps first door right and get us. Okay?" Sandy's voice went up an octave as she finished her directions to her room. She tapped the tops of her own knees. "Well, I'm going up to bed and I'll see you in the morning?" She stood and her small frame floated out of the room as quietly as it entered. Abilene's father came back in and stood in the middle of the room, tall, firm, confident. He crossed his arms.

"You sure you're okay for the night?" He raised his eyebrows again. Abilene nodded and reached for the top blanket. "Alright then, kid. The social worker is relieved you're safe, and I'm sure the cops will be, too. I'm a go up and I'll see you in the morning."

"Okay. Thanks." She didn't bother to remind him it was after 3 a.m., probably closer to 4, already morning. She waited until she heard his footsteps reach the top of the stairs before she unfurled the soft blanket. It smelled like it just came out of the washer, as if they were prepared for overnight guests. Abilene laid back in her shorts and shirt she had worn since she was at the hospital with Ashlynn over 24 hours ago. She stretched out her long, tanned legs and pulled the blanket securely over her feet and up to her chin as her head found the pillow. Abilene sunk into the couch. The white pillows reminded her of the motel's when they were freshly cleaned and fluffed. There was a slight scent of bleach as the pillow conformed to her face. She loved that smell.

Abilene drew in a deep breath and closed her eyes. She pictured the silent, dark world that existed outside of that living room, far from that couch. She pictured Julien driving alone, cranking Nirvana to stay awake. Shit, she thought. They had tickets to Lollapalooza in two weeks. She and Julien had plans for the first day of school. They had nights walking to Mazzy's, eating hot chicken in the parking lot, slushies on the river walk with nothing but the moon and memory to guide them. Julien would never be allowed to go to the music festival now that he stole the van and drove her hundreds of miles away and across state lines. "Ponyboy," she whispered into the night air. She wondered if Savannah was sleeping through the night. If Paris was healthy enough to leave the hospital the next day. If anyone did the dishes. If anyone made sure Dallas brushed his teeth. Where would her brothers go to school in a few weeks? What would they tell new teachers about their family? Their summer? Their mom? Then Abilene wondered what she'd tell people. Where would she go to school? How would a day unfold without Julien? Then Abilene thought of her mom and squeezed her eyes hard trying to get the picture of her in that bed out of her mind. She forced herself to tumble back further, years, trying to picture Ashlynn as beautiful and healthy, laughing. Abilene remembered a time when they were driving, and her mom found an old Beach Boys tape in the glove box of the station wagon they'd just bought. She pushed it into the player and cranked it. Her mom pounded her hands on the steering wheel and belted out "Wouldn't it Be Nice" and "Help Me Rhonda". She told Abilene her mom loved the Beach Boys, and she grew up listening to them while her mom cleaned the house on the weekends. Abilene could see her mom's face light up, her eyes shining brightly as her laugh filled the car. She nudged Abilene to join her. Abilene tried, but mostly concentrated on watching her mom and laughing with her. Abilene let sleep creep in as a tear leaked out. She was too tired to wipe it away. Sleep wrapped its arms around her and pulled her from the memory, the sound of the Beach Boys and her mom's radiance when she was happy. Abilene knew once she let go of the thought, let go of the moment in the middle of the night and drifted off, she'd soon wake in a brand new world, a world where her mom and laughs in a musty station wagon no longer existed.

# CHAPTER 11

Abilene slowly opened her eyes. She had the feeling she was being watched. Two blond girls with mussed up hair and wild blue eyes were inches from her face. They giggled.

"Hello?" Abilene said. The oldest, Krista's eyes grew wide. Kayla, who was three by now, put her little hand over her mouth to stifle a laugh. Abilene noticed their faces were smooth and looked like porcelain. There was no doubt they'd grow to be beautiful women.

"Good morning, Sissy," Krista said. "Mom says you're gonna live here now." She put her pinky in her mouth. Abilene could tell they were nervous, afraid she'd make a sudden move. Abilene slowly rose to put them at ease.

"Yeah, it seems I'm gonna stay for a bit." Abilene said. Kayla crawled onto the couch next to her and reached for her arm.

"Yay! I get another big sister. You stay foreber." The three-year-old squealed. Abilene couldn't help but smile at her. She hadn't really thought about it before, but Kayla was roughly the same age as Savannah. Abilene thought the two would be best friends if they had the chance. She swallowed a lump in her throat and wondered who was dressing Savannah and what they told her about Abilene not being there.

Both girls reached for Abilene's arms and pulled to get her from under the blanket just as Sandy appeared from the hallway from the kitchen.

"Breakfast, girls," she said with crossed arms and a grand smile. She didn't seem as small or quiet as she had been hours earlier. The presence of her two little ones made her automatically more commanding, Abilene figured.

As they ate, Sandy and the Sergeant leaned against the counter slurping coffee and staring at them. Abilene kept glancing around at the family she was thrown into, almost afraid if she spoke, she'd wake, and it would all disappear like a dream. She ate quietly, even though she was starving. The giggles made her both amazed at their inherent cuteness and jealous of their closeness, their seemingly normal daily existence. An existence she couldn't relate to.

"Listen, Abilene, I'm gonna call social services again and find out more about arrangements for your mom, and what will happen to the rest of the kids, okay? I reckon we'll have to go to court and sign papers to get things permanently arranged for you staying with us now. You understand?" Sgt. Matterly said, breaking the silence. Abilene nodded. Just yesterday, she was living with the idea of taking on more responsibility helping to raise another baby and worrying about who was going to clean up after the kids. Now today, she was a legal issue, something to sort out, sign for in court.

"I know this may be confusing, and I know you have a lot of feelings to work through, questions about what will happen next and all, but I promise you, we're gonna do all we can to make this easier on you any way we can." Sandy said as she lowered her cup. In the light, Abilene could see stains on Sandy's robe. Abilene swallowed a mouthful of cereal. Easier? Nothing ever got easier, Abilene thought. Why would it be now?

As the days flowed into each other, Abilene felt suspended between mourning her mother, laughing at her two new half-sisters' antics, and calling the house a few times a day to check in with the others. Jackson and Austin were all packed and set to leave with Butchy immediately after a service for Ashlynn. Abilene was both irritated and relieved by how excited they were at the thought of living with their dad forever. They barely mentioned Ashlynn and didn't seem to think of Paris at all. She wondered if Tucker had given them a chance to hold her, feed her, or bond with her. Savannah would get on the phone long enough to ask Abilene when she was coming home. Abilene would tear up, take the arrow to the heart, and tell her soon. Then, she'd look over at Krista and feel guilty as if she had traded one three-year-old for another. Dallas, he was a different story. He refused to get on the phone even when Tucker yelled at him to talk to Abilene. Abilene didn't blame him. She left him. Ashlynn didn't have a choice. Abilene was fine being the target of his anger. Better her than their mom, she thought. Abilene couldn't feel the floor in the kitchen when she was on the phone with them. It was as if half her body was in Holden in that tiny house next to the motel and the other half in this new world, new life, new family.

As hard as those calls and discussions of funeral arrangements to unfold in two days were, calls to Julien were the hardest. Several calls went unanswered. Julien's mom hung up on her once and his father gave her a fierce lecture about being a spoiled little snot who enticed Julien to steal the family van. Abilene thought it ironic to call her spoiled when she had a mom still lying in the morgue. Julien answered the next day, the day before Sgt. Matterly would drive her back for the funeral and meet with the state social services to make her full custody deal permanent. His voice cracked. Hers did too. Her heart felt it would burst and she couldn't imagine ever hanging up. They both talked a mile a minute about the last 72 hours without each other. Julien was grounded until school started again, and was solely responsible for his sisters. Abilene told him a thousand details about her new sisters and asked if he had seen hers. He hadn't given that he wasn't allowed out. He swore to get to her mother's service to see her. Abilene wondered how she'd make it through that without him if he couldn't.

The long car ride with her dad wasn't as awkward as she expected it to be. He had taken leave for two days to take her to Holden, attend the service, sign what needed to be signed and stay the night at a motel afterwards. She told him she didn't want them to stay at the motel her mom worked at. The memories of her there would be hard enough, but being within reach of her bedroom and the other kids would be too much. Just the thought of stopping there to get the rest of her stuff was making her stomach clench. After periods of small talk, he asked random questions about her life the last few years and filled her in on theirs. He told her countless stories of special ways Sandy made each house a home and made the moves easier on the girls. Little did he realize that was Abilene's job for twice as many kids over the last few years. As he shifted gears, then returned his hand to the wheel, Abilene saw a tattoo peek out from the edge of his t-shirt.

"What's the tattoo?" She said.

"Oh, I got this when we were stationed in Hawaii. It was kinda an anniversary present. She got one on the back of her shoulder too." He said as he reached over and pushed the sleeve to his shoulder. It said 'Sandra' in cursive, with hibiscus flowers and leaves woven in and out. It was quite elaborate, and Abilene hated to admit it was beautiful. She felt a pang of jealously, thinking no one had a tattoo like that for Ashlynn. Then her mind drifted to the boys. Maybe one of them someday would get one in memory of Ashlynn. "You like it?" he asked.

"Oh, yeah. It's actually pretty cool." She answered.

"Do you think all your stuff will fit in the car alright? I guess I should've asked that before we left, huh?"

"Yeah, I think so. I don't care about the furniture or anything. It's all just crap we got along the way, thrift stores when we moved from town to town. It ain't like I got a giant heirloom bed and matching dresser or any of that shit that I want to drag with me." She said. Abilene regretted the words as soon as she spoke them. Krista and Kayla probably had heirloom everything, or at least something. She noticed her dad looked away and swallowed. Maybe a sliver of guilt bubbled. As the words *sorry about that* crept to the tip of her tongue, she stopped herself. Maybe, she thought, he deserved a sliver of guilt for not making sure she had nice things.

"I paid support, you know. Every month, I sent your mother money to make sure you were taken care of." He said as he stared straight ahead. The urge to apologize roared back like a wave crashing on the beach.

"I know. I... I didn't mean it like that. Just well, honestly, we didn't have much. We'd move with whatever we could pack. No furniture. Then, we'd get to the new place and buy what we could."

"Plus, she had so many kids. I'm sure that made it harder to get nice things."

Silence crept back in for what seemed like a hundred miles. Abilene went back and forth from wanting to tell him to fuck off for mentioning her mom had so many kids like she was trash or something and wanting to beg him to step up and be two parents now, even though he had barely been one. She wanted him to love her as much as he obviously loved Krista and Kayla, love her beyond signing papers and putting a roof over her head.

"She was a good mom, you know. She did the best she could." Abilene said. Her voice cracked. She didn't want tears to escape, but they did.

"Hey, I know. I'm sorry. She loved you so much. I'm sure she loved all of you so much. I'm just sorry I wasn't there more. I wish I could've made her life easier."

"Did you love her? I mean, when you were together? I found a receipt from a hotel with both your signatures. Like a honeymoon or something when you married."

"Did I love her? My God, Abilene, I loved her. Everyone loved Ashlynn. She was beautiful, most beautiful woman I ever knew. And she was so funny, and kind to everyone. She could disarm a bank robber with her smile and the way she said 'hello'" He huffed and glanced out the window. "Girl, never doubt you came into this world cause of love. A part of me will always love that woman." He shot a quick smile at Abilene. She wiped the corner of her eye and stared straight ahead.

The funeral, Abilene's first, was a flurry of activity, noise, and borderline chaos. Part of Abilene found it fitting when she wasn't feeling consumed by numbness. Everyone from the motel was there, including the manager who was so quick to apologize to Abilene, as if lending her the car to get to the hospital was some sort of mistake on his part. The maids and the other manager all caressed her hair as they drew her in close with looks of sympathy, pity, really. The noise and chaos that kept sweeping through the service mostly stemmed from her siblings. Tucker held the baby close, and Savannah seemed comfortable running in and out of his legs. She was happy to see Abilene and dashed into her arms, but didn't hesitate to let go and resume trying to climb Tucker and touch her sister.

"Look at the baby, Abi. Look!" she shouted out a few times until Abilene would shush her and lean over to peek at Paris. Tucker patted Savannah on the head and nudged his mother to take her to the bathroom. Abilene was shocked to see he appeared to be a dad, maybe for show, but either way, he played the part well. He even tied Savannah's shoes at one point. As the

Sergeant stood near, telling Austin, Jackson, and Dallas stories about the Army, Tucker nodded her way.

"Hey Abi, you wanna hold her? My mom and I are taking them to Louisiana tomorrow." He said as he awkwardly offered the swaddled newborn into her arms. Abilene took her as she wondered if Tucker regretted how he had man-handled her moments before Ashlynn died, or instead of regret he was nervous she'd say something about it. Abilene moved her focus from Tuck to the baby he placed in her arms. She pulled the blanket down and Paris looked up at her. She had their mom's eyes. Golden flecks mixed in with light brown, almost a swirl, like a golden nugget with pieces of earth still attached in certain crevices. Abilene fought tears. The last she looked in Paris' eyes was when Ashlynn's arm went limp, and the doctor caught her as she slid to the edge of the bed. She could feel Tucker smile at her as her father came up from behind. Both men had loved Ashlynn in their own way, in their own sliver of time. Both Paris and Abilene were a product of that love.

Abilene stared into Paris's eyes, and everyone and everything faded into the background. She was suddenly transported to the hospital room. She heard her screams at her mom. Ashlynn's shock and response back. "I hate you." Played over and over in her head as tears ran down her face. She used her free hand to wipe her chin before they fell on Paris like some kind of cursed water that would make Paris hate their mother, too. She trembled and felt her dad's hand on her shoulder. Abilene was sure he was asking if she was ok, but his words were muffled, blocked by her own memories flooding her brain, her own voice booming just as it had at the hospital. Abilene realized no one but her and Julien knew the last conversation she had with her mom. No one else realized the truth Abilene had discovered reading those postcards. At least if anyone knew, they held her secret close to their own heart. No one else but Julien knew that Ashlynn died listening to Abilene scream at her, call her a liar, and declare she never wanted to be like her. Abilene was the forever keeper of that memory, a curse she'd have to bear, deservingly so. She handed Paris back to Tucker and ran out the front door of the funeral home. Abilene crashed right into Julien's chest. She instantly meshed with him and together they cried and hugged for what seemed years.

Once Abilene finally let go and pulled herself back to look at her best friend, she realized it seemed like a lifetime since they had seen each other, not days. He brushed her hair from her face and smiled at her.

"I can't do this, Julien. I can't say goodbye. I can't say goodbye to her and my brothers and sisters at the same time. And to you, too."

"You'll see them again, and me, of course. Your dad brought you here. He'll take you to see them too, right?" Julien said.

"Yeah, I guess he will." She said. Dallas appeared at her side. He reached up for her shoulder.

"Did you hear?"

"Hear what?"

"Butchy is gonna take me, too. I get a dad just like Jackson and Austin." Dallas said as he stood a little straighter. He looked like he grew in the last few days.

"Seriously, Dallas?" Abilene said. Tears sprang from her eyes again. "You get to stay with them? I was so afraid they'd stick you in some shitty orphanage or foster home."

"Nope. I'm getting a dad." He shrugged his shoulders to stifle what Abilene knew was genuine excitement.

"Well, you better be good for him, so he doesn't change his mind. You hear me?" Abilene said as a smile crept across her face. She felt a weight lift from her shoulders, knowing Dallas would be cared for, loved by someone other than her.

"I won't. You know me. I'm an angel." He said with a wink and a smile she didn't realize she missed until he flashed it at her. He then looked down and shuffled his feet. Abilene could tell he was wearing Austin's old dress shoes. "I'm gonna miss you, though. I miss mom, too." His shoulders shuddered, and Abilene drew him in for a hug.

Hugs, tears, and a few smirks between siblings were all they had left as they descended into the house for the last time as a family. They packed clothes into three different vehicles. A few boxes were earmarked for donations the motel would handle. One of the motel maids promised to clean the house after the furniture was given away. Abilene walked back to the bedroom she shared with Savannah a few days earlier. She sat on the bed for a moment and inhaled the musty smell, the dust and years of grime that had collected in a house lived in by countless families drifting through life. She closed her eyes and tried to hear the sounds that were normal a few days ago—the boys fighting, a shoe hitting the wall, Savannah whining for more paper to tear or to be held even though she knew she was getting too big. Then, smells came to the surface of her memory. The smell of microwave dinners, steamy and filled with salt, the sweet scent of the generic shampoo she used on Savannah's head and then she would dig her nose into the boys' hair in order to sniff out proof they had washed themselves. She tried to remember the rare smell of scrambled eggs when her mom was off work and made breakfast for them or had a craving, and begged Abilene to make her some for dinner. Abilene took a deep breath and glanced at the window she'd open in the middle of the night to talk to Julien or pull the sheer curtains and half-broke blinds closed to obstruct the view of whatever creeps were staying at the motel that week. The last few months in that room certainly weren't the longest she had stayed in one place, but it was the last place they'd ever have as one family. She'd never get that back. Abilene rose from the bed to walk out whether she was ready or not. There was no going back. She had to move forward to the next room, the next home, the next smells and sounds that hopefully would feel like home someday.

Once outside with the others, she watched with little fanfare or any formal announcement as Butchy and Tucker took their respective kids, promised to call each other and make plans for them to connect maybe next summer, buckled seatbelts, and took a few tidbits of advice from Abilene. She wandered over to the cars and she kissed the little ones and smacked the older boys on the head in their playful way. They drove away, separately but together. She wondered if Savannah understood or would remember anything of what they had, who they were together. Abilene stood in the driveway with the Sergeant, her clothes, her pictures, her tapes, her mom's boxes, and Julien. She watched in disbelief as the siblings she raised, fed, cleaned up after, shampooed, spanked, comforted, and helped with homework all left her alone, alone with her grief, her guilt and burden of truth, her emptiness. Even flanked by her dad and her best friend, she felt like her guts were pouring out and flowing down the road after both vehicles. She gasped as the cars went out of sight. They were gone. Her mother was gone. Every aspect of her former life, except Julien, was gone, and he'd be gone in a moment, too. While they promised to call each other constantly and visit, and of course marry someday if they didn't find anyone else by 30, she knew once she left, she didn't know when she'd be with him again. No days she could count down. She was losing her best friend. He reached over and slid a tape into her hands.

"Listen to that. That'll keep you cool. I promise," he said with that toothy smile. She laughed and rolled her eyes. He shuffled his feet and glanced all around.

"Your kind of cool, or a real kind of cool?" she said back.

"You're an asshole."

"You're an asshole, Ponyboy. Don't forget me, okay?"

Sgt. Matterly finished loading the car and waited by the door. Abilene wondered if he heard them call each other 'assholes'. Julien grabbed her arms and pulled her in for a quick hug. He squeezed the air from her lungs. Abilene thought a river of tears would explode from her eyes if he let her go.

"Don't worry. You'll find a new best friend in Georgia."

"Yeah, and a new girl will move to Holden and have much better taste in music, and you'll forget all about me."

"God, I hope so. You were a lost cause." He laughed. She knew before she got in the car, she'd miss that laugh. She took a step back and looked at him. That smile slid across his face. Abilene's heart ached, and she started to shake. She didn't know how she'd leave him behind and how'd she ever laugh again without him by her side. All their late nights alone together flashed through her mind. The thought of not being able to climb out of a window and be with him gutted her.

"What am I going to do without you? I can't go like this." she stammered as she fought tears. He reached for her hand.

"Yes, you can. You'll be fine. I'll always be right here, okay? We'll see each other again. I promise. And if I get out of here, maybe you'll look up one day and I'll just be there. We'll find our way back to each other somehow. That's what best friends do." He let her hand go. "Now, go with your dad. He'll take care of you." She nodded and turned to her dad. She couldn't look back at Julien as she got in the car and closed the door. Abilene held back the tears as she watched him in the mirror until she couldn't see Julien wave anymore from the street. Sgt. Matterly patted her hand. She felt like her insides, her heart and guts, were still on the street in Holden.

"You get used to saying goodbye, kid." He said. Abilene inhaled deeply.

"To who? My mom, my brothers and sisters, or my best friend? Or everyone all the time, over and over again, until I die?" She said. He didn't have a response. She didn't want him to find one. Abilene sat in the passenger seat and let memories of her short time in Holden float around in her head. Memories of the years before that crept in, too. She let them pass through realizing those memories, and the stacks of clothes and pieces of her life in the backseat and trunk were all she had left of her old life, her old family, her old self.

# CHAPTER 12

*Fall 1992*

Nothing surprised Abilene more than how quickly she adjusted to life on Fort Patten with her father and Sandy. School shopping with a step-mother, going to the park with her half-sisters who were practically a comedy duo, dinners she didn't need to make or even clean up after, and then going grocery shopping with someone who didn't need her input for meal-planning or cost saving instincts to make the food last as long as possible. Sandy would ask her taste preference, what she loved for breakfasts and what she hated, but didn't need her to be part of the process otherwise. Abilene felt odd observing a parent parenting without needing her as backup or confirmation she was doing it right. The level of responsibility on her shoulders wasn't measurable, other than being responsible for herself. It was the first time in her life no one expected her to step up and do any day to day parenting jobs, or at least be ready to step into the roll if duty called. This change of circumstance left her both oddly thankful, yet feeling left out as if Sandy didn't trust or need her there. Abilene kept reminding herself that to Sandy, she was an extra kid, not the built-in babysitter and co-parent she had been for years for her mom.

Abilene was still hesitant to ask the Sergeant too much about where he was all those years, why he never sent for her more, or if he worried about her at all. Partly because she didn't want to know his answer, and she didn't need it. Abilene had quickly realized his answers or excuses didn't matter all that much. She was there now, and that alone was more than he or she had ever planned for. Plus, she reasoned, whatever his excuse was, it couldn't possibly be her fault. He didn't know her well enough to reject her. Despite the kindness and acceptance that was a new normal for them all, Abilene still couldn't call him Dad all the time, and Sandy was just Sandy. Occasionally she called him Dad when the girls were part of the conversation and if she quickly yelled or asked for something. However, if the conversation was not spontaneous, she called him Tom or The Sergeant when talking to others. He didn't seem to mind, and she didn't care too much if he did. She cared he loved her and wanted her around, but took a realistic approach to how much. She figured she had gotten through life this far without him being right there, accessible every day or even every holiday. There was no need for getting overly comfortable or dependent on him, aside from a roof over her head now, of course.

Once the first day of school dawned a few weeks after her arrival, Abilene went through the motions of pulling up her red cowboy boots and waltzing into yet another new situation. Her numbness to the thought of standing up and yet again explaining who she was, where she came from, and some random standard tidbit most teachers insisted the new kid share quickly faded when she sat in her seat front and center. She always sat up front so she couldn't see the others stare at her, even if she could feel it. She shuffled her boots and waited for the usual 'stand up and tell us about herself' only to be thrown for a loop. The teacher read a list of names of all the other new kids. It wasn't until that very moment Abilene realized the greatest surprise of starting school on a military base. About half the class was 'the new kid'. Summers were when most military families got orders to move to a new post, new region, even new country. The kids were shuffled, rearranged, and discombobulated every few years. The cycle of moves simply meant a new kid was far from being the only new kid. There wasn't time or desire to have all of them stand and go through the process she had repeatedly been put through. The names were read, and hands raised. A simple and genuine 'welcome' was extended, and the day moved along. The relief Abilene felt almost made her cry. Her shoulders instantly relaxed and a wave of being just like the others in the room washed over her. Abilene realized she wasn't ever going to be THE new kid again. She'd simply be one of many new kids. Not standing out was the happiest first day she had experienced anywhere.

She couldn't help but glance around and wonder if they all, or anyone, felt the same relief she did. She noticed everyone looked different, not like carbon copies of each other trying to fit in or appear part of the well-established cool kids' club. They all seemed to have a confident air, dressed exactly how they wanted to with styles and accessories from all regions, countries, life experiences that set them apart yet tied them to each other at the same time. They were all different yet could relate to each other being in the same boat, but independently rowing and all totally cool with that fact. It was the best boat she had ever climbed into. She smiled, took out a notebook from a new backpack Sandy bought her and settled in for her first day of her junior year. She wondered if Julien was okay without her and felt a pang of sadness, thinking he was in a boat filled with kids he had always known, yet he was alone.

When the lunch bell went off, Abilene found herself like a bee buzzing with a group of other girls clustered together as part of a natural hive. They gathered their trays, sat at a long table and seemed to do what they must do every few years—a rundown of basic stats, where they came from, last place stationed, favorite place stationed, dad or mom's MOS, which Abilene realized was an acronym for job title, and rank. Rank seemed to be the only distinction resembling class. They shared stories of this or that bullshit teacher or coach at Fort so-and-so, parties at underground clubs in Germany or Guam or Italy, and weather in whatever region—bullshit snow at Fort Drum and bullshit heat at Fort Sam Houston. Then came Abilene's turn. While her story was slightly different—first time at a Department of Defense school and living on a post because mom died and soldier dad got custody—no one stared like she was a freak, a misfit, or too poor, or too weird to be bothered with. They nodded, got her hesitation to share, and took it all in as just her story, nothing more or nothing less, nothing to judge or hold against her, nothing to illicit eye rolls or laughs, just acceptance. She soaked it in and let it soothe the sting of past first day experiences that still haunted her.

By the end of day one, one girl took Abilene under her wing. It was her third year at Fort Patten High School. As luck would have it, she would most likely get to spend all four years of high school in one place. She was a rarity in that regard. Her very presence was another reason she stood out. Alyssa Hale was one of those mixes of physical beauty, unabashed kindness, and a sense of humor most beautiful people never bothered to cultivate. They already had the world eating out of their palms, so why try to be funny, too? But for Alyssa, it all just came naturally. She held Abilene and everyone else spellbound, without seeming to notice or care. She had straight, shiny blonde hair, large blue eyes and was short. Alyssa had a refined look without trying. Her makeup was spot-on, trendy but not overdone. As delicate as her features and gait were, her laugh was hearty like an old, round comedian, with a smoke dangling from his lips. It took up all the space and made everyone else laugh harder because it was unexpectedly boisterous.

Alyssa decided Abilene was going with her to the football game on Friday night and shopping on Saturday. Abilene realized Alyssa would not take no for an answer, and she had no desire to miss out on a moment spent in Alyssa's presence. She was too fierce and alluring to resist, and everything about her fascinated Abilene. Yet, Alyssa didn't project or command dominance in a way that intimidated anyone. She simply attracted those who needed kinship, protection, the exiled who sought a place of acceptance, and acceptance was what Abilene needed most. Something about being with her also made Abilene feel like she did when she was with Julien, a sense that friendships were real, and some people were just meant to go through life side by side. Every time Alyssa made her laugh, she felt a twinge of missing Julien. During sparse phone calls to his house in Holden, she'd ramble on and on about Alyssa. Julien would say he was happy Abilene found a real friend, and Abilene knew he meant it. She kept wishing he'd find the same. Guilt followed those twinges of missing him after they'd talk. Guilt that she left him behind. Her world opened up, and she enjoyed the normal teenage experiences she had missed because of being a de facto mom to her other siblings. His had stayed the same—shitty and stuck in Holden without a real friend in the world.

She had a brand-new existence—a new friend to navigate a new school, two new little sisters that made her time at home more fun than she could have ever expected, and two new parents who let her be her and adjust accordingly. It all helped make her junior year float more effortlessly than Abilene could've anticipated. There were moments late at night after finishing homework and listening to Tom and Sandy banter back and forth over what to watch on tv that night that she felt slightly guilty about adjusting so quickly. Abilene would have moments where she cried, thinking about her mom. Mostly right before she'd fall asleep in the room Sandy had decorated for her, a room that used to be Krista and Kayla's playroom, she'd glance around and let a few tears escape. She'd replay her mom's last day in her head and hear the shouts, see her mother's face, her mouth, her arm go limp, and wonder if there was anything she could've done in those seconds. Maybe if she had stopped her damn screaming and ran to the nurses' station when her mom said she had a headache still. Maybe if she had talked to the doctor more about her mom's blood pressure situation or had asked more questions. Maybe instead of spending her days that summer at a dirty pool or walking to Mazzy's in the middle of the night for slushies and hot chicken, she could've been reading about preeclampsia and could've possibly prevented the entire event. Event. That's what Abilene had referred to it as. It was an event that happened and had changed her world.

There were other nights she played with the girls, read them stories to give Sandy a break, even though Sandy insisted she didn't need her to, nights Abilene fell right to sleep, slightly excited for the next day. Those were the nights she dreamt of her mom and her siblings as if they existed together in some alternate universe, still throwing shoes at the wall, tearing up her homework, and Abilene was still somewhere doing dishes or making whatever her mother craved. The nights of falling to sleep easily led to mornings where tears crept up or a wet pillowcase from crying in her sleep. She preferred crying in her sleep, blissfully unaware until the next day.

Alyssa seemed to understand her loss without truly having ever felt it. Abilene figured that was just the nature of an Empath, someone who felt it too without having gone through it. It was the way she listened, too. If they were shopping after school or walking around base and Abilene would mention her mom, worries about her other siblings, or anything about her old life, Alyssa would look her dead in the eye and tell her to keep going, keep talking. She didn't let Abilene gloss over it or try to soothe it quickly to keep the process of grieving from touching her like Sandy and Tom did at times. They didn't mean to, but Abilene could tell they thought that was the best way to help. Change the subject, encourage a good cry, then move on. Sometimes crying wasn't enough. Alyssa let Abilene take the lead on what was enough, when the tears were finally drained, when the words were exhausted. She didn't let Abilene let herself off the hook or stuff it down because it might be inconvenient for others at the table. Abilene treasured the freedom to grieve, to not grieve and not feel guilty about it, and to just be. As the year progressed, Abilene knew she hit the friend jackpot once again.

# CHAPTER 13

*Christmas 1992*

Christmas at Fort Patten was unlike anything Abilene had ever experienced before. While she knew her mom did her best to make Christmas great for all of them, decorations and public parties weren't really part of their traditions. The Army post looked like a full-blown Christmas movie set. Even the tanks that sat in the center of the main traffic circle on post had giant wreaths placed on front, with massive red bows that swayed in the breeze. Lights were everywhere. Each house on the post seemed hell-bent on outdoing each other. There was a Santa at the Post Exchange and neon holiday liquor signs hanging at the Class 6, the post liquor store. All that was missing was snow, which was something Abilene had never experienced, but she wondered if the Army could truck it in for effect, like it seemed to do with the endless lights. There were endless parties too, parties for the adults, the teens, the little ones, families whose soldiers were deployed somewhere, parties for each unit and company. It seemed like Sandy and Tom were out at one function every few days. The kids' parties left Krista and Kayla covered in frosting or some other form of sugar. The hot cocoa flowed everywhere, and candy canes were attached to every gift and treat. It was as if the north pole itself engulfed Fort Patten.

Sandy loved Christmas, which was obvious with the number of totes she had in the garage solely dedicated to holiday décor. Abilene thought some of them were a little cheesy at first, but as the weeks rolled by, they grew on her. Seeing Kayla and Krista beaming with delight and wonder helped. Each squeal from them also made her miss Savannah and wonder what kind of Christmas she and Paris would have with Tucker and his family. The phone calls she placed to him to have him put Savannah on the phone spaced out more. At first and into the fall, Abilene called every week just to be sure the girls were safe. She'd also call Butchy each week to talk to the boys, to make sure they were staying on track. She also liked to hear their voices to be reminded of Ashlynn, of their life together as a family. The boys would stay on the phone less and less, always hurrying out the door to play soccer, run the streets, or whatever else boys their age did. Butchy would assure Abilene they were adjusting fine, and to Abilene's pleasant surprise, he'd ask her how she was, how school was, how life with the Sergeant was. Despite the fights, the leaving, the side of the story Abilene always got from her mom, she always sensed Butchy loved his sons and in some small way, he loved the rest of them too. Abilene wondered after each of those calls what life would have been like if he had stayed with Ashlynn. There was no doubt in her mind Ashlynn would, at the very least, be alive.

Abilene woke Christmas morning to Krista's high pitch voice telling her to get up. They couldn't go downstairs and open presents until Abilene came down with them. Kayla pulled on her arms as Krista climbed onto her bed and leaned down close to her face.

"Get up, Abi. You gotta walk us down to see what Santa brought," she said with a sweetness that made Abilene smile.

Together, the three of them walked into a living room overflowing with gifts piled up onto the couch, flowing across the entire floor. The giant tree was nearly hidden. Abilene stopped to take it all in compared to Christmas' of the past. The pangs of missing her 'old family' caught her off guard. She stifled the urge to cry. She knew it would upset Sandy or make her feel she hadn't done enough, as if one more wreath or gift would have made it all okay. The girls let go of Abilene's hands and rushed to the scene to unwrap gifts in a frenzy of excitement. Abilene forced a smile and sat on a free spot on the floor.

"You can sit up here. You want coffee or anything?" Tom asked as he scooted over and tried not to spill his. Abilene nodded.

"I'm fine," Abilene said. Sandy stood and wrestled an enormous gift from the back of the pile. It was a flat rectangle.

"This is yours, honey," Sandy said in her soft voice as she slid it out and propped it up on the edge of the couch.

Abilene smiled and peeled the red and green striped paper to reveal a large corkboard with a white frame. Her name was painted across the top in pink cursive. Abilene couldn't remember having anything with her name on it.

"Thanks, this will look cool on the wall above the desk," she said as she ran her fingers across the frame.

"There's a box of tacks too, but I didn't wrap those," Sandy said with a laugh. "I wasn't sure you'd like it, but I saw it and thought it would be nice for you to pin up pictures of your brothers and sisters and those postcards, too." Sandy shrugged her shoulders.

"My postcards?" Abilene said.

"Yeah, I see you spread them out on the bed sometimes and read the back. I figured they must be important. Thought maybe you could hang them up to see every day." Sandy smiled and her eyes grew wide as she waited for a response.

Abilene gasped. She didn't realize anyone noticed her taking her mother's postcards out and reading them over and over, trying to feel what Ashlynn felt or trying to make sense of it all. She'd stare at them some nights in anger over the lies, the lost promise of a home, a place out there that was theirs, their heritage, their past, their lineage. There was no grand family home called Swenson House, no future tea on the balcony or walks by the lily pond. There was no longer a grand plan to drive there, declare the home hers complete with some long-lost family waiting with open arms and apologies for discarding Ashlynn. The postcards were a mixed bag every time Abilene got them out, and all along Sandy had been observing and never asked. Abilene wasn't sure if she should cry, throw the corkboard, or calmly explain how the postcards were her only proof of her mother's lie, of her myth, the only thing she had of her mother's at all. Abilene's cheeks grew red and tears exploded from her eyes before she could speak. Sandy stood and placed a hand on her shoulder.

"Oh my, I didn't mean to upset you. I thought—"

"It's okay, Sandy. Abilene, what's wrong?" Tom said as he set his cup on an end table. Kayla and Krista froze mid-unwrapping frenzy. A quiet fell over the entire Christmas wonderland. All eyes fell on Abilene as she slowly rose. She leaned the corkboard against the other presents and then wiped her tears with her hands. She drew in a deep breath as she stood in front of them in her pajamas.

"I'm sorry," she muttered. Abilene made her way over the pile of wrapping and bows. She gingerly stepped and broke into a full sprint once she reached the stairs. Abilene made it to her room just as sobs made words impossible. She closed the door and let it all out. Abilene melted into her bed and thought she'd drown in tears. She was crying for 10-year-old Ashlynn, a dying Ashlynn, the kids left behind, the foolish plan to drive to Abilene with Julien one day and claim what was hers, what would never be hers. It all felt like bricks crashing through the ceiling, crushing her. Gasping for air, she pulled out the cards from the middle drawer of the desk Sandy bought for her. She laid them across the bed. Abilene forced herself to look at each picture. They each felt like a dagger jabbing into her heart, piercing through her repeatedly.

"Hey, kid." Tom said in a whisper from the door. Abilene drew in one deep breath.

"I'm sorry. I just—"

"It's okay." He said as he made his way to her bed. He reached down and picked up the postcard with the dining room table on it. Tom turned it over and read it. "What are these about, anyway?"

Abilene handed him the rest. "She told me this was her childhood home, and we'd go back there someday. But it was all a lie." Abilene told him about the newspaper article, how Ashlynn was only ten and got these from her parents, and how Abilene found them all when she was searching for his address and number right after her mom died. She told him how she grabbed them all and now it's all she has left of her mother. Tom read and reread each of them. She could see tears come to his eyes.

"My God, kid. I had no idea she told you any of that. I knew her parents had died when she was young. She was raised by her grandparents. But, damn, I didn't know about these, about this house, none of this." He exhaled and looked up at the ceiling. Tom sat next to her. "She wanted to name you Abilene because she said it sounded beautiful and it was a cool town. She never told me any of this, I swear."

Abilene relaxed her shoulders. She leaned her head on her father's shoulder. He tapped her knee and leaned over to kiss the top of her head.

"You don't have to hang these up or anything. Sandy will understand." Abilene took the stack of postcards from his hand and held them up to her heart.

"Dad?" she said as she sat straight up and stared ahead.

"Yeah, kid."

"Was anything she ever told me true? Anything about her life that wasn't bullshit? Anything about me that wasn't a lie?" Tom smirked and stood up in front of her. She always forgot just how tall he was until she was sitting and he was standing in front of her. He pushed his hands in his pockets and smiled down at her.

"Yeah, marigolds. Marigolds were her favorite flower," he said. Abilene could see in his eyes he was thinking of her mom and some wonderful, sweet memory that he had held dear all these years. She wanted to ask more but didn't. For now, for that Christmas, knowing marigolds were her mom's favorite was enough of a gift. It was enough of a truth to take the edge off the lies. Abilene decided she'd hang up the postcards. They were beautiful, even if the truth wasn't.

Christmas gave way to a mild winter and early spring for Georgia. Abilene and Alyssa took advantage of every hot sunny day to wander the post after school. They giggled easily, told lame jokes, and just enjoyed aimlessly walking sidewalks, woodsy trails, and hanging out at the base coffee shop and PX. While she still tried to call Julien every once in a while, they rarely got to speak for long. They'd play phone tag, then one would give up trying. Then another month would pass and another call would happen. A few minutes of catching up, checking up, teasing, and a few laughs would then lead to an awkward silence. Abilene missed him, but no longer needed him like she did in Holden or when she stood outside the gate that night last summer. She mainly thought of him when she'd hear a certain song, or the family would leave post and come back in through that gate. Abilene often wondered what her life would be like if she and Julien had just kept driving, or if she insisted he come with her instead of going home. She played the tape he gave her some nights when she was bored or lost in the past, the what ifs.

On the hottest day of spring, a Saturday, Abilene and Alyssa wore their shortest shorts, combat boots, and flannel tied around their waist and headed out for a day of nothing in particular as Sandy took the girls to the commissary. Abilene loved when she and Alyssa dressed alike without trying. She felt people might mistake them for sisters if she wasn't so much taller and had hair that sprang out in every direction, unlike the perfectly behaved hair that swooshed Alyssa's shoulders.

"Hey, the ice cream stand. It opens up today." Alyssa said mid-sentence, interrupting herself, as she did often.

"Alright." Abilene said as they stepped off the curb to cross the street that led away from the housing area. They walked past the high school and made a few jokes about the vice principal, who was the most vile woman they dealt with on any given day. The girls stepped in unison across the traffic circle and tapped the tracks of the tanks as they passed. They could see a line already forming at the ice cream stand. It stood alone at the edge of an intersection. It was a small shack no bigger than a food truck, with picnic tables peppered all around it. A giant sign on top seemed bigger than the actual stand. It was right across from the barracks. They got in line behind G.I.s and families with kids running in circles and climbing the tables. Once they got cones, they snagged a spot on a picnic table facing the barracks. While Abilene had been on post for almost nine months, she hadn't paid much attention to the soldiers living and training around her. She really only saw her dad, his friends, and the neighborhood dads in uniform each day coming and going to work or in school picking up a sick kid. They all blended into each other—just dads wearing the same uniform. Sure, rank and patches set them apart, but from a distance they all looked the same except for a few height extremes. Abilene licked her cone and noticed a group across the street. They were in front of the barracks in PT shorts and not much else tossing a football. It was the first time Abilene gave much thought to how many of the soldiers on post were near her age, especially the single guys in the barracks. The group of five in the grass laughed and tossed the ball to the ground. Three of them reached down to grab shirts. One of the tallest with muscles that gleamed in the sun and sweat pulled his shirt over his bald head and looked her way. His eyes met hers as she took another lick of the ice cream that was melting into her hand. She felt a drip hit her knee and run down her leg. She fought the urge to look at it and lose eye contact with the soldier. As he and the others made it to the curb, he flashed her a smile that hit her like lightning. Electricity coursed through her entire body and the hair on the back of her neck rose. Goose bumps trickled from her forearms to her legs. She couldn't speak or breathe. His smile and eyes paralyzed her. The boys in school were boys. They teased her, flirted in their own way, but this was a man and, for that moment, he was the only man in the world. He looked carved like a Greek god statue, and she felt a pull towards him. Everything around her, the families in line, parents demanding to know what flavor kids wanted before they ran off, the other teens from school flanked lazily on other picnic tables, the other soldiers pulling their wallets from pockets, and even Alyssa talking faded into the background. Everything was under a sea that kept them all muffled and barely visible under the surface, a surface that contained only her and him as he stepped closer. His eyes never looked away from her. He was absorbing the whole of the world around her. Time stopped. The breeze stopped. He stepped from the curb without looking away from her and seemed to glide across the street. The closer he got, the more she was sure he'd pull her into his orbit and hopefully never let her go. She drew in a deep breath, hoping to smell him as he got closer.

"Abi!" Alyssa broke into the cocoon she was in. "Abi!" she yelled, with a nudge to her side. Abilene shook her head.

"What? Wha—" Abilene stammered as she searched for his eyes again.

"I said I'm getting a drink. What do you want?"

Without moving an inch, Abilene stared straight at the approaching soldier and let a giant smile slide across her face. "I want one of those. That one, to be exact."

# CHAPTER 14

*Summer 1993*

A midnight drizzle covered a quiet Holden as Julien kept his head down and walked to Mazzy's. His house was trashed by another fight between his parents. His sisters huddled under blankets and finally drifted off after the melee. Working for Chris for another summer would give him some refuge, but not enough, especially when the sun went down and the steam rose from the hot streets. He was counting down the days to senior year because it would provide another distraction, another reason to be away from home. This year, he thought, he might join a sport or a club just to be away more. But for now, lonely escapes for hot chicken and slushies spiked with whatever he could steal from his mom's stash in the middle of the night would have to be enough. He turned the corner he avoided most nights and glanced around and up to the dimly lit porches tucked away from the street. A voice he dreaded pierced the silence.

"Hey Julien, where ya going?" Charlene said in a quieter than normal voice. Julien tensed his jaw and stopped for a second. He waited for her to hurl an insult or say something about his crazy mom. Julien swallowed and clenched his fist in anticipation of having to tell her to fuck off.

"You hear me? Where ya going?" She repeated.

Julien turned his head to see her at the bottom of her porch steps. She was alone, which was rare as Charlene was the leader of her pack and rarely left to her own devices or to entertain herself.

"You know where I go. I'm just walking to Mazzy's. Why? You got something smart to say about that?" He said as his pulse quickened.

"Nah, I was just wondering if you want company is all," she said. Julien watched her take a few slow steps closer to where the streetlight cast a glow over her.

"You? You wanna walk with me to Mazzy's?" He scoffed and put his hands in his pockets. "I didn't think girls like you set foot in places like that." Julien walked away. He heard her coming behind him. Julien turned to walk backwards. "You gonna follow me? You just waiting to yell about my 'crazy' mom, as you call her or something?"

"No. I'm just... just bored, I guess. Ain't nothing else to do around here and I can't sleep in this heat or in that damned air conditioning my daddy keeps on full blast all day and night," she said as she quickened her pace to catch up with him. Julien turned to walk forward just as she reached him.

"Whatever. If you wanna come, come. I don't give a shit. But I ain't buying you a slushie or anything." He said into the dark drizzle.

They walked the last few blocks in silence. Julien let his guard down slightly but still waited for the joke, the insult that he was sure she spent the entire summer and last year of school planning in her spiteful mind.

"Can I ask you something?" She said. *Here we go*, Julien thought.

"What?"

"Do you miss her? Abilene, I mean."

"Yeah. I do. We try to talk here and there, but she's busy, so it's been a few months. We got different lives now, but she was my best friend. I know that's a joke to you and your little posse of followers. But she was anyway." Julien shrugged his shoulders. He swallowed a lump, thinking of how it was almost a year ago that he drove Abilene to Georgia. A year since they hugged after her mom's funeral. Their paths had diverged and showed no signs of crossing again.

"I'm sorry, ya know. Whether or not you believe it. I'm sorry her mom died like that, and she had to leave." A few moments of silence lingered between them. "And I'm sorry you lost your friend." Julien glanced at Charlene and was surprised to see genuine concern in her eyes. Part of him still expected her little gang of followers to spring from the bushes or from behind the trees just to laugh at him for thinking Charlene cared. Then another part of him, the part that can see people's intentions in their eyes, could tell she meant it. He realized she looked lonely, too. He never noticed before, but suddenly he could see being Charlene must not be a picnic at all.

"Thanks for that. I miss her, but whatever. She's happy with her dad and his family. She's good now." Julien said as Charlene nodded. "That's what matters most."

They both bought slushies and Julien bought hot chicken. Even if he wasn't hungry before he got there, the smell made it impossible to turn down. They didn't talk. They just walked. As they got close to her house, she slurped the last of her slushie.

"I guess I'll see ya in school soon. Senior year. Crazy, huh?"

"Yeah. Crazy." Julien said.

She turned to walk to her porch. Suddenly, she spun around to face him again.

"Hey, Julien. I'm sorry for all that stuff I said about your mom, too."

He nodded her way and walked away as he brushed away a rebellious lock of hair. The entire way home, he smiled, thinking he needed to call Abilene soon and tell her about Charlene becoming human suddenly. She'd get a real kick out of that. Even though they rarely spoke, he couldn't help but smile, thinking of things she'd love to hear. Most of the time, he never got the chance to tell her those things, but that didn't stop him from thinking of her first, anyway.

Julien balled up the bag with napkins and few bones and stuffed it into the garbage can at the end of his driveway. He noticed the lights were on. That was never a good sign in the middle of the night. Then the familiar sound of his father yelling at his mom filled the air.

"Shit. Not again," he muttered as he made his way to the front door. Julien walked into the usual chaos. Sheila was in the front hall, crying. Mascara rivers made her look like a tragic clown the circus threw off the train. Noah was at the kitchen entry with his arms slung above his head, clinging to the door frame leading to the living room. His face was red with pure rage and tear-streaked, too. A few of his bottles lined the counter behind him. Julien instantly thought of Sammy and Selena.

"Are the girls in their room still?" He said to his mom. Sheila nodded. Her eyes looked more wild than usual.

"Hey!" His father yelled as he slammed his hands on the door frame. Sheila shuddered and let out a small whimper. Julien just wanted to rewind the night and go back to the quiet streets and let the drizzle drown him or wash him away from Holden completely. "Look here, dipshit!" Noah's voice shook the house. Julien knew his sisters must be trembling.

"What, Dad?" He said in a quiet voice. Julien had been diffusing these kinds of nights for years. His mom wiped her face and walked to Noah. She reached up and tried to wrap her shaking arms around his waist.

"Let him go check on the girls, Noah. He ain't done nothing wrong except get home late." She said as she nestled her head into his sweaty white t-shirt.

"That's the thing, She. He's always wandering in late as fuck and not helping you at all. He's useless. A little smart-ass punk. Huh, boy?" He yelled out. Julien knew it might take more than a quiet voice and ignoring insults to get this night over the hump of drunken fights and madness. Years of insults and terror echoing through the house finally came to a head for Julien.

"I do a shit-ton here and all you do is come home and go after her until she's a slobbering mess and Sammy and Selena are scared shitless. You're the useless one here!" Julien yelled before he realized what he was saying. Fear drenched him like a bucket of river water after the words barreled across the room. Noah grabbed Sheila by the back of her head and peeled her off him. He slung her across the room with a quickness and smoothness of motion that Sheila didn't have time to react or even yell out. She hit the floor with a thud that echoed. Noah's eyes never left Julien. In that moment, Julien knew his mom, he, and his sisters were just a swarm of gnats to Noah that he could swat away and squash without a second thought. Sheila reached up and held her head. Julien saw blood as she looked back down at her hand. None of them had realized until that moment she hit the baseboard and cut herself.

The blood on his mother, the look on his father's face caused a heat to rise in Julien's gut. He felt like lava raced through him and his body would burst into flames. Julien lunged at his father without hesitation or a plan. He wanted to push him straight through the kitchen and wall to the outside. He wanted to pound his father out of existence for all the fear, pain, and tears he had caused. Then he wanted to shake his mother wildly until her senses awoke and she swore to get help, be healthy, be normal, love him and his sisters above all others, and stop thriving off the chaos she provoked. She called it passion. Julien wanted no part of it for another minute.

Just as Julien reached his father, his father drew back with one smooth, quick motion and propelled his fist forward. Pain exploded from the side of his face after the crack of contact. He fell back to the ground and his ears rang. Spots danced before his numb face. Double vision appeared for a few seconds. He couldn't talk. He touched the side of his face and winced. Of all the fights and chaos that had unfolded in that house for years, no one had ever touched Julien. There were slaps between his parents, threats of killing, and more things thrown at each other than Julien could count. Julien realized he had never been punched by anyone before.

Sheila crawled over to him and ran her hands through his hair as he sat stunned and afraid to move. He cringed at her. He blamed her just as much as he blamed his dad. Noah let out a deep hateful laugh that made Julien nauseous. Julien pushed his mom's hand away as she cried and muttered she was sorry. He pushed himself up from the floor, not looking at his dad, and staggered down the hall to his room. Julien looked in his mirror and saw swelling already taking place and what was surely going to be a black eye. Julien wanted to grab his sisters and run, burn the entire house down behind him. His mom didn't come to check on him. He knew she was probably already back in Noah's arms. He was probably gingerly cleaning the cut on her head. Julien realized they deserved each other. Julien peeked out the door. When he didn't see his parents, he dashed to his sisters' door and peeked in. They were in bed. Sammy gave a frown and a tiny wave.

"It's ok. We're all ok." Julien whispered. Sammy nodded. He closed the door and went back to his room. Julien undressed and crawled into his bed. He sunk into the mattress with just his boxers on. Julien closed his eyes and heard the faint sounds of his parents still fighting in the living room. He reached over and turned on his radio, rolled back over, and cried as the side of his face throbbed.

At work the next day, Julien's uncle saw his black eye and shook his head. He told Julien to let it be a lesson. There isn't any glory in trying to save his mom or change his dad. They were who they were, and he shouldn't have tried to get in the middle of it. Julien swore he never would again, and he swore his dad would never have the chance to punch him again. After work, Julien stood tall and marched across town to the Army recruiter's office. He thought all day about asking his Uncle Chris about his time in the Army and if he should enlist, or if he should just go to vo-tech or trade school to work on engines. He wanted his uncle's opinion, guidance as if Chris could be some kind of father-figure because God knows he couldn't ask his father. But as the day wore on, Julien kept thinking about how easily his dad punched him and how his mom would always reach for Noah and nestle her face in his chest. He knew it didn't matter if Chris advised him to enlist or just take off. Chris's opinion on anything wouldn't make a damn bit of difference. Nothing or no one could stop him at that point. After work, Julien didn't breathe or slow his stride until he walked through the glass door covered with a giant Army decal.

"Can we help you, son?" A voice boomed from behind a desk. The soldier stood. The word 'son' made Julien stop dead in his tracks for a minute. No one had called him 'son' in ages. He stood taller with his shoulders back with his eye socket still throbbing.

"Yes, sir. I'd like to enlist."

"You out of school? You graduate already?"

"No, sir. I start my senior year in two weeks."

"Alright, son. Have a seat and we'll talk about what you want to do once you graduate and how the Army can get you there. You know what you want to be yet? What Army career you're interested in?" The soldier motioned for Julien to take a seat as he sat back down behind his desk. Julien hadn't thought further than just getting the hell out of Holden, and he knew the Army was one way to do it. He looked up at the giant posters on the wall. Julien saw a soldier in his dress uniform with shining medals and colorful bars across his chest. He looked determined and fierce. His jaw was chiseled, and he had eyes like a warrior. The medals proved he was. He looked like the kind of man Noah wouldn't dare take a swing at. Julien pointed at the poster above the recruiter as he approached the desk.

"All I know is I want to be a soldier. I want to be one of those."

# CHAPTER 15

***Summer 1993***

Abilene walked through the door just as Sandy was carrying an enormous bowl to the dining room.

"I was wondering if you were gonna be home for dinner. You and Alyssa been running all around this post all day. You even eat lunch?" Sandy said as she passed by. "The girls wanna watch a movie tonight. You in?"

"Yeah. I'll watch something with them and yeah, I ate lunch at the PX." Abilene said as she slid off her flip-flops and followed Sandy. "Dad home yet?"

"Nope, not yet." Sandy said as she took a seat. She felt lucky her dad was home each night. Alyssa's dad had been deployed for the entire summer and might not be back by their graduation in May. Because he was gone, Alyssa's mom let Alyssa run wild most of the time. She had her hands full with Alyssa's brothers, who reminded Abilene of her own brothers she hadn't seen in a year. Michael and Joey were 10 and 12 years old. They both reminded Abilene of Dallas. Every time she went to Alyssa's house, and they sprinted past her to get outside, she felt a tiny pang in her gut and would wonder what her brothers were up to, if they were enjoying the summer, if they missed her, and of course, if they missed their mom.

Abilene scooped a plateful of spaghetti and ate. Sandy was staring at her.

"What?" Abilene said in between bites.

"Listen, I know I'm not your mom or anything, but I gotta tell ya, you need to be a little careful."

"Careful?"

"Yeah. Susie, next door, saw you and Alyssa at the bowling alley the other night with a group of privates. Now, I remember being 17—"

"18. I'll be 18 in October." Abilene said as she swallowed.

"Those guys, they ain't boys, honey. They're G.I.s and they all probably have girls back home waiting for them to take leave and marry them."

"We aren't doing anything, I swear. We just—"

Sandy held her hand up. "All I'm saying is to be careful. School starts next week. Your senior year. Focus on that. Focus on *those* boys." Sandy wiped the corner of her mouth and glanced at the girls. "Just watch, so it's not your dad coming across you and Alyssa. You hear me?"

Abilene nodded. She and Alyssa hadn't been careful at all. They spent the entire summer following the group of G.I.s they saw at the ice cream stand months ago. They sat on the same picnic table every Saturday and exchanged glances, which morphed into winks. That flowed into accidentally running into them at the bowling alley. The girls would get a lane next to them and giggle and bumble their way through a game. The winks turned into buying them nachos and a few laughs as they finally talked to each other. Abilene burned for Benny, and any sight of him only made it worse. His name was Benito Nash. While the other G.I.s called him Nash, Abilene called him Benny.

After a few Saturdays of playful flirting, they decided to all meet up at the movie theater. They sat next to each other in the dark and talked to just each other for the first time. Before the movie started and the popcorn was still full, they were all over each other. Abilene wanted to swallow him up. She wanted him to carry her out of there to his barracks and ravage her. She couldn't get close enough to him or couldn't touch him enough. Their mouths and tongues searched for each other for the entire showing of Jurassic Park. She never wanted anyone like that. It was pure lust. She wanted to explode every time their eyes met.

After the movie, they had to peel apart. Alyssa grabbed her arm and marched her around the corner from the theater. For the first time since they met, Alyssa looked furious. Her easy-going way of floating through their summer disappeared. Alyssa told her it was one thing to flirt with those

G.I.s, but that was too far, especially during a crowded premier where half the post was in the theater. She could get him kicked out of the Army. Alyssa yelled Abilene was still 17 and that G.I.s entire career could end if either of their parents found out. If anyone who knew them saw Abilene in that theater, it would be Benny and his friends who pay the price. Abilene hadn't thought about that. Even having those facts thrown at her now didn't faze her. She still wanted to run after Benny and have him take her right then and there on the street, if possible. She ached for him and didn't care who knew it or saw it. He was all she thought about and dreamed about since she first saw him across from the ice cream stand.

Abilene, lost in the memories of making out with him, nodded at Sandy and swallowed a lump in her throat. Her mind raced with everywhere she and Benny had met up during the summer. He tried a few times to tamp it down, avoid letting anything more than flirting happen, but he burned for her too every time he caught a glimpse of her. They hadn't had sex yet, mostly because of Alyssa's constant warnings that Benny would get kicked out for sure. But Abilene knew after she turned 18, there was no stopping either of them.

The phone rang. It startled Abilene as she tried to figure out new places to sneak away moments with Benny. Sandy pushed out her chair to answer it in the kitchen.

"Abilene, it's Julien," Sandy called out in her high-pitched voice. Abilene jumped.

"I'll get it my room," she yelled as she dashed up the steps, thankful for an end to the conversation.

Abilene threw herself across her bed and grabbed her pink cordless phone, a gift from Sandy on one of their shopping trips.

"Hey, Ponyboy! We've been playing phone tag for months." She said breathlessly.

"Hey, asshole. You haven't been home all summer when I call." Julien said. She noticed his voice was low, like he was hiding out in his room. She could picture him alone on his bed.

"I've been busy. There's so much to do here. I met someone, a guy." She lowered her voice to a whisper. "I'll tell you about him later." There was a long silence. "What's up with you? You sound bummed." She exhaled, thinking he always sounded bummed anymore. Abilene hated that part of her didn't want to hear why. Their last few calls had been strained because of the guilt she felt for being happy finally, being free to go to movies, sleepovers, games, shopping, and everything they couldn't do together in Holden. She felt herself pulling away from him, and she hated herself for it. As much as she wanted to move forward, hearing his voice reminded her she left him behind in Holden.

"Kinda yeah. Things are just shit here, Abilene. My parents, all of it. But I got a plan. I was telling Charlene the other night when we walked to Mazzy's—"

"Charlene? What the fuck are you doing walking with her? She hates us."

"Listen, she's different now, but that's not the point. I got into a fight with my dad. The fucker punched me, and then the next day I walked to the re—"

"Seriously Julien! After all she said about us? To us? To our faces? She's your new best friend?" Abilene felt tears well up. Her pulse quickened and her temples throbbed. She gripped the phone tighter. Her guilt about moving on without him turned to anger that he was moving on without her.

"Stop. This isn't about her. I decided—"

"It is about her. How can you be friends with her after all she said about your mom? And walking with her Mazzy's? That's our... our place." She bit her lip and knew it wasn't about Mazzy's being their place. It was about Julien being her friend, not Charlene's.

"You know what? She's about the only friend I got here. You left. Everything went to shit last year and this summer, too. You never call me back. Ever. Shit, I called you every week for months. We ain't talked in forever and when we do, it's all about how happy your life is now and all the cool shit you got from your new family. How do you think that makes me feel? Did you even hear that my dad hit me? The fucker punched me in the face. But you just wanna give me shit because Charlene is my friend now? She's different. We're pretty close, actually. She's even kinda my girlfr—"

"Fuck that. I left because my mom fucking died! Did you forget that? It's not my fault I've been busy this summer, you know. I had to move on and make a life here. You want me to feel like shit because I have a little bit of happiness now and a decent place to live, decent parents, places to go and shit? I had to leave there. Remember? It wasn't a choice to leave you. But you sit there and try to make me feel guilty while you cling to Charlene, the biggest bitch in Holden? That's fucked up." Abilene realized she was yelling. She reached up from the bed and pushed the door closed with her foot before Kayla and Krista walked in.

"You don't even care what I've been going through here, what my dad did or anything. You only care that you think I replaced you with Charlene. Fuck that, Abilene."

Abilene slammed the phone down. "Asshole." She burst into tears. She hadn't heard his voice in so long. All she could hear was him saying Charlene's name over and over again. Abilene rolled over and looked at her boom box. His tape was still in it. She hadn't listened to it since she started sneaking around with Benny. She hadn't even told Benny about Julien, about how he was the best friend she ever had, how he saved her from a life of misery in Holden, how his hug saved her after her mother died. Abilene barely told Benny anything about her past, only that her mother passed away in childbirth. She didn't tell him about their life moving around, her siblings' names, seeing Ashlynn fade away as Abilene yelled she hated her. That was all bound with twine in her heart. She had no plan to unwrap it and hand it to Benny anytime soon, if ever. Julien was the only one who knew her then, knew the real her. And now Julien had replaced her with the one person they called an empty shell. Abilene pressed play and rolled on her back to stare at the ceiling. Nirvana filled the room. Then Pearl Jam. Release Me played, and she cried. Abilene cried like a girl who just lost her best friend.

Abilene wiped away tears with her forearm and let the music fill her room, her perfect room with perfectly new bedding, posters, a phone, and even a small tv, all the things she never dreamed she'd have. It was a cocoon of love, safety, of belonging to a normal family like she'd seen on tv. She had the normalcy she secretly envied, but hearing Julien's voice made it all seem fake, like she was acting the part of a normal teenage girl with two little sisters who made her laugh, a new mom who loved taking her shopping, and a dad who wanted to know how her day went and what she wanted to be when she was out of school. This family, the Matterlys, had absorbed her, plucked her from Holden as her world fell apart, but part of her still clung to that version of Abilene in red boots, walking home to a tiny brick house next to a sketchy motel. Part of her needed to stay connected to that girl, that time in her life as shitty as it was. Julien was the only connection left there. She squeezed her eyes shut as she realized that's why any talk of him doing things differently, getting close to someone else, bothered her so much suddenly. Even though she had moved on to a new life away from that town, that summer, she needed him to stay the same, even though she knew that wasn't fair. To stay there waiting for her, unchanged. Holden is where she lost everything except him. She hated that his life was horrible there and for pulling away from him as hers got better. Abilene knew it wasn't right to want him to stay frozen in that existence just so she could stay connected to that time. A time when she had her real mother, her siblings, and her best friend. If Julien moved on, it would be the final break away from all she once had.

Abilene exhaled and shook her head as she sat up and stared at the boom box on her perfect white dresser. Guilt overwhelmed her. He deserved to move on, be happy, find friendship, hell, even find love. He deserved to get away from his parents and find his own sense of normalcy, peace, stability, and everything she had at Fort Patten. She swallowed a lump. Abilene glanced at the phone. She thought of calling him back and apologizing, maybe even asking how Charlene had changed. Then she felt a pit in her stomach. Maybe she'd call another day, but not today. But someday.

Someday turned into weeks, then longer. All summer, she and Alyssa had been mixing up clothes, trying to put together the unique looks. Once they both realized they missed out on seeing Pretty in Pink when they were in junior high, they rented it from the video store, then became obsessed with clothes. Alyssa even sewed a chunk of lace along the bottom of her favorite flannel. They realized afterwards it looked ridiculous, but it sparked more ideas. Together, they decided their senior year would be the year they set the trends, take risks, and pull off the unique looks.

Abilene and Alyssa walked into school the first day of senior year liked they owned the place. Alyssa did, since she had been there the longest. After a summer of being inseparable and sharing every secret, Abilene walked confidently beside her. While she and Alyssa swore it was the year to mix it up, go bold with style—clothes, hair, makeup—there was one thing she had to wear the first day, her red cowboy boots. Those boots made her walk taller, prouder, even at moments when she wanted to slither into a corner of a random classroom and be invisible. Those boots were from her mom. It helped that Alyssa thought they were cool, too, because they were authentic. Abilene needed something authentic in her life, something that felt permanent. If Julien couldn't be that, or her new family, or even this school she'd be leaving in a year, at least she could look down at her feet and feel connected to something that was uniquely and wholly hers.

Everyone in school, new and old, tried to pretend their lives were normal and not some strange experiment in what happens to adolescents who are part of military families being uprooted every two years or so. They had homecoming, football games, pep rallies where half of the kids were so new they could hardly keep track of what the mascot was at their current school. But, Alyssa and Abilene had something the others didn't have—they had plans and outside interests that didn't include pretending they were in a small town normal high school where everyone belonged, where homecoming queen crowns shined, and favorite teachers lasted for generations. Their outside interests included racing out of Fort Patten High School as soon as the bell rang and heading to the ice cream stand or the bowling alley once the stand closed for fall. Abilene had one mission each day as they tossed books in backpacks and slathered on more makeup in the bathroom before leaving the building. That mission was to find Benny. He was usually on duty until four or five if he wasn't in the field for a few weeks. When he was in the field the last two weeks of September and into October, she thought she'd go insane not seeing him. They were a thousand times more careful after Sandy's lecture, but not seeing him at all wasn't an option.

While Alyssa warned her and would point out a few new guys at school, it was no use. Benny consumed her mind every second he wasn't attached to her lips. Homework was an obstacle she tackled to keep her parents from grounding her if her grades went south. Going to school at all was simply a ruse to keep up the illusion of following the rules. Plus, she couldn't see him during the day, anyway. Abilene smirked at the thought that if Benny was around during the day, she'd probably skip school more than she cared to admit. Going through the motions at school, coordinating clothes with Alyssa, giggling and passing notes, making small talk with other kids about where they came from and where they were headed next was all to just pass the minutes before she could sneak around the back of the bowling alley and let Benny run his hands all over her or sit at the picnic table at the ice cream stand while he sat a table away and exchange knowing glances, knowing they'd sneak off once the crowd dispersed. She had a close call one afternoon as Benny walked past with his ice cream and ran his hand up her thigh as he passed her by. Just as she felt the heat of his quick touch, she glanced up and saw her dad drive past. He did a double take, and Abilene waved wildly to appear as innocent as she needed him to believe she was. The last thing she needed was her father to notice Benny and potentially notice him again while picking her and Alyssa up from the bowling alley or the PX.

Abilene had it all planned out. She had dreams about it, the night she'd tell Benny not to hold back. There was no real danger once she was 18. While they couldn't openly date because her father would surely kill Benny, there were no legal ramifications if they got caught. Sure, the Sergeant could make his life hell, hers too, but Benny wouldn't get kicked out or anything. Plus, Abilene told herself no one would find out, anyway. More each day, with each stolen kiss and glance, and brush of his hands, she believed this had to be love. There was nothing else it could be. It was like a fire inside every time she even thought of him. Time stopped when he was within sight. Her focus narrowed, and the world around her didn't exist anymore. Only him. There wasn't room for anything else. Sandy caught her off guard a few times, asking questions or trying to trip her up, or, worst yet, trying to entice her to date guys from school who lived in their section of the housing area. Sandy would throw a name out at dinner or when she'd pick up the girls from a football game. Sandy's voice would climb as she said a name and asked the girls if they knew him, what they thought of him, if they knew his father's rank. Father's, and sometimes mother's, rank was the opener to most conversations about any new kids, both amongst the kids and especially the parents. The last thing any parents wanted was a love story gone wrong between two kids whose parents were severely unequal in rank, especially if one was an NCO and one was an officer. That could be more awkward for parents than for the kids. Alyssa and Abilene would muster up enthusiasm and agree with Sandy that so-and-so was cute, nice, sweet, smart, athletic, funny, or whatever, just to lead Sandy to believe they noticed and considered pursuing so-and-so. While Alyssa flirted and considered dating a few of the high school "boys" as Sandy called them, Abilene was purely pretending. Benny was always in the forefront, on the tip of her tongue, in her heart.

He was away for her birthday. Abilene went to bed that night lonely yet trying to hide it as she blew out candles and let her sisters pick the best pieces of cake. She went to bed just as she woke up, a virgin. She laid in bed imagining him with her, next to her, on her, in her, part of her forever. Then, for the first time since she met him, she seriously wondered if he felt the same or thought of her as much. Their actual conversations were far and few between. They joked, laughed, teased, and talked about places they lived, but never really about each other and what this meant in the long run. It struck her like lightning that she envisioned giving herself to him and never really thought past that point. Would they stay together once she graduated? He told her bits and pieces of his childhood in Colorado, the views, his parents, his sister, and such. She shared the bare minimum. Abilene didn't tell him about her namesake, Swenson House, or her mother's last moments. She didn't tell him about Julien. She was ready to give him her virginity, but not those pieces of her soul that she guarded with her life. Abilene wondered what part of him did he guard. Then, as she drifted off, Abilene thought maybe after they made love, she'd give that part of herself too, and he'd give her the same. They'd be bound together forever. They'd become open books and love each other and never want to be apart for a second. Until she graduated, they would hide their love. Then once she went to college, he'd visit, and their families would see them as an ordinary young couple who fell in love one summer on Fort Patten. No one would ever know the stolen moments that piled up a year before that. It was perfect. Hopefully, she thought as she drifted off, Benny would think so too. Sparks like the ones she felt when he entered her mind, her atmosphere, her physical space, had to mean something. Passion like that couldn't just fade away or disappear. And it certainly couldn't be anything less than love.

She thought of her mom and the men she brought around. Ashlynn cried for men, yelled at men who yelled at her, then ran into their arms, but that wasn't the kind of heat that made sense. A raw passion based on nothing. After all, Ashlynn's men always left her as a puddle on the floor or in the driveway as they pulled away into the night. They left her babies both in and out of utero. They left, taking a piece of her with them. Those men tore chunks of her soul out. Then when she died, they took those babies away. Abilene swallowed and realized she hadn't thought of her mom for her entire birthday until that moment. She hadn't thought of her other siblings in a while, either. All she had room for in her mind and heart anymore was Benny. She weighed him against all the other men she'd known—her mom's obsessions, and her dad. Benny was different. Benny wasn't a yeller and as far as Abilene could tell, he wasn't a leaver either. What more did love really need to be?

# CHAPTER 16

*Fall 1993*

Benny came home from training two weeks after Abilene's 18th birthday. It felt like an eternity. Once they met up at the bowling alley on Friday night, Abilene told him she was ready, and she didn't plan on waiting another day. She wanted him to be the one. The smile on his face told her he didn't plan on putting up a fight.

"You sure you want it to be me? I mean, you can't go running around telling people about us still. Even though you're 18 now, your dad could put an entire world of hurting on me." He tilted his head and gave her that smirk that first caught her eye at the ice cream stand. "You gotta remember, you might be of age, but you're still in high school and that's all that's gonna matter to certain people, including on my side, too. Shit, my CO might beat my ass if he hears I'm messing with some high school kid."

"I'm not a kid." Abilene said as she nudged his side. "And stop being so paranoid. We've all but done it, anyway." She gathered up her long, wavy mane and pulled it to one side. She gave him a wink and leaned closer to his ear. Abilene glanced around quickly to be sure no unexpected soldiers or school friends wandered into the bowling alley. "What about the park, by the track, you know, the one by that baseball field and concession stand?"

Benny's eyebrows rose. "Nah, too many cars drive by there. The headlights shine across the whole park." He lightly brushed her knee and dragged his fingers up her thigh. "I could just sneak you in the barracks."

Abilene laughed, then glanced around again. "Hell no. That's just asking to get caught." She realized she laughed too loud as she noticed a few kids from the basketball team looking her way. *Shit,* she thought to herself.

"Alright, I got it. There's a bridge past the track. You know where the trail goes through the woods. That bridge, I don't know, is kinda secluded. It's hidden, tucked away where you can't see it if you don't know it's there." He bit his bottom lip. At that moment, Abilene would've done it right there if he said that's what he wanted. The fire inside her spread at just the thought of being alone with him and not stopping. She never wanted him more. Her heart raced.

"Ok. Sounds like a plan. I'll get Alyssa to drop me off at the start of the trail. You get a blanket or something?" She glanced around for Alyssa.

"Hold on there, girly. I don't mean right now. How about tomorrow night? You gotta relax, sweet thing." He leaned back and pulled his hand from her thigh. Abilene swallowed a lump in her throat.

"Tomorrow." Abilene said.

Abilene barely slept that night. She tossed and turned, thinking of nothing but making love to Benny under the stars. She plotted what to wear, what to say, what time to have Alyssa pick her up, how it would feel, and what they'd do after she graduated. Abilene had images of Benny visiting at college, taking her home to meet his family, Sandy and the Sergeant. beaming with pride that she was dating a soldier, a good soldier, with his entire career in front of him. Her dad would be apprehensive at first but come to see Benny as a respectable man, much like himself. Sandy would shoot her knowing looks, but would never tell Tom she knew Abilene had been sneaking around with Benny before graduation. It would bring them even closer, this shared secret that would cause no harm. As she drifted off, trying to calm her nerves, she thought of Julien. She wondered what he was up to at that very moment. She wondered if he would like Benny, approve of them being together. Would he shake hands and say 'take care of my best friend' or would he be suspicious of Benny's motives? Would he warn Abilene to wait or tell her to go for it if she loved him? She drew in a few deep breaths and admitted she didn't know what Julien would think of Benny. They hadn't talked in months, since summer. Every once in a while, she'd be reminded of him and contemplate calling at night, after school. But when the time would come, she'd stare at the phone and freeze just trying to think of what she'd say. The longer she didn't talk to him, the more he faded into a lost chapter in her life, one that wasn't as clear as it once was. One she wasn't in a hurry to revisit. Part of her hoped Julien felt the same way. Another part of her hoped he thought of calling her each day and that he would tomorrow. Every time the phone rang, a quick pang of hope still filled her chest. She knew it was stupid and selfish to both want him to call her and not want him to out of fear of what they'd have to talk about.

The next night, with hands shaking, Abilene yelled bye to Sandy as she helped Krista and Kayla put in a movie in the VCR. It was family movie night. Sgt. Matterly was in the kitchen watching the popcorn in the microwave and yelled out to her just as she reached the door.

"Home by midnight!"

"Yes, sir!" she yelled back as she pulled the door closed. Abilene paused on the porch, looked up at the sky, and took a deep breath. She smiled. After tonight, she'd be a woman. She'd be different and Benny would never want anyone else. The two of them would spend their days and nights all over each other, never more than a few feet apart, until they got old. This kind of passion, love, she thought, would only get hotter and the rest of the world would only be background noise. The two of them would be bound for life. Alyssa's beep shook her from her fantasy on the porch.

Abilene made her way from the corner streetlight to the trail. Alyssa gave her a small flashlight and told her she'd pick her back up at the shoppette in two hours. Abilene crept along the dark trail. She never noticed how quiet the woods were at night, except for a few scurries and birds rustling. After she got to the bridge, the trees opened up above her and she could see stars. She heard a whistle. Benny was off to the side of the bridge on a small patch of grass. He was on a blanket smoking a cigarette. The red end sizzled as he drew in and patted the spot next to him. Abilene felt a rush of adrenaline and made her way off the trail. He never looked so good sitting waiting for her. Abilene kicked off her shoes and scooted beside him. He leaned back and looked up at the stars. He pointed out a few, but his words didn't register. She felt tingly and suddenly scared they'd get caught or worse, he'd change his mind. She leaned over and kissed him while he was mid-sentence. He rolled over toward her and was on top of her before she had even come up for air. In a matter of seconds, his hand was caressing her under her shirt, her bra, and his other hand was behind her neck. He was pressing into her as she fumbled for his shirt to pull it up. They both fumbled, moaned, and tried to swallow each other whole. She moaned "Benny" as he slid her pants further down. Besides that, there were no words, just a hunger for each other as quickly as possible. Once he was inside her, she let out a deeper moan. It was uncomfortable, but not as painful as she expected. He started slowly, but quickened once she pulled him closer and faster. It grew painful, but she didn't want him to stop. Abilene opened her eyes and saw the stars above her as he thrust into her. She exhaled and held onto his shoulders. It was everything she'd hoped it would be as he collapsed onto her. His weight pressed her into the grass under the blanket. He was sweating and she could feel his heart beating through his chest. She wondered if he could feel hers. His breath was ragged as he kissed her neck. She didn't want to move. Abilene didn't want to reenter the real world, the world off that path and away from that bridge. A world where she couldn't sit on his lap and kiss him without being absolutely sure no one was around. She wanted them to lie there with him inside her forever. He peeled away from her, and she saw the muscles of his back as he turned to remove the condom. Seeing him shirtless made her want him more, again. She reached up and touched his back as she sat up.

He turned back to her. "So, was it everything you wanted? You feel ok?"

Abilene smiled. "Yeah, it was. I'm good. It was definitely good." She stared at him for a moment as he hunted around for his pants and boots. "Hey, Benny," she said as she reached for him again. "I love you." Her voice cracked. He turned to her and leaned down again. Benny kissed her gently as he caressed her cheek.

"I love you, too." He said in a quiet voice. It was the sweetest thing she ever heard. He laid back down and pulled her arm to his chest. She laid down next to him. They watched the stars in silence for what felt like days. Their breathing and his fingers running up and down her outstretched arm were the only sound and movement. Abilene could've slept right there next to him, next to that bridge forever. He sat up after a few minutes and lit another cigarette.

"You want one before you gotta meet Alyssa?"

"Nah. I'm good." She sat up and leaned her head on his shoulder. Abilene wanted time to stop. She couldn't imagine leaving that trail, going back to school, sitting through class, sitting through movie night with her family, shopping with Sandy, or being anywhere else but beside Benny feeling the heat radiate off his body and the touch of his hand on her leg. She wanted him that close forever and couldn't imagine peeling herself away from him, pretending they weren't madly in love.

"Hey, so what will we do after I graduate?" Abilene asked. She regretted breaking the silence.

"I dunno. That depends on where I get stationed, I guess." Benny said. He kissed her forehead. She had pictured him visiting her at college nearby once she was settled. Her dad had a few more years at Fort Patten, so she'd go to college close enough to drive back for holidays. She and Alyssa had talked about going to UK just over four hours away. She assumed Benny would be at Fort Patten, too.

"But you've got time left here, right?"

"Technically, yeah, but they're shifting a lot of us around lately. Not sure what'll happen." Benny said toward the sky above them. "We'll cross that bridge if we get to it." He bit his bottom lip.

The word 'if' felt like a punch to the gut for Abilene. Why didn't he say 'when we get to it'? She wondered. Benny looked at his watch.

"Shit, you better get up the trail. It's almost time to meet up with your ride." He said. Abilene's heart sank. She didn't want to walk up the trail alone, in the dark, like it was all a secret, something to hide, even though it was. She suddenly went from feeling blissful, connected, to feeling lost. Her eyes filled with tears.

"Hey, hey, don't cry. You can't cry after your first time. I'll feel like shit forever." He nudged her and pulled her face close to his.

"I'm sorry. I just didn't think you'd be leaving here, or I'd be leaving sometime too. I'm just—"

He pulled her closer. "Shhh. We'll be fine. Don't worry. We got something special here. I promise. I ain't going nowhere yet, you got that? Don't get all teared up about something that hasn't happened, ok?" He kissed her and pulled back to look into her eyes. Abilene nodded and wiped her eyes. Even though she believed him, the word 'if' floated in the air. Her daydreams of life with him visiting her in college, taking her home to meet family, staying in her dorm, all seemed harder to see. She tried to replace 'if' with him saying he loved her too. Abilene wanted to kick herself for letting one tiny word make her doubt herself, doubt Benny. It was one word. She squeezed her eyes and forced herself to replay the other words said moments ago. There were so many other wonderful words, wonderful smells of him, sensations of him collapsing on top of her, breathing into her neck. The stars, the blanket, the kisses on the forehead. All of it was perfect, beyond what she had fantasized alone at night for months now. All of it was exactly what she wanted. It all felt true, real, passionate. She had had the perfect night alone with the most incredible, hot, and enticing man she'd ever laid eyes on. The last hour was what every girl dreamed losing her virginity would be like, yet that one tiny word planted a seed. She wanted to rip it out of her mind, replace it with the others, but it latched onto her, embedded in her heart. If.

After that night and for many more, anytime Abilene could sneak off into the dead of night to be alone with Benny, she did. Stealing moments with him overtook every other thought and desire in her mind. While Sandy pushed her to apply to the local colleges and took her on tours, Abilene only wandered blissfully touring schools with visions of Benny visiting. No more hiding or ducking behind the bowling alley into his friend's car, but freely walking around campus, going out to dinner, hanging out with her new college friends. Despite that little seed of doubt he planted in her mind and heart, she let daydreams of being out in the open with him carry her through her senior year.

The end of March changed everything. After sneaking a few beers with Alyssa, Benny, and his newest cohort, a guy they called Ant, Abilene realized she was late. As she sipped cheap beer behind the concession stand of the little league field and giggled, teasing Alyssa for being a lightweight, she suddenly had a flash of a memory of Valentine's Day when she and Alyssa sent each other roses at school. It was all part of a ploy by Alyssa to get the attention of a guy in their class who wouldn't give her the time of day. She got her period that day. She hadn't had it since. As the other three laughed, Abilene's eyes darted around, trying to picture a calendar. She figured it was only two weeks. Odd, but nothing crazy. Maybe just stress from high school winding down. Abilene shook her head and rejoined the conversation.

Two weeks turned into three weeks. Abilene was never that late. She grabbed Alyssa by the arm as they left school on a Friday and told her.

"We gotta get you a test." Alyssa whispered as they pressed their heads together. "Don't panic. We'll go straight to the PX."

"The PX? Hell, no. What if Sandy or your mom walk in? We gotta go off post." Abilene's voice cracked. The thought of buying a test, much less taking one, made her nauseous. As they left school, the April air, normally still light and smelling sweet of fresh flowers and the first cut grass, was suddenly heavy. As they plotted to borrow Alyssa's mom's car to get fast food and look for dresses for prom, Abilene felt like she was walking through thick fog. Alyssa's words sounded muffled. She didn't know if she'd throw up or faint before they got to Alyssa's to sweet talk her mom.

"You're fine. Get it together before we go in the house." Alyssa said as she grabbed her elbow.

"I can't be—"

"You're not." Alyssa jerked her arm. "But if you are, we'll get it taken care of. You hear me?"

Abilene nodded and tried to push back tears, desperate to stop them from falling. She couldn't process the idea of being pregnant. Together, the girls entered the house, put on smiling faces, pretended to be enthralled with the idea of scouring the mall off post for prom dresses. The words pink satin, black lace overlay, purple tulle all swirled above her head. A lump formed in her throat. She pushed it down and nodded with a fake smile every time Alyssa's mom asked her anything.

The girls darted into the first pharmacy off post, then raced to the mall. Abilene was sweating. The thought of telling Benny anything made her heart pound. For reasons she didn't understand, she suddenly wanted to call

Tucker and see how Savannah and Paris were doing. Last summer, she had been good about calling every few weeks to listen to Savannah ramble on about pre-school and her baby sister. Savannah called her 'Pari'. Tucker would take the phone and ask Abilene how she was doing, how was school, and for about five minutes act like a concerned parent. While thinking of him still made Abilene queasy, there was something about those few minutes, forced, faked, or whatever that made her miss them, all of them. The boys, Savannah, even Tucker and Butch. They were bastards to her mom, and her mom sure as hell wasn't an angel to them either. But something about them, the feeling that they were still her family in some way, would wash over her and make her ache for them. She hadn't talked to the boys in months, either. They weren't much for talking on the phone. They'd ask a few questions, mostly about the Army, then fight amongst themselves before Butch would take the phone and say they had to go. Abilene wasn't even sure at this point what they looked like. They had to have grown. Boys that age grow fast. Krista and Kayla had grown so much in the last nearly two years she had lived with them. Even though they were fun little sisters and seemed like they couldn't remember a time when Abilene wasn't their sister, she didn't feel as close to them as she did her other siblings. The others she remembered as babies. She had changed them, fed them, bathed them, cared for them beyond what an older sister usually did. She had mothered them.

Ashlynn. Thoughts of her mom flooded Abilene's mind. She wondered if her mom felt the same panic and dread before taking a test when she was pregnant with Abilene. Abilene couldn't believe they had gotten so careless recently. She began to shake and cry in the passenger seat. Alyssa reached over and grabbed her hand.

"Hey! We got this. You're going to be okay." She squeezed Abilene's hand.

With the bag from the pharmacy in her hands, Abilene ran into the stall at the mall bathroom. Alyssa paced outside the metal door with names and initials etched into the old blue paint. There were puddles on the floor. With hands shaking even more violently, Abilene peed on the stick. She came out and placed it on the counter as she washed her hands.

"Breathe" said Alyssa. She rubbed Abilene's back as she dried her hands. Two minutes seemed like a lifetime. Thoughts of her mom, her brothers, sisters, her dad, and Sandy swirled. Her dad would kill Benny. Or would he kill her? Or both of them? It was time to look at the stick. Both lines appeared with the swiftness of two tiny daggers ripping her flesh open. Abilene's knees buckled. Tears broke free from the dam she tried to hold earlier. Panic rushed through her veins. Alyssa kept holding her, rocking back and forth, declaring they'd get it taken care of. Everything would be okay, but none of it calmed her. For the first time in forever, the only thing that came to mind was Julien. She needed Julien, and she didn't know why. She wanted to be back in that minivan with him, with peach schnapps, the light of the dashboard and tape player, him standing under a streetlight making sure she got home alright, just the two of them against the entire world. Now it was just her and the world was spinning too fast, crashing around her. His name escaped her lips through spit bubbles in between echoing sobs in the mall bathroom. He was the only who could steady her, and he was nowhere in sight.

# CHAPTER 17

*Spring 1994*

Benny Nash got down on one knee and asked her to marry him seconds after she told him. Abilene had an appointment to terminate the pregnancy and thought that was the simplest path, the most certain solution that she and Benny would both want. But at that moment, seeing the hope in his eyes, love seemed to shine through. She swallowed a lump and told him he didn't have to marry her. She'd be fine. His unexpected response made her dizzy. He pulled her down to the ground in front of him, right across from the ice cream stand where she first saw him a year earlier.

"I know I don't have to. I want to. I've got orders for July. Come with me. Let's do this." He drew her hands to his lips. "I mean it, Abilene. Marry me."

Abilene nodded and stopped shaking. "But I'm only 18. I don't think I'm ready for this. I've got college and all." Since she took the test, her mind raced from panic, fear, despair, anger that they weren't more careful, and yet she would lie there at night and wonder if somehow this wasn't meant to be.

He stood, pulled her up and into his arms. "We can get married right after you graduate. Then we can go. You can still go to school whenever or wherever. I know we're young, but we can do this. I want us to do this. I don't want to leave here without you. I'm sick of living in barracks and being alone." He paused and searched her eyes. "We can be a family." Family. That word meant so many things to her. Maybe going with Benny and having this baby could be something, someone of her very own. Maybe this was the family she could belong to forever. A family where she'd really belong from the very beginning. A family no one else could take from her.

"Ok. Let's be a family." She said through tears, a smile that hurt her cheeks and a flutter in her gut. Abilene's head spun, and she couldn't believe the words that flew out of her mouth. She knew she wasn't ready to be a mom, but the thought of going to bed and waking every day next to Benny was heaven. It was all she dreamed about since she first laid eyes on him, just not in the timeframe she ever imagined.

Together, they told Sandy and her dad. Moments of rage, fury, betrayal, threats of ruining any career Benny might have, red-faced spittle-filled threats of killing him and burying his body in several locations on post where no one would notice, threats of calls to commanders, and ripping his heart out of his chest while still beating, all quickly gave way to fallen shoulders, more tears, and heads in hands. Abilene stared in disbelief as the weight of disappointing her father bore down on her. He was the man who picked her up in the rain at the gate in the middle of night and tried so hard to be a good dad to her. In less than two years, he stepped up to be the most honorable and selfless man in her life. He crumbled as his threats of violence gave way to apologies for not raising Abilene from the start, for failing her as a father, and sadness for lost years. Before she could absorb all his words and feelings, and Sandy's tears and regrets too, she hugged her trembling dad. He cried into her wild tumbleweed hair and small shoulders.

"It's not your fault, dad. This is my fault." Abilene said.

"No, Abi. It's my fault. Sir, I promise you I'll take care of her. I love her." Benny piped in from the doorway to the living room. He stood tall as his shoulders fell back and he crossed his arms. Krista and Kayla appeared at the landing of the steps. Sandy tried to shoe them away, but the tears, shouts, captivated them and so did seeing this stranger stand in their house apologizing to their dad.

"It's my fault, Tom. I knew she was sneaking around with someone. I should've done more to stop it." Sandy said through tears. She shook her head and hid her face. Abilene thought back to Sandy's warnings. She felt as if she had betrayed Sandy. She spent months smiling and pretending to be interested in every other boy Sandy mentioned or pointed out. Abilene lied to her repeatedly about going to the movies with Alyssa, to the bowling alley, shopping for clothes. It was all a cover to be with Benny. And all for what? To finally bring him around to face the wrath, the shame of being part of Abilene's lies. It wasn't fair for Sandy to take any blame. It wasn't fair to anyone. Everything they created for her, saved her from, was crumbling away and it was all her fault. She ran to Fort Patten in the rain looking for a family, her dad, some place to call home, and they gave that to her. And she repaid them like this. Abilene wondered if she'd ever deserve their trust again, their love again, if she hadn't lost it.

An hour of regrets, accusations, frustration, and planning what's next led to dinner. Abilene's head was spinning. Benny held her hand through it all. He stood firm, determined to prove to the Sergeant and Sandy he'd make this right, make Abilene happy. A wedding in June was decided. Two weeks after graduation. Then, Abilene would head to Fort Bradley in upstate New York with Benny. They'd start their life together after driving to Denver to meet any of his family that couldn't make it to the wedding. Until the wedding, they were to keep their relationship quiet to avoid any repercussions for Benny if superiors found out, especially before she was out of high school. Alyssa would be her maid of honor. Krista and Kayla would be in the wedding too. Her dad would give her away. He had only just gotten her. Butch and the boys and Tucker and the girls would be invited. It would be small, intimate, almost secret, but done. She'd be with Benny forever.

Abilene was afraid she was showing at graduation, but Sandy kept assuring her no one could tell. She had a baby doll high-waisted dress, combat boots, and a choker necklace that distracted from everything else. Benny wouldn't come for obvious reasons, but he was invited to dinner afterwards off post. It was after that night that the nightmares started. Nightmares of being in labor but seeing her mom in the bed next to her. Her mom was always holding Paris and her arm would slide away from the baby. Paris would tumble to the floor, and Ashlynn would fade away, just as she had done two years ago. A baby slipped from her womb and minutes later, her life slipped away too. Abilene would wake in a panic, sweating, crying, and convinced karma would take her when she gave birth because of how she had yelled at her mom as her life ended. Despite the fear in her dream, she always sensed she deserved it. Like she had it coming. Abilene told no one about the nightmares.

Tucker and the girls came to the wedding held in a small event hall off post. They had a room at a motel down the road. Butch couldn't make it with the boys, but they called her that morning and told her to stay in touch, send pictures of the baby, the wedding, New York, everything. Dallas seemed to care the most. Abilene could tell by his voice every time she spoke with him that even though Butch took him to raise as his with Jackson and Austin, Dallas still felt like an outsider. He still found it difficult to behave like the others. His teachers, Butch, and others just had no patience for the likes of Dallas. No one did but Abilene. Her heart broke thinking how the world didn't get him.

When Savannah saw Abilene, she ran into her arms and squeezed her neck as she always had when Abilene would pick her up at Ashlynn's work. Paris was almost two. She waddled and had hair like Savannah's untamed, brown springy curls, blowing in the wind. She wouldn't go to Abilene. That was fine, Abilene thought. She didn't know her. She had only spent a few minutes with her and that time was filled with rage as Abilene called their mother a liar and told her she hated her. When Abilene looked into Paris's eyes, all she saw was the tiny infant that slid from Ashlynn's arms as she died. Abilene didn't try to pick her up or even look at her for too long. She didn't want to resent Paris, or herself, more than she already did. She had no connection to Paris, other than that one tragic day and the funeral that followed. That was enough.

Sandy came into the dressing room of the hall to help Abilene finish her hair and attach her veil before the ceremony.

"You look gorgeous, sweetie," Sandy said with a warmth Abilene was thankful for.

"Thank you." Abilene said as she adjusted the veil some more. "Sandy, I'm so sorry for lying to you." She looked down and twisted her fingers.

"Hey, hey, it's ok." Sandy said as she came up behind her and touched her shoulders. "You love him, right?"

"Yeah. I do. He's amazing." Abilene said as she touched her abdomen. She remembered the first time she saw him. A smile slid across her face. For the first time since finding out she was pregnant, she felt maybe somehow it would all be okay. None of it was ideal. School would have to wait. But the fact that she was marrying Benny and going to be a family with him seemed to make sense for the first time. They could do this. She deserved the chance to have a family all her own.

"Hey, listen, I know I'm not your mom, and I'm sure you're wishing she was here, but Abilene, I love you. You know that, right?" Sandy said. Her voice cracked as if the idea of saying it out loud caught her by surprise as much as it did Abilene. Abilene nodded. "And I want you to know you can come home anytime. You hear me?" She leaned down and reached her arms around Abilene. "You've always got a place with us if things don't work out. This baby too."

Abilene drew in a deep breath. She looked in the mirror at their reflection. They looked nothing alike, but she knew Sandy meant every word. Sandy never said anything she didn't mean. As much as she missed Ashlynn, she was glad Sandy had come into her life. Or rather, Abilene crashed into hers.

Ashlynn. As if she hadn't been on Abilene's mind every time she closed her eyes and images of childbirth and death pierced her brain. Now, as Abilene looked at herself in a wedding dress, she realized her mom only married once, when she married her dad. Abilene wondered what her mother was thinking on her wedding day, as she, too, was pregnant. Was she hopeful? Was she nervous? Was she desperate for family or blissfully giddy with the thought of being with the Sergeant forever? Everything she told Abilene about those days, about getting kicked out of Swenson House and running off with the Sergeant because her family couldn't accept her not marrying a fellow socialite was all a lie. What had the truth been?

"Dad," Abilene said as he slipped in the door.

"It's about time. You ready?" He stood in his uniform. She knew Benny would be in his too. These two men, these two honorable, noble men, both doing the right thing. Abilene smiled at him. It might've taken years, unveiling lies and myths, and taking a chance of showing up while in the midst of chaos and grief, but she had made it to her dad and loved him. His love filled her up the moment he got out of his car in the rain at the gate.

He took her hand. "Yeah, I'm ready." He led her to the door as Sandy left to be seated. Tom turned her toward him.

"You look beautiful. Are you sure about this? You're only 18, honey. There are other ways. We'll take care of you." His blue eyes pierced through her.

"I know you would. I want to marry him. I do." She let a tear slip out. "He's a good man. I love him."

"My god, looking at you right now." He touched her cheek and teared up. "You look so much like your mom did." He swallowed a lump. "You know, I loved her that day and for many days after that. But you, you were the best thing that came out of those years. I wish for your sake she could be here."

"Me too. But if she was here, still here, I wouldn't be here with you." Abilene said. Tom gasped. He wiped a tear.

"I'd like to think I would've smartened up and gotten to know you even if she was here."

Abilene took his hand. "Well, you're here now. We found each other. You and Sandy, you've given me a home. I just hope I haven't disappointed you."

"Never, Abilene Marigold Matterly. Never." He hugged her. She pulled away from him.

"Dad, my hair." She smoothed her locks. He laughed.

As the ceremony unfolded, she looked up at Benny. Benito Nash. Tall, steady, broad shouldered, with a smile that still made her feel electric. She worried if 18 was old enough to know if it was love, but then told herself it was. It had to be. She couldn't imagine wanting anyone more, burning for anyone more. He'd be a good husband, a good father, and they'd make love day and night throughout their new house, relishing in each other until they were old and grey. When it came time to kiss, she could've melted into him. His touch felt like sparks. His lips soft and engulfing hers. Tonight, they'd be alone in a hotel room and in a week, they'd head for Denver for a week, then Fort Bradley to start life together all before the fourth of July.

After the reception, Sandy took Abilene back to the house to change and get her bags to stay with Benny in town for two nights. Abilene walked into her bedroom with the white dresser, white bed, pink blankets, posters of Boyz II Men and Mariah Carey, boom box, and desk with pictures of her and Alyssa pinned on the corkboard above it, along with her mother's postcards. She fiddled with a wedding ring as she stood in the bedroom of a teenager. Abilene slipped out of her dress and pulled open her drawer for jeans. She placed the dress gently across the chair of her desk, where just months earlier she sat doing homework and panicking over the thought of telling anyone but Alyssa she was pregnant. She spotted the tape cassette on the floor between the nightstand and desk. It was Julien's tape for her. She thought about calling him a thousand times to apologize, to catch up, to keep him in her life. She reached for the phone repeatedly only to walk away, afraid of what she'd say, what he'd say. There was so much she wanted to tell him, but once it piled up to a certain height, it seemed too insurmountable to tackle or rattle off, or explain. She had never even told him about Benny. She never told Benny about him either.

Abilene buttoned her jeans, noticing they were getting tighter, and pulled a black tank top over her head. Sandy yelled if she needed help with her dress.

"No, I got it. I'll be down in a sec." Abilene said into the abyss of the otherwise empty house as she reached for her red cowboy boots. She slid them on. They were like getting a hug from herself and who she used to be. Before thinking or planning what she'd say, Abilene leapt onto the bed and reached for the phone on the other side. She dialed his number, amazed she remembered so easily. Her pulse quickened, and she nearly hung up. Once it rang a second time, her stomach dropped. She suddenly needed to hear Julien's voice like she needed oxygen. Abilene needed to tell him she was pregnant and just married a soldier. She needed him to tell her it was all good and would work out.

"Hello?" Noah, Julien's dad said.

"Oh, hi. Um, it's Abilene Matterly. Is Julien home?" Abilene was whispering, afraid Sandy would hear.

"Oh yeah, I remember you." He slurred and snarled.

"Is Julien there? I really need to talk to him." Abilene felt as if time stopped and nothing else mattered except for hearing her best friend's voice.

It was like she was still right down the road in Holden, as if no time had passed.

"Nah, girl, he ain't here. That little shit done left Holden, and he ain't coming back." Noah fumbled with the receiver.

"No, no wait, where is he? Where'd he—"

The click echoed. She could tell he was drunk. "Ain't coming back" played on a loop in her ears. Sandy yelled up again. Where could Julien have gone? Did he enlist or go to school somewhere? Why wouldn't he call her and tell her his plan? They promised each other to always keep in touch. She realized she didn't keep up her end of the bargain and she couldn't blame him for not keeping up his end, either.

"Julien, where are you?" She whispered into the air. She should've called him. Abilene should've dialed his number every day, especially when she heard Kurt Cobain died right after she discovered she was pregnant. She should've driven to Holden to see him last summer after they fought. She should've made it right. Now he was gone, and she couldn't shake the feeling she might never hear from him again. Their last hug, him saying they'd find each other again, he'd appear in front of her somewhere someday, all seemed like teenage promises that get left behind once the adult world crashes in. Abilene stood and picked up the small duffle bag she first showed up at Fort Patten with. She wiped tears she didn't know escaped and glanced around once more. She was leaving all she knew, and all she thought she'd always have—her past, her life in that room. All of it would just be a memory once she went downstairs and went with Sandy to the hotel where Benny was waiting. Just as when she climbed out her window in Holden and ran to Julien's house with her mother's postcards in the bottom of that duffle bag, there were those moments she could pinpoint where one life ended and another began. Abilene slung the bag over her shoulder and closed the door behind her, knowing this was the moment a new life would begin.

# CHAPTER 18

## Winter 1995

Fort Sherman was a hellhole. Everyone knew it. But, to Julien, any place that wasn't Holden, South Carolina was heaven, or at least purgatory. He hated saying goodbye to Charlene, the tears in her eyes, the disdain in her parents'. They were grateful he was leaving so she could go to college in North Carolina with no distractions. She swore she'd write, drive to Louisiana to visit him over semester break, and think of him every second. He let her make promises he knew she wouldn't keep. Julien was a realist. He knew she'd find someone at college that first weekend at a frat party, football game, or stupid icebreaker event for her dorm. He was fine with that. Julien had a life of his own to find, a life far from his home. He said goodbye to Uncle Chris and his sisters, who sobbed as he peeled them off his waist at the bus stop, and then to his parents. Sheila wiped away a few tears and hugged him tight. She whispered she loved him as he pulled back from her. Noah shook his hand, but showed no emotion. Julien wasn't surprised. Noah only showed emotion when Sheila had him off the rails with anger or passion—which Julien was wise enough to know was the same thing to the two of them. Julien promised to come home when he was done with basic training, spend a week or two before heading off to his next duty station. He didn't. Once he graduated basic training, he went straight to Louisiana. His uncle was the only one who came to graduation, which didn't surprise him either.

The water smelled like rotten eggs, and he was still getting used to not having long, thick locks of hair to run his hands through when he was anxious or nervous. Yet, he was happy. He was getting the best night's sleep in the Army. Having a drill sergeant wake him in the middle of the night with banging on trash cans was preferable to waking to his sisters crying, mom screaming for help, and dad throwing furniture. All followed by the sounds of his parents violently making love minutes after threatening to call the police on each other. He also preferred having a roommate in the barracks that didn't ask questions about his family or ask why he didn't call anyone on weekends or get mail, except the occasional letter from his sisters. He was free. Free of Holden and the fear that he'd be trapped there forever and destined to end up like his parents.

It was once he tasted that freedom that he understood why Abilene never came back and why it was hard for her to call. The longer he was out of Holden, the more determined he was to keep his distance. He tried to call home a few times, hear his sisters' voices for a few minutes, then he'd hang up. But he had no desire to return in person. Just as he predicted, by Christmas, Charlene was in love with an all-star football player. A junior at UNC who was headed to law school in a few years. She'd surely follow him after she graduated and be the perfect lawyer and lawyer's wife, just like her mom. At least she had the consideration to call instead of write. She cried. Julien knew the cries were to lessen the guilt she felt. He reassured her he'd be fine and wished her well. She wanted the dramatic ending, one she could eventually tell her daughters about—the time she left a sweet, small town, boyfriend turned soldier and how it hurt her more than him, but she had fallen in love with their father and couldn't help but wonder if that broken-hearted boy ever got over her. He did, immediately of course, but he let her have her fantasy of crushing him as she wailed into the phone and made him promise to call if he ever needed to talk. He gave her a few sniffles to round out the show.

A bar right off the back gate of Fort Sherman was the refuge of choice for Julien and the small group of girlfriend-less soldiers from the barracks. They'd head there after duty hours on a Friday night and on Saturdays for the live music and chips and shitty salsa that was free until 7 p.m. Julien didn't have many civilian clothes, a few pairs of jeans and a couple of old band t-shirts. His favorite was his Nirvana shirt, nearly translucent after years of washes and wearing at his uncle's shop for work. The neck seam was separating from the rest of the shirt, but that didn't stop him from pulling it on almost every weekend. When Kurt Cobain died in Spring of his senior year, he wanted to call Abilene immediately. He didn't. He waited for her to call. She didn't. Every time he pulled that shirt over his head, he wondered if she kept that tape or thought of him when Kurt died. He almost called her before he shipped out to basic, but again didn't. He missed their talks, the laughs, just the sense of being near someone like her. But lately, he wondered how much alike they really were. After all, Abilene lost her mom and gained a stable family, stable as far as he knew. Julien had no such luck. The only thing they seemed to have in common was that they both left Holden and neither would look back. Even though it had been over two years since he dropped her off at the gates of Fort Patten, his mind would wander, and he'd try to picture what her life was like. She was probably in college now, in a sorority, with much more in common with Charlene than him. He looked in the mirror and splashed on some cologne. Julien barely recognized himself. He was certain Abilene wouldn't recognize him, and he probably wouldn't recognize her.

A honk outside the window told him Smith and Banks were ready to go and snapped him from his daydream of those nights walking to Mazzy's with his first and only best friend. Smith and Banks were also small-town guys with no attachments back home. The three of them had spent Christmas eating Chinese off post and drinking the night away playing video games in Banks' room. Smith's girlfriend dumped him the same weekend Charlene dumped Julien. They were all three of the mindset that the fewer attachments they had, the better. They had all joined to escape where they came from, didn't know where they wanted to end up, and gave little thought past the next weekend. They all three were confident in their abilities to be great soldiers and saw the other guys as being held back, distracted by girlfriends back home, families always asking them to take leave for this event or milestone. For Julien, the thought of being free to pack up and move to a new duty station with no strings attached was exactly what he wanted. He would follow along and go wherever the Army sent him, as long as it wasn't close to Holden.

"Come on, Mac! Hurry up. I heard there's a sorority from the college hitting JJ's tonight." Yelled Banks from the passenger seat as Julien pulled a flannel over his shirt. He climbed into the back seat and slammed the door shut.

"Sorry, guys. Let's go." He said as he tapped the top of the headrest. "Where you hear that, anyway? Your dreams maybe?"

JJ's was smokey and sticky. There was a thickness, a fog in the air day or night. Julien wasn't a smoker, but did when he was there drinking. Smith was never without a cigarette in his mouth. His eyes were permanently squinting from smoke rolling up his face. Julien always teased it made him look like some deep revelation was about to escape his lips and nicotine-stained fingers. Banks was a health nut and prided himself on being the fastest runner in their unit. He had been a state champion long-distance runner back home in Pennsylvania. He had scholarship offers from east coast colleges, but always dreamed of being a soldier. His mom cried when he enlisted. She had lost an older brother in Vietnam and only associated serving in the military as an eventual death sentence. He promised her he'd always stay safe and maybe go to college someday. He was the only person Julien ever knew who ran for fun, when no one else was on the track or trails around the post. Even on a few nights after drinking with them at JJ's, he'd lace up his sneakers and go for a run in the dark if the urge struck him. Julien admired that about him and understood the urge. It reminded him of when he'd walk to Mazzy's alone at night. The sense of being in the darkness, in the quiet, with the rest of the world asleep was empowering, especially for a kid who held no power in the daylight. Julien figured it was the same for Banks. He was the only black kid in his school in small town Pennsylvania and told Julien and Smith about the feeling of perpetual loneliness mixed with the constant feeling of being watched, judged, held to a higher standard. His parents pushed him to excel as a way out of that town, but Banks knew it was also to gain respect. Being respected and revered as an asset to the school, the community, also meant an element of safety. No one would hurt the black kid who was winning and bringing home a state championship title.

They walked in the door with green paint peeling all around the rusty door handle and cut through the haze. Julien coughed and reached for his wallet. They chose seats right by the door rather than wander too far in. It was already crowded even though it was early. They heard the distinct giddiness of young women wafting through the bar. Julien smiled as he ordered a round of draft beers for the three of them.

"Hey, I gotta piss. I'll be right back." He said as he put $10 on the bar in between Smith and Banks. Julien used his shoulder to press through the crowd as he slid his wallet into his pocket. He felt a thud on his side as he was looking at the ground. Julien only saw a flash of black. Black hair, a black tank top, black jeans and boots as a voice squealed.

"Sorry! Oh my God, did I hit you?" The voice said as she rubbed his side. Long black hair whipped across his field of vision and revealed her tanned face, too dark lipstick, and the brightest eyes he had ever seen. She squeezed his arm. "You okay?" Her squeal had turned to a soft purr, nearly silent. Julien shook his head. The world stopped and went into a dead silence. She was all he could see or hear. She was barely over five feet, but seemed to take up his entire field of vision.

"Yeah, yeah, I'm good." He said as she moved her silky hair behind her ear. Her smile bore through him like a missile. He held his hand to his chest for a second. "Did I hit you?"

"No, silly, I bumped into you." She blinked, and he was sure she could hear his heart pounding. "I'm Vanessa." She said as she held out her hand. He was afraid to touch her as if she'd disappear. He noticed her long red nails.

"I'm Julien McCulley. My friends call me Mac." He touched her soft hand and felt a bolt of lightning go from his toes to the top of his head. He shuddered.

"Well, hello there, Mac." Vanessa tilted her head and raised one eyebrow. Julien thought he was trembling right before her eyes. He was unsteady, as if he had been drinking all night. Words were stuck in his throat and the room was spinning. She pulled her hand back. "Where were you off to in such a hurry?" A friend bumped into her, and she pushed her away, followed by a deep glare and sneer.

"Um, the pisser. I mean, the bathroom." He stammered.

"It's okay," she said with a laugh and another raised eyebrow. "Just make sure you find me later, then. You know, before you leave." A smile slid across her face as she glanced up and down at him. "Like your shirt."

Julien told her thanks and squeezed past her and her friends to the bathroom. He needed to get some space so he could catch his breath. When he left the bathroom, he saw her standing on the bottom rung of a barstool, leaning over the bar and laughing with the bartender. He shook his head and felt a slight pang of jealousy for no real reason. Once he rejoined Banks and Smith, all he could hear was her laugh floating through the air, finding him no matter how loud the music was or what Smith was saying. The sight of her long, shiny hair swishing back and forth across her nearly bare back was like a pendulum hypnotizing him. All he could focus on was the idea of that hair falling across his face if she was above him, floating, laying, making love to him. She kept glancing his way. He knew she was making sure he was paying attention from across the bar. She would raise that eyebrow at him or wink each time she caught him looking. He kept swallowing a lump in his throat and trying to focus on Banks and Smith as they bitched about PT and their first sergeant.

"Dude, just go over there." Banks said as he finished his beer and tilted the glass toward the bartender before putting it down. "Seriously, man. You haven't stopped staring all night."

"Nah. She's a bit too much, if you know what I mean."

"Damn right she is. A girl like that," Smith said as he pointed her way with his cigarette, "she'll rip your heart out right before your eyes and giggle the whole time. You don't mess with girls that hot. They'll be the death of ya. Trust me."

Banks laughed. "Yeah, like you have experience with a girl like that." He rolled his eyes and slid a ten to the edge of the bar while the bartender placed three sweaty beer glasses in front of them. "Hey, Frankie, who is that anyway?" He nodded his head toward Vanessa's group of friends.

"Oh, them?" the bartender nodded their way too. "They're townies. I think a bunch of them go to the beauty school in Lafayette." He leaned his elbows on the sticky bar. "They come in from time to time. But watch out, guys. They're a rowdy bunch."

"Rowdy wasn't the word that popped into my head, I tell ya, Frankie." Smith said. He pointed with the stub of a spent smoke. "That one with the long black hair. I think she's got my buddy here all verklempt."

"Shut up, man." Julien said. "All she did was say 'hi'."

"And look at you? You can't even focus on anything else." Banks said, punching Julien in the side. "Go on, Mac. If she ain't got you under some spell, prove it. Go up and ask her to come over or dance or something and see if you can peel yourself away from her afterwards."

"Shit, I ain't dan—" Vanessa hopped down from the stool and buzzed over to Julien before he could finish his sentence.

"You ain't what," she said, then sipped her beer as some sloshed from the rim to the floor.

Their eyes darted around at each other as if they had been caught stealing someone's wallet. Julien shrugged his shoulders. Frankie laughed and said, "Good luck," as he pushed himself back from the bar.

"Dancing. I ain't dancing." Julien said. His voiced cracked. He sipped and averted his eyes.

"The hell you ain't, soldier." Vanessa put her drink in front of Smith, took his newly lit cigarette, and took a long drag. Then she gingerly placed it back between his fingers as she let the smoke roll slowly toward Julien. Vanessa reached out and took his hand. He stumbled as he followed her to the dance floor in the middle of the bar. She slid each hand up his arms and interlaced them behind his neck. He licked his lips and looked up as he tried not to laugh. He placed his hands on her hips, leaning down to reach her. Indian Outlaw by Tim McGraw came on the jukebox.

"This isn't a slow song; I hate to tell ya." He said as she swayed her rounded hips.

"It is now." Vanessa whispered as she tickled the back of his neck. Julien drew in a deep breath and then let every morsel of air escape his lungs as he exhaled. It was the slowest breath he had ever released. He looked down at her eyes and knew he couldn't peel himself away if he tried. She smelled like vanilla and beer. His mouth watered as he inhaled, and heat rose between them as she pressed against him. She stood on her tiptoes and barely reached his mouth. He lifted her to meet him and kissed her dark red lips. He never felt anything so soft, yet so fierce. After a few more songs, Julien couldn't remember how it felt to not hold her close, to not have her lips teasing his, to breathe without Vanessa in his arms.

They were inseparable. If she wasn't at the barracks entangled in his blankets after a few beers at night, they were walking hand in hand down the main street of Lafayette when he was off duty. She would finish classes for cosmetology and shower, put on something tight or barely there, and race to meet him at JJ's. He'd get off duty, change out of his uniform, and meet her. He didn't stop racing through the day until his eyes met hers. JJ's was the only bar that they could drink at without question since they weren't 21. Going any place nicer wasn't an option. But occasionally Julien would get a six-pack bought by Smith and take it to sit with Vanessa by the water. She liked to fish. He liked to sit back and watch her cast the line, then jut out her hip and wait. Then, they'd make love on the banks, collapsing into the dirt and grass afterwards, followed by running for more beer, and making love in the car or her apartment at the end of the night. Even mixed with beer, sweat, and sex, he could still smell the vanilla in her hair every time he closed his eyes and inhaled. Each night when he closed his eyes in his barracks, he pictured her next to him, on him, or him on top of her. He couldn't see anything but Vanessa's face, her eyes, her hair, her shimmering tanned arms and legs wrapped around him. She was part of him now.

He started spending entire weekends at her apartment. Rosie, her roommate, wouldn't mind as long as he put the seat down and paid for the drinks at JJ's all night. Rosie and Vanessa were childhood best friends and were both in cosmetology school together. Rosie was studying to be an esthetician and was obsessed with trying different face masks on everyone. She'd smear one on Julien and make him stand still while she timed it. He wasn't allowed to laugh or smile, which would prompt Vanessa to dance in front of him, to tempt him to crack the mask. He never made it more than a minute before grabbing her, pulling her onto his lap, and kissing her, smearing green or gray mud on her face, too. Rosie would roll her eyes and call them 'fuckers' as they all opened more beers.

After a night of masks and sex, Vanessa peeled herself off his chest and pulled her hair behind her ears. Julien reached up and traced her lips with his finger.

"Hey, let's go to New Orleans next weekend. Just us walking around, going in a few voodoo shops. Shit like that?" He said.

Vanessa cocked her head to the side and smiled. "Yeah, ok. Then we can go back in a few weeks for Mardi Gras?"

"Yeah." He said as he reached up and kissed her.

"My mom used to take me down for Mardi Gras sometimes. Just to see the parades and shit, nothing crazy." Vanessa's eyes grew wide. "Mac! You gotta meet my mom. I told her all about you. When we get back, we'll have dinner with her, ok?"

"Ok."

"And when you go home, I'll meet yours, right?"

"Someday, I guess. I haven't gone home in a long time. But someday."

Julien suddenly felt between two worlds. He had thrown himself into Vanessa's world full force without looking back. He realized it had been Christmas since even called home. His sisters begged him to come see them, and Sheila whispered how much she missed having him there to help take care of them and his father. Julien remembered rolling his eyes, thinking it shouldn't be on his shoulders to take care of them. He sent the girls a lot of money in their birthday cards since he rarely spent any of his pay. But besides that, he didn't want to take care of anyone. He was tired of taking care of others and he wasn't even 20.

Vanessa talked about her mom nonstop. Her father was gone, divorced, but still called her from time to time. Vanessa's mom, on the other hand, was only one town away. She was Filipino, the daughter of immigrants who made their way to Louisiana as fishermen, which made sense to Julien why she looked so natural, at home standing along the water. Vanessa had her mother's skin tone and facial features. She had light eyes like her father, though. A soft green with flecks of grayish blue. To Julien, she looked like a painting, something someone carefully composed as they tried to capture a unique exoticness not found casually. He loved watching her every move, the way her eyes and skin looked different in certain lighting. The only thing he didn't like was when she yelled, screamed actually. Julien learned over the course of a few short months that Vanessa had a temper, an explosive fuse that was ready to ignite at the slightest mishap or misunderstanding. At first, he thought it an odd, attractive, exciting, and an intriguing form of passion. It made her hot in his eyes, seeing her get worked up and rattling off Filipino phrases. She was fiery, and he couldn't look away when she was in a rage. It always passed quickly, sometimes minutes. It was worse when she was drinking, but then again, they were always drinking. He wondered if Vanessa's mom was as much of a temperamental firecracker. Then Julien pictured taking her home to his family. Memories of midnight fights and furniture breaking, his mom crying with smudged mascara, his father, beer in hand, sputtering insults at her, at all of them. Maybe, Julien thought, Vanessa would fit in too well.

# CHAPTER 19

*Spring and Summer 1995*

In New Orleans, a night of drinking and petty jealousy over Vanessa flirting with a group of guys to get into a piano bar in the French Quarter turned into an all-out brawl. Julien sustained a punch to the face and gut. His nose was bloodied and ribs bruised. Vanessa helped him hobble and stumble to the hotel room as he bled through a handful of bar napkins and dripped all over the dirty streets cluttered with beads and bottles. Once the bleeding stopped, the screaming began. Vanessa said he humiliated her and ruined their chance at getting into the bar. She said he was a loser, weak, for not holding his own against the bouncers outside. If he had been a real man, he would've let her flirt her way in and get them free drinks all night. He was battered on the outside and inside. She threw the lamp in the hotel, then went out on the tiny balcony and screamed below to tourists. The rage and uncontrollable anger no longer excited Julien. Watching her reminded him too much of his parents. He watched her until it was out of her system. Only then did he realize it would never be out of her system, just as it was never out of his parents' systems. It would always be right under the surface, ready to be unleashed once the beer bottles were opened.

As they pulled into Vanessa's apartment building lot after a long quiet ride, Julien leaned over and kissed her, then sat back and stared straight ahead.

"Listen, I think we should take a break from each other. Just to regroup. I don't want to fight like that again." He said, then held his breath.

Her eyes filled with tears. She wiped one away. He could see anger start to rise from her collar bones on up. She shook her head and her long hair fell in front of her face.

"Fine, whatever, asshole." She said and reached for the door handle. Julien had the urge to grab her hand and pull her close, kiss her again, and love her enough to quell her rage. He didn't. She slammed the door, then opened the trunk to get her bag. She slammed that, too. He watched in the rear-view mirror as she stomped her way to her door. Just as he placed his hand on the door handle to jump out and run after her, she turned and flipped him off. She screamed something he didn't understand and disappeared in a flash. He knew she was crying. He was on the verge of tears as well. But he needed to let her go. He needed the quiet, the break. He needed the peace he had before he met her that night.

Days went by and thoughts of Vanessa never waned. Banks, Smith, and others tried to get him to go out at night. He spent his nights in the barracks playing video games, watching tv, and laying in his bunk staring up at the ceiling. He kept replaying their fights, the drunken screaming, then the passion that would consume them afterwards. Her hair, her eyes, her smell was all he could think about. Three weeks after she slammed his car door and cursed him in Filipino, he rolled over and grabbed his phone. He dialed her number, then immediately hung up. He dialed it again. She answered.

"I know it's you, dumbass." She whispered into his ear. He smirked and rolled his eyes.

"Hey." He said.

"Hey."

"I'm sorry."

"Yeah, me too, Mac." She said. He could tell by her tone she didn't mean it and was probably rolling those big, sparkling eyes, but he didn't care.

He was under a spell, knew it, and knew he didn't have the strength to break away from it too long. Julien rationalized that if she kept getting crazy when they drank, they'd drink less, or he'd just stay away from her on those nights. He could cut out early and go home to sleep in peace. He saw himself being the voice of reason, telling her to slow down, maybe just agreeing with her while drunk, then reasoning with her in the morning. He could just go along for the ride, apologize when need be, anything if it meant being with her. As she talked, he forced himself to remember the times they made love at the river, the laughing fits in the car, watching her cook for him. The smell of her hair when she was asleep under his arm. He hung up the phone and exhaled. Julien knew he was in for a hell of a ride, but he also knew at this point he had no choice when it came to Vanessa. He was exhausted by her, physically and mentally, and figured that must mean its love, or at least a lust he can't ignore.

Julien and Vanessa spent the summer swimming, drowning in an insatiable appetite for each other, and drinking. He met her mother and whole family. They were all firecrackers, but the love they had for each other was unlike any he had seen in a family. They yelled, but they hugged afterwards. Julien couldn't remember his father ever hugging him or his sisters after a night of drunken violence.

One humid night in July, they had been out to eat and fought about Julien smiling too much at a waitress. She drove off and left him in the dark, sticky night. He called Banks for a ride.

"Dude, don't you get tired of that bullshit? You guys are either going at each other's throats or you're going at it, if you know what I mean," Banks said as they pulled out onto the highway toward post. Julien just kept shaking his head. "Come out for a run with me tonight. Clear your head."

"Alright. Maybe that'll work. I'll run until this crazy chick is out of my head." He said with a laugh. Banks shook his head.

"I sure as hell don't have the time or energy to keep up with a run that long."

The two of them changed into PT shorts and sneakers and headed for the trail that led to the track near the back gate. Banks was like a bullet. Julien knew he was at least a full lap behind him. The thick, still air was suffocating, but he ran anyway. The longer he ran, the longer until he was tempted to call her to find out if she was over it yet. Even though he didn't know what 'it' really was. It never had to be about anything. Banks stopped at the path leading back to the barracks. He bent down, putting his hands on his knees.

"Let's call it a night, Mac. I'm spent. This heat is killing me." He huffed.

Julien slowed to a walk as he met him. "Yeah, it's brutal tonight. Let's head back."

As they walked back and fought to catch their breath, Banks slowed even more.

"Mac, you gotta get it together. This Vanessa stuff is gonna drive you crazy."

"I know. Man, I can't shake her. I love her. But, well, you know."

"Yeah, we all know. Does she know you'll be outta here next summer at the latest? I mean, what's your plan then? Just cut and run or what?"

"I don't know. Take her with me if she'll go. Marry her. What do you think I should do?"

Banks shook his head and wiped sweat across his forearm.

"No idea, man. You got your hands full with that one. You want a lifetime of that?" Banks said.

Julien stared straight ahead. "It wouldn't be boring." They both laughed.

"Got that right. A girl like that will never be boring. But seriously, just be careful. Girls like Vanessa will eat you alive. She could be the death of you, you know."

"That's what keeps it interesting, my man." Julien said. Banks shook his head.

Julien showered, fell into bed, and clicked on the small tv that teetered on a stand they found left over in the housing area. That was the best place to grab furniture. Anytime families moved, they tossed perfectly good furniture to meet the weight limit for moves. Julien's tv stand, small coffee table, and stand for his phone and keys next to the bed were all thrown out the summer before. He drifted off to sleep feeling exhausted mentally and physically, and thankful that he didn't call her. He also had a pit in his stomach because she didn't call him either.

By the next night, she called and said she was outside the gate at the all-night diner. He briefly thought of hanging up, but he couldn't. Hearing her voice made his pulse race, and he couldn't help but smile. He threw on sweats, grabbed his wallet, and headed to the diner. A few hours later, they were back in his barracks, tangled under the sheet. She was purring and nuzzling his neck as they laughed. They had grabbed a 12 pack of beer and it was nearly gone. The smell of stale beer from his nights alone without her and now from being back with her filled the room. They drifted off with the light of the tv casting shadows around the room. Despite the chaos of the push and pull between them, Julien slept better with her next to him, and she with him holding her hip and nestled into the back of her head.

Julien woke in the middle of night and glanced around at his life in his small corner of the world. It wasn't much, but with her next to him, it felt like everything. Despite the magnetic pull of being next to Vanessa, he was restless, like he was growing up in Holden. He sat up and lifted himself up from between Vanessa and the wall. He pulled on his sweats and a t-shirt over his head. Julien shook of the half-drunk feeling swirling in his head as he searched for his shoes and keys.

"Hey, Mac, whatcha doing?" Vanessa said with a sleepy smile.

"I'm gonna go for a walk. Get something to eat, I think." He whispered.

"Oh, you want me to come?" She said as she rolled over to the edge of the bed.

"Nah, you know I like to walk alone at night."

"Yeah, but it's still fucking weird. I'll come if you want."

"Nah. Go back to sleep, love." He said as he tied his shoes, stood, and leaned down to kiss her head. She smiled up at him. He wished she'd always be that soft, smiling, and at peace. He huffed, thinking if all their interactions occurred at this hour, when she was half-asleep, they might be alright.

Julien made his way through the parking lot and sidewalk to the track. He did half the loop before getting off and walking down the road to the shoppette. It was open 24 hours a day, but rarely busy in the middle of the night. Even the toughest soldiers needed sleep. The bright lights made him squint. He instinctively ran his hand over his head where his blonde mop had once lived. He still couldn't get used to having no hair. Julien made his way to the prepared food case and ordered some hot chicken to go. He slowed down in the liquor aisle. A small bottle of peach schnapps caught his eye. He laughed and picked it up.

"$6.00? That's it. I knew this stuff was cheap, but damn." He said to no one. Julien took the bottle to the counter and grabbed napkins for his chicken. The smell of the chicken placed on the counter made his mouth water. He paid and walked back outside into the July heat. The air hit him like a brick. For a moment, he wished he had stayed in bed with the fan blowing on him. He looked up at the sky and noticed it was clear, with stars tossed in every direction.

Julien took the wooded trail from the track instead of staying on the sidewalk. He held a chicken leg in his mouth as he opened the peach schnapps. The sticky liquor got on his hands. Julien stopped next to a giant boulder that marked the half-way point between the track and barracks parking lot. He ate, drank, licked his fingers, and ate some more. He wondered why he ever thought peach schnapps was ever good. It was like syrup mixed with the hot sauce dripping from the chicken. He laughed, thinking of those nights in Holden. Those nights walking to Mazzy's were his salvation. He thought that was the height of sophistication, good chicken and good drinks. What he really missed was his best friend. Julien wondered how one summer of nights walking, talking, eating, and sneaking sips of the cheap shit could be so burned into his mind. He had friends at Fort Sherman. He loved the talks with Banks and Smith, the runs when he could keep up with Banks. They'd talk about life, their pasts, and Banks was right. Running helped settle his mind, take him out of the chaos often caused by Vanessa, and egged on by him, if he was honest. As crazy as things got between him and Vanessa, he had to admit his part in it. He was the one who kept going back for more, knowing she wasn't going to change. Running helped him escape, quiet the noise, and regroup. When he thought back to those nights with Abilene, he realized it was the same—an escape to quiet the noise and regroup. He realized it was three years since he dropped her off at Fort Patten. Julien had no idea where she moved on to, where she was, or with whom, but something in him told him she was safe somewhere. He wondered if she had a friend out there to talk to, to calm any storms. Julien regretted not calling her more, especially before he left for the Army. He felt like shit for not trying harder to keep in touch with her. The last time they talked, she was yelling about Charlene. He smirked. He never really thought about Charlene even though he lost his virginity to her, and she was the first girl he said he loved. She was a blip in his memory compared to Abilene. He sipped the peach schnapps and remembered their one kiss. Her laugh when they pulled away from each other and sloppily realized how absurd it was that they thought to kiss each other. Abilene's words echoed in his head, yelling about replacing her with Charlene. She was right. He tried to replace her with anyone. He didn't want to spend the rest of his time in Holden alone, like he had before Abilene came.

"Abilene Marigold Matterly, where are you now? I hope you're happy wherever it is." He said to the clear sky above. He sipped again and picked up his bag of leftover chicken. Julien headed back to the barracks to wash his sticky hands and face before crawling back into bed with Vanessa. She moaned and took his arm and pulled it around her waist. He smiled and let the alcohol and contentment of a sleeping Vanessa settle his mind. He looked at the top drawer of his dresser where he had a ring he bought months ago. It was tucked in a corner with the hair scrunchie Abilene left behind in his mom's minivan the night he dropped her off. When he found it the next morning, he decided since it was all he had left of that summer with her, it would be his official good luck charm.

He leaned in and smelled Vanessa's hair. As chaotic as life could be with Vanessa, the feeling of her next to him in the dark, the vanilla smell, gave him hope things could always be this good if she came with him. The thought of leaving her behind as he drove away from Fort Sherman seemed impossible. He drifted off, knowing he'd ask her to marry him and leave Louisiana forever. Maybe, he thought, driving away together and a change of scenery was all they needed to calm any storms and be happy together. It was certainly better than being alone.

# CHAPTER 20

## Fall 1997

"Hey, you forgot your coffee!" Abilene yelled out the front door as Benny left for work. He turned back, grabbed the travel mug, kissed her on the cheek quickly, and winked at her. His wink and touch still made her heart jump. She shuddered as she pulled her robe closed, pulled her hair back behind her ears, and looked up at the sky. The heavy, gray clouds told her snow was a possibility even though it wasn't Thanksgiving yet. Abilene had lived in northern New York at Fort Bradley for three years and still couldn't get used to the cold and snow. While she loved it the first year, it was a fleeting appreciation as the winters wore on. Benny loved it and he loved to take their daughter, Bitty, sled riding. She ate up the attention from her father. Abilene did too.

It was a few weeks shy of Bitty's third birthday and Abilene was still in the middle of planning a birthday party. She envied the moms who had spring and summer babies who could all have outdoor parties at the park and base pool. Abilene was regulated to either the movie theater on post or a party at home. As much as she loved her Army wife friends and all their little ones, the noise and chaos of birthday parties always sent her packing up early, only there's no early escape when it's your kid's party.

Bitty was smart, carefree, and needier than Abilene cared for. She named her Elizabeth Ashlynn but called her "itty bitty" from day one. The name Bitty stuck. Abilene wasn't sure when was the last time she or Benny called her Elizabeth or Lizzie, as Benny's family insisted. Even though they had been married just over three years, Abilene had only met Benny's family a handful of times. They drove to Denver right after the wedding so she could meet his sister. Then, his parents and sister all visited for Bitty's birth, then her first birthday, along with Tom, Sandy, and the girls. For Christmases, Benny and Abilene took turns visiting her family, then his. Benny's sister, Angelina, flew out on her own the summer between her high school graduation and freshman year of college. She helped with Bitty and drank beer with Abilene at night as they watched movies and played cards. Benny was away in the field for two of the four weeks Angelina stayed. Even without seeing her often, Abilene came to see Angelina as a sister to her, too.

Aside from Angelina, Abilene found making friends with other Army wives easy. Living in military housing made it impossible to not find someone to connect to. There was a small playground directly across from their unit and all the neighborhood kids and moms hung out there when the weather was nice. In the three years since moving to Fort Bradley, she saw several good friends move and several arrive, along with a few she didn't mesh with. She found it hard to say goodbye to the ones she grew to love, and easy to watch the moving van pull away with the belongings of others. The constant moving in and out, families on the street changing, and revolving friend groups were all par for the course as an Army wife. She found it an easy adjustment because of the few years at Fort Patten as a teenager and moving all over with her mom before that.

Currently, her best friends and neighbors were Monique, Casey, and Shawna. They would gather at the park after lunch, shop together on the weekends, and call each other for hours when the weather was too crappy to hang out outside, which was the norm after October. Monique was two doors down and a constant presence. They walked into each other's homes like family, told each other's fears and dreams, cried together, and laughed until their sides hurt. Monique had two boys and a girl who was a few months younger than Bitty. Abilene loved the fact that Monique's daughter, Sissy, and Bitty were like little best friends, holding hands and sharing snacks. It took away the guilt Abilene felt for not having another baby just yet. Benny wasn't the only one putting pressure on her to have another. Shawna and Casey would mention now is the time to get started before Bitty started school. Abilene told them she was confident she couldn't have more kids. She hated lying but did what she could to shut down those conversations when the subject came up. She told them Bitty had been a rough pregnancy and labor, and the doctors warned her that having another could be dangerous. Only Benny and Monique knew the truth. Pregnancy and labor with Bitty unleashed debilitating panic attacks. The attacks started when she started to show about five months. Nightmares of being in labor plagued Abilene, blood pouring from her body, and Ashlynn hovering above her, calling her a liar and telling her she hated her—just as Abilene had done as her mother lay dying.

The nightmares morphed into night sweats, daytime shaking and sweating, followed by a racing pulse and heart rate. Benny insisted she tell the OB at an appointment shortly after they settled at Fort Bradley. The OB listened as Abilene cried and retold her experiences as her mother died after having Paris. Benny knew Abilene's mom had died after childbirth, but didn't know the details. The OB insisted on therapy to help Abilene keep her panic attacks under control for the sake of the baby and to ease her fears of impending labor. Therapy worked mostly until labor. As Abilene lay in the Army hospital bed, she was convinced she'd die as soon as Bitty slipped from her womb. She even wrote letters to Benny, her dad and Sandy, and her newborn, just in case. For a full day after labor, she paid more attention to her heart rate than the baby in her arms. Even with a team of nurses and her doctor assuring her she had a perfectly normal delivery, heart rate, pulse, O2 level, and everything else, she feared a stroke at any moment. It wasn't until she was home with Benny and Bitty that she slept and stopped waiting for death to knock. Abilene stopped therapy after that. Panic attacks subsided until Bitty's first birthday. From then on, it was every birthday without fail. Benny kept insisting she go back to therapy to deal with the trauma so they could eventually have another kid and not put her through nine months of attacks, but Abilene found it easier to avoid getting pregnant at all and avoid what she still feared her destiny would be—death by giving birth. Worse than thinking she could die that way because of some genetic issue was that dark fact that Abilene felt she deserved that kind of ending. She deserved to be pulled away from Bitty and Benny, to hear how much they hated her as she slipped from earth, just as her mom had suffered. Deserving that fate was a feeling, or certainty, that she kept to herself.

Now, just weeks before Bitty's third birthday, Abilene dressed Bitty in a sweater and light coat to walk to the park to meet up with the others. She knew there wouldn't be too many chances to spend so much time outside as the weather was surely turning.

Her three friends smiled and waved as she approached.

"Hey, Abilene. Which day is Bitty's party again? We're heading to Sam's family's between Thanksgiving and Christmas this year instead of the holiday to snag cheaper tickets." Casey said as she pulled her silky black hair into a bun on top of her head. She always looked like a model with her long, lanky legs, flawless ivory complexion, and thick black hair that seemed to fall into place exactly as any woman would plan.

"The sixth. That's the plan now." Abilene said as she pulled her hat over her ears. The wind was picking up and her ears stung. "Damn, it's colder than I'm ready for this year."

"Yeah, but girl, you're getting orders soon, so you might avoid the worst of it." Shawna said as she walked back from the slide. Shawna could be heard from anywhere.

"We ain't heard nothing yet. Been three years this summer, so who knows? I wouldn't mind getting stationed back down south, to be honest. Last winter almost broke me." Abilene said with a laugh.

"Yeah, southern girls like you can't take too many northern winters." Shawna said as she settled on the bench next to Casey.

"Plus, if we get down south, I can see my half-sisters more. If we get close to them, I can have them stay and help with Bitty."

"And your other siblings? What, there's like eight of them?" Casey said with a smirk that somehow made her more gorgeous.

"No," Abilene laughed. "Five. Three brothers and two sisters. I haven't seen any of them since my wedding. The boys are all together and the girls are with their dad. I talk to them here and there, mostly on holidays, but that's it." She looked down at the dying grass. She had told Casey and Shawna the basics of who was who, but not much else. They all knew her biological mom had died, and they split the kids. They were respectful enough not to ask for more details. When she first met Casey and Monique and exchanged life stories, they commented on her siblings' names—Austin, Jackson, Dallas, Savannah, and Paris. Without planning or thought of consequence, she told them they were all named after the city they were conceived in. She rattled off her mother's lie so easily, it scared her. Sweat slathered her palms. A lump formed in her throat, and she was sure they could tell she was lying and would instantly shun her from their circle. They nodded, commented on how cool that was, and never mentioned it again. Abilene hated herself for lying and hated herself for how easy it was to stick to the story. She hated her mom for that lie and yet fell right into keeping it alive. Part of her rationalized she didn't want her new friends to hate Ashlynn, too. Considering Benny still didn't know the details of their names were a lie, she believed it was simply best to keep the ugly truth to herself.

The day before Bitty's birthday party, Benny came home with news they'd get orders for Fort Grant, Kentucky. A mix of emotions flowed through Abilene. She hated the thought of saying goodbye to her friends, but was also overjoyed to call Sandy and tell them she'd be so close to see them more often. The Sergeant had retired the year before and took a civilian job on Fort Patten. He and Sandy bought a house off post, a small brick ranch. After so many years as an Army wife, Sandy loved being able to paint rooms any color she wanted and to dig up land for winding flower gardens. She had a different color in every room and was never happier. She and Abilene talked nearly every week, especially about motherhood. Questions Abilene had, health concerns, preschool advice, she'd call Sandy and talk her ear off. Despite the circumstances that landed her in Sandy's life, Abilene was grateful to have her as a mother figure. She even referred to her as 'mom' when talking to her dad and sisters. Sandy was the first person Abilene called when Benny told her that by May, they'd be heading to Kentucky. Alyssa was the second. Alyssa had gone to college for two years before taking a job doing marketing for boutiques in Louisville, Kentucky. Abilene would be about an hour from her high school friend. While they didn't talk much, they called each other for the big stuff. For a fleeting moment, after she hung up with Alyssa, she thought of Julien. She hadn't thought of him in forever, but he crept into her mind without warning.

Anytime big news came her way, he seeped into her consciousness for a moment. Abilene looked at the phone perched on the kitchen counter, then looked at Benny as he picked up Bitty from the floor and wondered who Julien had. Did he have a kid too? A wife maybe? Charlene? Did he get out of Holden for good? *God*, she thought, *I hope he got out of Holden for good.*

The morning of Bitty's party, Benny kissed Abilene's forehead as he grabbed his keys to pick up the cake.

"You sure we just need the cake? I won't have time to go back out." Benny asked as he tied his shoes.

"Yeah, just the cake." Abilene said as she opened a bag of streamers to tape to the archway between the kitchen and dining area.

"Hey, you sure you're okay?"

"Yeah, why?" Abilene asked as she fumbled with a giant "3" balloon tied to the head dining chair.

"You know. Every year, you get yourself worked up. I don't want to leave you alone if you'd rather me be here." Benny said. She stopped fiddling with the decorations and looked up at him.

"I think I'm okay. At least for now." Benny walked over to her and took her hands.

"By this time next year, your family will be so close they'll be at her party. Maybe we'll have another one on the way, too." He kissed her forehead. Abilene's eyes welled up.

"You know I'm not ready for that. I can barely make it through thinking about that day without a panic attack, and you think I could go through another delivery?" She felt her cheeks get red.

"Hey, listen. I told you repeatedly to get therapy again. You don't have to live like this. We don't have to live like this. I mean, really, we're never going to talk about having another kid because of this? Maybe if you actually deal with it, got over it, we can give Bitty a brother or sister." His voice grew louder than she knew he wanted. She swallowed a lump in her throat and fought tears. He let go of her hands.

"I can't help it. You know that." Abilene stepped back and folded her arms.

"You could if you got help. Maybe, I don't know, maybe you're just using that as an excuse not to have another kid." Benny shot at her. Abilene drew in a deep breath.

"You know that's not it. Dammit."

"Do I? The doctors have all said what happened to your mom had nothing to do with genetics and there's no danger to you having another." Benny put the keys in his pocket and looked down at her. "Listen, I know it sucked that she died like that. But you gotta let this go and live in the present. We gotta move forward."

"You think I don't want to? I wish I could. I just don't feel—"

"Feel what?"

"Feel like you get it. She didn't just die. I lost everything that day. Everything. Everyone. Everyone who really knew me."

"You have me."

"Do I? I mean, come on. You wouldn't have married me if I wasn't pregnant. Jesus, Benny, I'm not sure you were really in love with me before that, anyway. We spent a few months sneaking around, but I don't think you loved me, not the real me, anyway." She looked down. "We just couldn't keep our hands off each other. That doesn't mean you were in love with me. You were a soldier with a girl who would do anything to get with you, following you all around post, stalking you, really. That's not love." Abilene regretted the words as soon as she said them, both because she knew they were mean, but also because she feared they were true. She let the tears slide down. Benny walked out and slammed the door.

Abilene slid into the chair and stared at the giant gold "3" balloon, waving slightly by an invisible breeze. Just over three years of marriage and she felt they were both just playing house. The nights were lustful, sensual, and she still burned for him when they touched, but they never laughed. They never joked or teased each other as she saw her friends do with their husbands. It felt like a gut punch to her when she saw Monique and Joey laugh at an inside joke. She and Benny didn't have inside jokes. They had Bitty. They both loved her but had no connection to each other besides behind the bedroom door. Maybe, Abilene figured that was all marriage needed to be. Loving each other through the night and raising kids. Jokes, knowing nudges, playfulness were what friends were for. She was good at making friends. She told herself that was enough. What more did she expect from Benny, anyway? He got her pregnant, married her, took great care of her and Bitty, supported her plans to start school when Bitty was a little older. He was faithful, he was a good man and a good soldier. She tried to be a good wife, a good Army wife at events, and a good mom. Abilene had avoided the fate of being a single mom. She just needed to hide the panic attacks and life would be as perfect as it could be for a girl who got carried away with a soldier who caught her eye at the ice cream stand a few years earlier.

After the holidays, and with a move pending, Abilene did what all military wives do—downsize and clear out the clutter. Each move had weight stipulations and soldiers were allotted only so many "household goods" to move with each new duty station. While they hadn't obtained a lot, between totes she still dragged with her from high school, Benny's collectible baseball memorabilia, and clothes Bitty had outgrown, they had plenty for her whittle down. Abilene started with her closet. She bagged up her maternity clothes. Abilene put those at the bottom, hoping Benny would never notice. She also bagged up some of her clothing creations from high school that she and Alyssa constructed after watching Molly Ringwald and Brat Pack movies over and over. A few got hung back up. She couldn't bring herself to purge them all, even though she spent most of her energy dressing like Phoebe from Friends now. Abilene glanced down below her dresses to see her boots. Those red cowboy boots were like an appendage. She smiled, knowing wherever she moved, they'd be coming with her even though she hadn't worn them in a few years. She tried them on under her flowing peasant skirt. They still felt like a hug.

Abilene moved on to Benny's closet, which was mostly Army uniforms, one suit, a few dress shirts and pants, and various shoe boxes he insisted on keeping. Any time he got a new pair of shoes, he kept them in the box. It was an odd, yet endearing quirk that took up too much room in his closet. Abilene pulled the step stool over to reach the top of the closet. There was another box. There wasn't a shoe brand on it or anything else. It was a small record or file folder-type box. It looked a little rough around the edges, not new, certainly over three years old. Abilene stared at it and tried to place if she had seen it before. She shrugged and thought maybe it was filled with childhood or high school certificates and such. Benny's mom had his trophies and awards still displayed all over his old room, the room they slept in anytime they visited Denver. Abilene smiled a little and tied her hair in a scrunchy. It warmed her heart for a moment, thinking Benny was a little like his mom, a hoarder of every accolade, and maybe he'd do the same for Bitty someday. She reached up and pulled the box to the edge. It was lighter than she expected, considering its size. She stepped down from the stool with it and placed it on the bed. She slid off her boots and scooted onto the bed next to it.

"What are you hiding, Benny?" She said as she untied a leather string wrapped around it twice and tied in a bow on the top. There were letters inside, all in addressed envelopes, and a few cards scattered at the bottom. Pictures under those. Abilene scrunched up her nose and briefly thought about tying the box back up and placing it back on the closet shelf. Something in the pit of her belly told her to leave well enough alone. Benny was a good man. They had a perfectly good life together. Why look for trouble when there is none? Benny also had a right to privacy. But the delicate cursive writing on the envelopes was too much of a temptation. Abilene reached in and pulled out the first letter, opened it, and read.

*New Year's Day 1994*
*Dear Benito,*
*I can't believe you're really leaving again! I already miss you. Last night, our third new year's eve together was incredible. Every time with you is. God, I can't wait to marry you. Every night I look at my ring and wish you were right next to me. Two more years, babe, and I'm done with college and will join you, just like we always talked about in high school. Once I'm done with spring semester, I'll fly out to Georgia and spend a few weeks, and it will be just like heaven, like the cure song that I sang to you at that stupid junior high dance! Haha! The last two weeks with you home only make me love you more. It's you and me forever, my Benito.*
*Love Sarah*

Abilene's hands shook. She blinked and looked at the date again. Benny had flown home to Denver over Christmas, two months after she lost her virginity to him. Abilene pulled another letter from the box.

*March 1994*

*Benito,*

*My plane ticket is all set, babe. I'll be there in June. We'll go to that lake you told me about, make love all day, be alone, FINALLY! No parents, no sisters or brothers barging in or following us. God, I can't wait to live with you. I miss you so much. I hate how much the long-distance calls are or I'd call you every night before I go to sleep. You're all I can think about. Our life together is going to be beautiful, babe.*

*Forever,*

*Sarah*

March 1994 hit Abilene like a lightning bolt. That was the month she got pregnant with Bitty. Weeks later, she huddled in Alyssa's arms in a mall bathroom crying hysterically when she took that pregnancy test. She was petrified of Benny's reaction, her family's reaction. Abilene shook more. Tears ran furiously down her face and splotched the letter. She felt sick to her stomach and dizzy, just as she had when she found the postcards from Swenson House to a 10-year-old Ashlynn. Nothing made sense. Abilene fought to get the paper back in the envelope. It tore. "Shit!" she yelled out. Abilene took a deep breath and sat back on her heels on the bed. Her mind raced. "Breathe. Just breathe." She whispered to herself. She drew in another deep breath and placed the now-torn letter in the box. Abilene glanced at the lid. Her mind told her to tie it up, place it in the closet, and forget the letters. Her heart pounded and urged her to read more. Abilene grabbed another.

*June 1, 1994*

*Benito,*

*I can't believe this. We just hung up. I've never been so devastated. I am sitting here with a ticket on my desk and my heart torn into a thousand pieces.*

*I can't believe you got some girl pregnant after all we had, all we talked about. You said we were forever up to two weeks ago. Me and you against the world. Dammit. If she agrees to get rid of it, I still don't think I can get over this. I really don't. I know I said on the phone we might have a chance if she does, but now I'm not sure. Fuck fuck fuck. How could you fuck this up so bad, fuck us over, ruin us? How? Over one night drinking too much with the guys? One night and you ruin years of our love? You broke the one promise I never thought you would. You broke us, Benito. We could have had it all. We did for years. I don't even know what to do with myself now. My parents, your parents, all the plans they made for a wedding in two summers. You threw us away for one night with some drunk chick at a bar. One night and we'll never be the same. We'll never be us, never again. God, I know I told you I still love you and you said you still love me when we talked tonight, but I don't think I can do this. I can't.*

*Sarah*

Abilene pictured herself on June 1, 1994. She was standing in the living room as Sandy hemmed the dress they found for her to marry Benny two weeks later, exactly one week after her high school graduation. Benny had asked her to marry him. She had told him he didn't need to. He was the one who insisted they could make it work, that he wanted to make it work. The words *get rid of it, one night with some drunk chick, you said you still loved me,* jumped out from the letter in her hand, over and over again she read it. Each time, her heart beat harder. There was an ache in her chest and a pit in her stomach. She thought she'd vomit all over the bed. Her mouth watered and sweat broke out across her forehead and nose. Everything was spinning.

She feverishly read through the rest at the bottom of the box, noting the dates, struggling to remember where she was at the time. The June letter was the last. She read them in reverse, all the way back to Benny's high school days with Sarah. The night they both lost their virginity together after a football game. Plans for prom. Poems she wrote about his dark hair and eyes. Fights they had. Break-ups that lasted weeks with panicked letters of when to meet after school to talk it out. Vows to never talk again. Vows to love until they were both dead and buried. The night he left for the Army. The night they snuck off to a hotel the weekend before he left for basic. Letters detailing their love, their fights, their passion, their inside jokes about their friends. Inside jokes. The letters were filled with them. Code names, nicknames, making fun of each other's fears and phobias, embarrassing stories that would have made anyone else laugh along with them. Anyone but Abilene. She didn't exist in their world of letters except the last one—a drunk chick who might get rid of it. That's all she was to Sarah. There were pictures too. Pictures of them in photo booths, dances, her sitting on his lap at someone's house party, in their graduation gowns, skiing at Breckenridge Colorado with Benny's family, kisses on his cheek, kisses on her forehead, photos they took of each other laying in bed tangled in sheets together. Smiles. Connection. Love.

Bitty cried from her room, having woken from her nap. It was a faraway echo in Abilene's head as she searched each letter for something, anything, of the Benny she knew. She felt like an outsider who stumbled across secret letters from the previous homeowner. Letters outlining a grand love story, a true love story, only this wasn't evidence of a love story that warmed her heart. It was a love story thrust in her face that showed tangible proof she didn't have what they had. Smiles. Connection. Love. None of it involved her. None of it was her life. She gathered up the letters and tried to arrange them as they were. She tied the box closed and climbed the stepladder. Her legs were shaky and her hands were sweaty. She slid the box back on the shelf and briefly thought about lighting it on fire, along with everything else in his closet. She climbed down, wiped her eyes, smearing mascara across her cheeks. Abilene suddenly felt invisible in her house like a strange, foggy apparition. Invisible in her marriage, her life, or what she thought was her life. Every moment since she met Benny suddenly seemed like a lie, an act he put on while away from his "forever Sarah". She replayed every moment they spent together at Fort Patten at the bowling alley, the PX, parking lots, the track and bridge along the trail. Every glance, touch, and kiss.

Abilene let numbness settle in her bones as Bitty's cries grew louder. She took Bitty to the kitchen to get her an afternoon snack, then she reached up to the top of the fridge and grabbed the bottle of tequila they used for margaritas when they had card games with the neighbors. She took a swig, gasped at the burn in her throat and stomach, took another and let more tears fall. With shaky hands, she put the bottle back. She didn't have time to get drunk and forget what she saw and read. Abilene had dinner to cook and bags of old clothes to place in the trunk to donate tomorrow. She had a daughter to care for, a life to live even if it was all based on a lie, Benny's lies to her and to his "forever Sarah".

As the minutes ticked by and Bitty got preoccupied with a coloring book on the dining room table, Abilene felt like she'd explode if she didn't tell someone what she found. This was the second time in just a few years that rummaging through a closet had upended her entire life. The last time, after finding the truth about Ashlynn, she threw her things into a bag, climbed out her bedroom window, and ran straight to Julien to help her find her dad. There was no running away with a three-year-old in the picture. She entertained the idea of calling Monique but knew once she told her, Monique would look at Benny differently, at her differently, too. Monique's husband had cheated on her when he was overseas and she was pregnant with her youngest. It tore her apart and telling Abilene was cleansing, but Abilene could tell it still haunted Monique. The last thing she wanted to do was burden her friend with this and remind her of what she'd been through. Abilene called the one person she could tell who wouldn't say anything to Benny or anyone else—Sandy.

Sandy was off work and answered on the first ring. Before she could get out any kind of greeting, Abilene spit out what she found, details, and dates. The tears came rushing back as she said it all out loud.

"Abi, Abi, honey. Slow down," Sandy pleaded. Abilene took a deep breath and described the pictures to Sandy.

"Oh girl, of course he had a girlfriend back home. Most of those young soldiers do. I told you that when you and Alyssa were sneaking around your last year of high school. But you're married now. He married you."

"But you don't understand. June 1ˢᵗ, Sandy. He was still telling her he loved her. They were still in love. What am I supposed to do knowing that, huh?" Abilene said. She swallowed a lump in her throat, afraid of Sandy's answer.

"Looks like you have two choices. You can tell him you found the letters and ream him out. Call him out on lying to her about you, lying to you by not telling you he had someone. Then pack up Bitty and get your ass back home to us. Or you can bury it. Accept he had a life and yes, love, before you and after meeting you, but he ultimately made a choice to marry you and take care of you and Bitty."

Abilene drew in a deep breath again. She huffed into the receiver and wiped her eyes again.

"Listen, Abilene. Take it from me. Every man has a past, women too. She might have a piece of his heart forever. God knows, and I hate saying this, honey, but I thought for years your dad still had a thing for your mom. She was gorgeous, and no man could look away from her." Sandy said with a slight laugh. "I know part of him still loved her. But I loved him. I loved him enough for the both of us in those early days. Now, I know your dad loves me, don't get me wrong. Jesus, he's got my name scrawled across his arm. But, back then, Ashlynn was in the middle of our marriage, whether or not he even realized it." Sandy exhaled loudly. "I know this sucks but honey, you got a good man, a wonderful dad, a good provider and soldier who will always do right by you. Bury it. Keep what you read tied up and hidden in that box. It's the past. Bury it."

Abilene shook her head and loosened her grip on the phone. She glanced around the kitchen and watched Bitty at the table, coloring and humming to herself.

"Okay. You're right, Mom." She exhaled and looked up at the ceiling. "Imma go start dinner."

"You sure you're okay?" Sandy said.

"Yeah, I'll be fine. Thanks for talking me down. I love you."

"Love you, Abi. Kiss Bitty for me and call back if you need me," Sandy said.

Abilene hung up and held onto the counter with both hands. The words 'bury it' replayed in her head. Her mind knew that was the easiest thing to do, the least disruptive. But she couldn't shake the words she read. She was sick of having half a marriage, an existence with no genuine connection or love. No inside jokes. Besides her wedding picture, she wasn't sure there was one picture of her and Benny smiling and laughing. She wanted what Benny and Sarah had in those pictures and letters. Abilene realized in those moments she may never have that. She'd bury it like Sandy said and try to bury her desire for more along with those letters. The piece of him she had, the piece of her he wanted, had to be enough. After all, having part of Benny and this tiny family was still better than leaving and following the path her mother took—a destiny Abilene was determined to avoid repeating. Ashlynn was constantly chasing more, the next guy thinking that would make everything okay. Thinking that would fill the hole the death of her parents created. It never did. Sometimes, as Sandy said, a good man is good enough. She'd bury the desire for more and keep it locked away and out of sight, like Benny's box of letters.

# CHAPTER 21

## Summer 1998

Boxes were stacked to the ceiling in the kitchen and living room. Benny had to report to his commander, leaving Abilene to handle the unpacking. Maintenance was on the way because the air conditioner had gone on the fritz. Abilene forgot how humid a southern June day could be. It had been four years since she left Georgia for upstate New York—the snowiest Army post in the United States. While she was excited to be in Kentucky and closer to family, the sweat pouring off her face and dotting the cardboard boxes that contained their lives was making her momentarily miss her days up north. Bitty played with dolls she traveled with from room to room. Abilene took a box cutter to each box and sliced the tops. She scraped her knuckles, regardless of how carefully she opened each. Her goal was to get her kitchen and baths in order before Benny got home. He'd move the heavier furniture into place for them. As she put the coffeemaker on the counter, there was a knock at the door.

Abilene opened it to see a woman waving wildly with a bottle of wine and flowers.

"Hey, I'm Roxanne. I'm not much of a baker, so no cookies from me, but I thought I'd say hi and bring over something. Welcome to Fort Grant." She said. Her hair was the brightest blonde Abilene had ever seen. It was a short pixie cut. It beautifully framed her delicate face, and it made the clusters of freckles on her nose and cheeks stand out more. She was shorter than Abilene, maybe a smidge over five feet. Yet her edgy look and gritty voice made her seem ten feet tall.

"Thank you so much! I'm Abilene, and this little thing clinging to my leg is Elizabeth, but we call her Bitty." Abilene reached behind her and tugged at Bitty's arm. Bitty smiled and moved her hair from her face as she looked at Roxanne. Roxanne smiled down at her and gave a tiny wave.

"Abilene? Like the town in Texas, huh?"

"Yep. You want to come in? Boxes are still everywhere, but I just unpacked the coffee pot." Abilene said as she opened the door more.

"Sure, my oldest, Emily, is home with the little one. She's 14. I have a 4-year-old, Maya, who would love to meet this one soon." Roxanne said as she sauntered in through the narrow hallway that led from the living room to the kitchen and dining area. As Abilene followed with Bitty right on her heels, she could tell instantly she and Roxanne would be fast friends. She was right.

The summer unfolded in days of sweltering conversations on porches, following the little ones as they rode tricycles and wobbled on training wheels. Ice cream smiles for the kids and iced coffees for the moms cooled them all down after soaking up the sun most days. Abilene taught Bitty how to swim at the base pool. She'd lounge with Roxanne, and Roxanne's circle of friends watching their little ones running, diving, vying for attention to see who could stay under the longest. Abilene also got to see her dad, Sandy, and Krista and Kayla a few times as they came up for the fourth of July and she took a trip to Georgia to spend a long weekend at their house. Time was flying as she wondered how Bitty was nearly four and would go to a full day preschool in the fall.

Roxanne and her husband, Miles, asked Benny and Abilene to join them at the NCO club on a Friday night for karaoke one night before school started. They wanted to take advantage of having Emily free to babysit all the younger ones before she got too busy with school and cheerleading practice. Abilene hadn't been out without Bitty in ages. She struggled to remember the last time she and Benny were with only adults, and it didn't involve a military function. Much to her surprise and with a pang of jealously, Bitty ran to Emily at full speed and crashed into her legs when they dropped her off.

The four of them ate appetizers and drank beer, sang, and laughed at the guys' military stories. Benny reached over and grabbed Abilene's hand while telling a story about his friends in the barracks getting caught with a keg. She laughed and felt butterflies. Abilene watched his eyes, his smile, the way his tanned skin crinkled when he laughed. She loved watching him when he didn't notice. Abilene finished her beer as the waitress put another one in front of her. Roxanne and Miles got up to do a duet they promised would liven up the room.

As Meatloaf blared through the speakers and Roxanne took a serious stance as if she was auditioning for a video, Abilene laughed and drank more. She noticed Benny looking at her.

"What?" she said while cracking up more at Roxanne.

"Nothing. I just forget sometimes how beautiful you are." Benny said with that wink that always made her weak. She smiled and felt her pulse speed up.

"You're quite the charmer sometimes, honey." She said as she cherished the morsels of affection he rarely gave. That was thing about morsels of affection. You always end up hungry for more.

"If we go to Denver this Christmas, I want to take you and Bitty skiing. I used to go to Breckenridge every New Years. I think Bitty is old enough to try. She's certainly brave enough, right? That little shit has no fear." Benny said as he swigged.

"Skiing?" Abilene said. She swigged more and the letters and pictures flashed through her fuzzy mind. "Like you used to do with Sarah?" Abilene gasped as soon as the words left her mouth. *Shit, shit, shit.* She thought as panic welled up from her stomach to her throat. She couldn't breathe.

"What? What did you say?" Benny asked. His cheeks grew red as he placed his beer on the table. His eyes were burning through her.

"I... found that box when I was clean—"

"You went through my stuff? What the fuck, Abilene?"

"I didn't mean to. It was when we were getting rid of stuff to move here." She looked down and fought tears and tried to focus. She had too much to drink to get her thoughts straight.

"You had no right, Abilene. That's just a box of shit from high school. Nothing you needed to go through." He gripped his beer and his knuckles turned white. She regrouped her thoughts and remembered the dates of what she read that day.

"You can be mad at me for going through it, but how do you think I feel?"

"What do you mean, how you feel?" Benny cocked his head to the side. Anger spread across his face.

"You told her I was just some drunk chick you knocked up. You were still with her after I got pregnant and told her you loved her. Were you lying to her or me?"

"What the fuck does it matter? That was years ago. Yeah, I was with her when we met, but I broke it off and haven't heard from her in years. You got pregnant, we got married. What more do you want?" He said through gritted teeth.

"When I lost my virginity to you, when I was getting fitted for a dress to marry you, you were telling her you'd be together forever, and you loved her. So, which is it, Benny? Did you love her or me when we got married?" Abilene slurred. Benny pounded his fist on the table. Abilene jumped.

"Her. There. Are you happy now?" Benny looked straight ahead as Roxanne and Miles made their way back to the table. Roxanne shot Abilene a look as Abilene fought tears. She finished her beer.

"Hey, Abi, want to get another?" Roxanne asked. Abilene nodded and stood. She followed Roxanne to the bar and told her not to ask. Abilene could tell by the look on her friend's face she knew something was wrong. Roxanne nodded back at her and ordered the beers. Abilene drank it, then another, and another, barely remembering the ride home and changing into pajamas with Benny's help. Her last memory before she closed her eyes was seeing Benny walk past their room carrying Bitty to her room. Abilene exhaled and tried to fight off the spins as she told herself *he's a good dad. A good man. Bury it, Abilene,* even though she knew it was too late.

Abilene woke with a killer hangover. She shielded her eyes walking into the kitchen. Benny was getting cereal for Bitty. He asked her if she wanted coffee. When he handed it to her, he met her eyes. Benny gave that wink and turned back to Bitty. Abilene knew in that minute they'd never talk about what they said last night. He'd never say another word about it. She'd never ask again. They had buried it and she was too exhausted to think about digging it up anytime soon. Pretending it was okay was the path of least resistance, the option that meant nothing would change. Abilene sipped the coffee and resolved to be a good wife and mom even if meant not being the love of his life. She'd swallow her pain, her longing to be more, longing for inside jokes, and a connection and settle for contentment. Abilene would settle for being still, not running or seeking anything more. She knew how it would end if she did.

Summer faded into fall. Bitty's birthday came and went. She managed to stifle a panic attack because of the comfort of family being there. Krista and Kayla stayed for a long weekend. Abilene took them shopping, stayed up late watching movies, and felt part of her little family. Benny pulled her close on nights after a few beers and they made love feverishly, drenched in sweat, and tangled up in each other. She'd kiss his chest. He'd kiss her forehead and drift off to sleep afterwards. She settled for the fact that he wanted her in his bed, even if she drifted off wondering if he had her in his heart. But then again, she'd reason, what difference would that make in her daily life, anyway?

At Christmas, they flew to Denver, skied with his family, and sat by fires at night drinking wine and beer, cuddled next to each other, talking with his parents and sister and her boyfriend late into the night. They'd make love quietly, and she'd push out images of him with Sarah on those very slopes. The past was buried. He was in her arms here and now.

After being in Kentucky for over a year and Bitty starting kindergarten, Abilene reflected on what she wanted to do for herself. She had met up with Alyssa a few times, spent most days talking with Roxanne, who worked at the post bank, and on the phone with others. Abilene enrolled in a few classes at the community college off post. Benny kissed her forehead and told her she'd do great. She felt like she was carving out something for herself. Roxanne told her they'd go out to the bar and celebrate her next step. Abilene got dressed in her old cowboy boots, best faded jeans, and a black velvet shirt that had cap sleeves. She kissed Benny and told him not to wait up.

Roxanne and three of her friends closed in around her at a table close to the bar and jukebox. Abilene loved going out with the girls. She and Roxanne had started a tradition of going out together once a month to get away from the kids. Roxanne nudged her as one woman squeezed a chair into the group.

"I think that's Olivia's hairdresser," she said as she pointed to a short woman with a bright smile and long black hair. Olivia worked at the bank with Roxanne and was an Army wife too. She had met them out a few times. Abilene smiled at the woman and took a swig of her beer. The woman waved back and reached across the wet table.

"You must be Abi!" Abilene reached out and shook her hand, noticing her long red nails, which perfectly matched her earrings. "I'm Vanessa." Abilene was enraptured by her beauty. By the end of the night, she was enraptured with her wit and ability to drink more than any other woman at the table. Vanessa would chug, do a shot, howl, and unleash a smile that made anyone in the room fall in love with her. Abilene wished she could be more like this wild, gorgeous, free spirit hair dresser. By the end of the night, they ended up in the bathroom together. Abilene came out of a stall and was already feeling fuzzy, vowing to get a glass of water.

"So, you live on post too?" Vanessa said as she reapplied red lipstick that made her full lips look even more enticing.

"Yeah, on Liberty Lane. You?"

"I'm on Anderson, other side of post. My husband, Mac, is a tank mechanic. Yours?" Vanessa said.

"Oh. Mine, Benny is in security, cyber security. You got kids?" Abilene asked as she washed her hands.

"Nope, only been married three years. I'm not ready for all that yet," Vanessa said with a laugh as she put her lipstick away. "Plus, Mac had a shitty childhood, so he isn't all keen on having kids yet. He says I'm not mom material yet, not till I calm down at least!" She winked. Abilene laughed with her. Vanessa was like a wild colt she couldn't look away from. "Hey, Abi, I can tame those curls for you with a serum I use in my shop. You should come see me sometime."

"Yeah, of course. I just bounce around from salon to salon really since I moved here." Abilene followed her out back to the table. As she watched Vanessa walk in front of her, she knew this new friend would make life interesting. Vanessa was the type of woman who made everything more interesting, especially girls' night out as she watched Vanessa go right past the table to the dance floor. Vanessa threw her hands in the air and commanded attention from everyone.

"She's a trip, huh?" Roxanne said as she pulled out Abilene's chair.

"Yeah. You can say that. She's pretty wild." Abilene said as she slid down in her chair without taking her eyes off Vanessa, who was hypnotizing a half-dozen men watching from the side of the dance floor. Abilene took a drink and thought maybe someday she'd be that hypnotizing and maybe Benny would notice. Abilene hoped the kind of energy and sensualness Vanessa oozed was contagious. Even if it wasn't, she knew Vanessa was the kind of woman she wanted to be around more. She was pretty sure everyone who ever crossed Vanessa's path probably felt the same way.

# CHAPTER 22

*Christmas 2000*

"Alright, sit back and let's see what we want to do with this hair. You want the usual?" Vanessa said as Abilene looked at herself in the salon mirror. She had always loved her wild wavy locks but two summers of Kentucky humidity made looking put together more of a battle than she cared to wage with a kid six-year-old in tow—a six-year-old who acted just as wild as Abilene's hair.

"I think I want it straight and maybe short for once." Abilene said as she tilted her head and tried to see the girl she had once been. She still saw her, but she noticed bouncing back from girls' night and drinking too much at late night card nights wasn't as easy as it once had been. She had also started smoking when out with the girls. Vanessa smoked, only it didn't show on her face like it did Abilene the next morning. Maybe the effects were just in Abilene's head and not so much on her 24-year-old face.

"Short like Roxanne's?" Vanessa asked with wide eyes.

"Maybe. What do you think? Will that look okay on me or no? You're the expert. I trust your gut." Abilene said, looking up at her friend in the mirror.

"Hmm." Vanessa said as she gathered Abilene's hair back and leaned down next to her shoulder.

"It'll be one hell of a surprise for her going-away party Saturday night. I say let's do it." A wide smile came across Vanessa's face as she picked up scissors.

As Vanessa washed, combed, and snipped Abilene's hair, they talked about the surprise party at the Mexican restaurant right out the back gate and gossiped about a few girls they knew in common.

"Damn, I'm gonna miss Roxanne. She's so cool and her husband is cool with her going out with all of us, unlike Olivia's. He's an ass." Vanessa said.

"Yeah, that's what I hear. Mine doesn't mind me going out with you girls as long as I get home safely. Hell, we've been together since I was 18, so I never got to go out much with girlfriends before having a kid, you know?" Abilene said, realizing she missed out on college parties and bar hopping on her 21$^{st}$ birthday. But she smiled thinking about Bitty in her arms and thought to herself that she'd do it all again. "How about yours? Mac, right? You never mention him much."

"He's cool. Mostly. As long as I don't come home drunk, starting shit." She laughed. "We have had a few knock-down drag-out fights when I drink, but I can't help it. He just, well, everyone, as you know, can get on my last nerve when I have one too many." They both laughed as Abilene remembered Vanessa getting them kicked out of a bar across town a few months ago because she climbed on the bar and started dancing. The bartender and owner tried to help her down, and she threw her beer at him and tried to keep dancing. It took all four other wives to get her down and out the door before the owner called the police. They never went back to that bar. It mortified Abilene. Only now months later was it funny. When she told Benny about it, he told her to watch out for that one. Wives like that can ruin a soldier's career. Abilene could almost see when Vanessa reached a point of no return, when shit would hit the fan if someone looked at her wrong or said the wrong thing to any of the other wives. Abilene felt sorry for her husband for having to rein that in regularly.

"Hey, once Roxanne moves, Benny and I will need more players for our poker nights. You and your husband should come over sometime." Abilene said, then instantly pictured a drunk Vanessa climbing on top of her kitchen counter, stripping and yelling. She had only been out with Vanessa a few times in the last year and a half, but each of those seemed to lead to a drunken incident.

"Oh yeah, we'd love that. Mac is leaving for training until May, though. He leaves in a few weeks, so yeah, once he gets back."

"Oh man, I'm sorry. That sucks." Abilene said, remembering when Benny was gone for months training and how lonely the nights could be. The days were a breeze, but nights alone dragged on.

"That's okay. I'm heading home to Louisiana for two weeks after he goes, and God knows the salon keeps me busy and outta trouble." Vanessa said as she put some mousse in Abilene's hair. "Well, what do you think?" she said as she spun Abilene around.

Abilene's eyes grew wide when she saw herself. Her tumbleweed hair was now shaggy, short, bright, and so, so different. For a moment, she saw Ashlynn's face staring back at her from a time when Ashlynn chopped her hair off to look like Madonna in the Papa Don't Preach video after Butch left her. Abilene's eyes welled up.

"Oh my God, you don't like it?"

"No, no. I love it. It's just different. Truth be told, it reminds me of my mom who passed away. For a second, I thought I was looking at her." Abilene said through misty eyes. Vanessa reached down and wrapped her arms around Abilene.

"I didn't realize you lost your mom." Vanessa said. Abilene gave her the abbreviated version—died from preeclampsia, went to live with dad, all ended up okay. She unwrapped herself from the cape and hugged Vanessa for making her look and feel beautiful. She felt taller with short hair, older too. Abilene saw the woman looking back at her in the mirror, no longer a young mom and wife, but a woman. She smiled as she paid Vanessa.

"Okay, honey, I'll see you at the restaurant."

"Yep, I'll be the hot one looking punk with my new do. Oh, and May. When your guy gets home, you're coming over to play poker. We play for real money, so be prepared." Abilene said with a laugh.

Benny loved the hair style. He ran his strong hands through it and gave her a kiss when he came home. Bitty couldn't stop touching it, either. The last two years at Fort Grant had turned Abilene and Benny into an actual couple on the outside, even if there was still a distance between them. He treated her like gold, never raised his voice, never complained, and supported her as she took various classes off post. She was only a few credits shy of an associate degree in marketing, even though she didn't know what she'd do with it. She had dreams of going into advertising, maybe marketing for fashion companies, much like Alyssa had stumbled into. Benny took

Bitty off her hands when she needed to study or had a test, or late-night study group at the community college about 30 miles from Fort Grant. Abilene often wondered if he was so accommodating to make up for not being madly in love with her. As if he owed it to her to support her dreams since he had taken one vital one from her—real love. She never brought it up, the distance and quiet between them. She knew he cared for her and physically desired her behind closed doors. Abilene did everything he wanted in bed to keep his attention when she had him alone. She took those heated moments of passion and lust as a sign that, even if he wasn't madly in love with her, he definitely wanted her and wouldn't go fishing around for anyone else. They were comfortable with each other and with the little family they had.

Now and then, she'd see him staring off, though. She instantly wondered if he was thinking about Sarah. She'd swallow a lump in her throat when she could see the answer in his eyes. Abilene never told Benny, but he said Sarah's name more than once in his sleep, mostly when they had a trip planned to Denver to see his family. When they would be there for holidays or most recently for Angelina's wedding, she'd notice him looking around wildly, searching every time they went out in public. She knew in her heart he was always looking for her. Abilene tried to imagine what he'd do if he saw her off in the distance at a store, the restaurant, or down the street as they walked with Bitty. Her gut seized at the thought of their eyes meeting. While he wouldn't run off and abandon her right there, part of her wondered if he'd at least consider it. She had nothing that kept him by her side except for Bitty and his sense of honor toward her. Bitty was the only thing that she knew bound them together no matter what, no matter what past ghost may wander around his head or heart. She was smart enough to know she wasn't the one, but she also slept well at night knowing to Benny she was someone he valued—the mother of the kid he loved to pieces and a partner he wanted in his bed. For now, that was enough for Abilene.

# CHAPTER 23

*June 2001*

Benny got the card table cover draped and smoothed the green velvet while Abilene cut up a lime for drinks. She poured herself a splash of bourbon, added some ginger ale, and let an ice cube swirl around the glass.

"Is Bitty all settled in with a movie?" Benny asked as he grabbed a glass for himself from the cupboard. They had monogrammed glasses Benny's sister gave them as gifts for being in her wedding last year.

"Yep, she's all tucked in and happy with popcorn. She's watching Monsters Inc." Abilene said as she headed for the fridge to get the cheese plate and veggie plate out. Benny grabbed her arm and pulled her back toward him after she placed them on the counter. He spun her around and kissed her. "What's that for?" she asked as her voice went up and a smile crept across her face.

"Nothing. You just look sexy, that's all. I know I don't tell you that enough." Benny said as he bit his bottom lip and pulled her close again by her jean belt loop.

"Nope, you don't tell me enough, Sergeant Nash." Abilene stared into his eyes for a moment before he kissed her again. Her heart fluttered. "But thank you." She whispered, surprised by the moment. He released her and went to the cabinet to get the cards. Abilene paused for a moment and watched him walk away. She couldn't believe that after seven years, he could catch her off guard with those morsels of affection out of the blue. The doorbell rang. Abilene heard Benny open it and yell, "Hey man! Come on in guys. Abi, it's the Thompsons."

"Oh hey, Marcy!" Abilene yelled out as she arranged the snacks on the kitchen island. "Come on in and mix a drink." The Thompsons moved in across the street right after the new year. They were the same age and loved cards, too. Marcy came in and poured a glass of wine from a bottle she brought with her. She threw some pieces of cheese and crackers on a small paper plate and sat on a stool across from Abilene.

"So, who else is coming tonight?" Marcy asked as she chewed.

"My hairdresser and her husband. Army couple. She works at a salon off post. They live here on post. No kids. Our age. Her husband just got home a few weeks ago, I think. Her name is Vanessa, and he's Mac. Haven't met him, but she's cool." Abilene put some cheese on a plate for herself. "A bit of a handful when she drinks, but fun. Nothing is boring if Vanessa is around." Abilene said as she took another sip of bourbon. The doorbell rang again. "Must be them," she said as she put her glass down. The timer for the oven went off.

"Got it!" Benny yelled out from the living room. She heard the door open, voices, introductions, and Benny telling them Abilene was in the kitchen, to wander in and get a drink. Abilene heard Vanessa's distinctive southern drawl. Abilene slid on over mitts and turned to grab dip from the oven. She spun around to see Vanessa entering the kitchen. She shot her a smile and placed the dip down.

"Abi, this is my husband, Mac." Vanessa said as he peeked out from behind Vanessa with Benny coming right behind him. Abilene froze. Her throat closed, and she felt her heart would burst through her chest.

"Ponyboy?" escaped Abilene's lips. She struggled to make sense of it as she gasped for air. She felt as if the wind was knocked out of her. Everything was spinning. How could Julien be standing in her kitchen after all these years? Julien's jaw dropped, then a wide smile took over his entire face. His eyes squinted as that familiar, toothy grin appeared. *There you are,* flashed through her mind. That alone caught her off guard.

"Abilene?" He said in a whisper. "Is that really you?" Abilene shook her head as if she was hallucinating. Then a smile and laugh bubbled up out of nowhere as she ran past Vanessa and jumped into Julien's arms. He lifted her off the ground and squeezed her. Her oven mitts grasped his shoulders as he lowered her. He was taller than she remembered. They stared into each other's eyes, searching for an explanation, both trying to make sense of how they ended up in front of each other all these years later, just as he told her they would someday. Silence fell over everyone else. The room, time, life stood still for what seemed forever.

"I don't understand?" Abilene finally said. She scanned every inch of his face and let the mitts fall to the floor. She ran her hands across his shaved head. He tussled her short hair in return. "You... you enlisted? Vanessa is your—"

"Wife, yeah. I'm sorry, Abi, but how do you know my husband?" Vanessa crossed her arms and jutted out her hip. "What is this Ponyboy shit?" Abilene swallowed a lump in her throat as Julien shoved his hands in his pocket and took a step back from Abilene.

"We were best friends in Holden, South Carolina. That is until Abilene's mom passed away and we... she left to find her dad." Julien said almost in slow motion, as if he needed to be sure Vanessa understood. Abilene could instantly tell Julien must take this gentle tone to diffuse Vanessa frequently. It was obvious he was choosing his words carefully. Benny stepped forward next to Julien and cleared his throat.

"I'm sorry. I'm not following. Vanessa is your hairdresser," Benny said as he pointed to Vanessa, "but her husband is some high school friend from South Carolina?" Benny said as he drew his hands to his hips and looked at Abilene.

"I didn't know her husband was Julien. I haven't seen Julien since— God. Julien? I can't believe you're here. You're right here just like you said you would be someday." Abilene shook her head again. "Vanessa always called you Mac."

"I'm Julien McCulley. Everyone calls me Mac. Well, everyone in the Army. Abilene knows me as Julien." Julien said to the room while looking into Abilene's eyes again. "Vanessa called you Abi. It never occurred to—"

"Apparently you go by Ponyboy, too?" Vanessa said as she glared at Julien.

"Yeah, just a nickname Abilene gave me back when, never mind. That was long ago." Julien hastily looked around the room as everyone stared at him and Abilene. "I guess you married a soldier?"

"Yeah, we have a daughter, too. Bitty. She's seven." Abilene said, without taking her eyes off Julien. She had so much to tell him. "I'm so sorry I didn't keep calling. That last time we talked, and I hung up because of Charlene. The things I said. I was such a brat. That was so stupid. I... I called after we graduated and your dad—"

"My dad's an ass. Well, you already know that. I should've kept calling you. I always regretted not calling back. I was just so pissed you were having an easier time of it. I was stupid. My God, I always wondered what happened to you." He released a long breath and looked around at everyone. "This is crazy."

"Crazy is one word for it. Small world, I guess," Marcy said as she scooped dip onto her plate. She hadn't missed a beat of eating while the rest of the room stood blanketed with confusion.

Abilene and Julien got lost in each other's eyes. Abilene didn't feel invisible for once. She couldn't explain it to herself, much less to anyone else, but she suddenly took a deep breath and felt a sense of relief that Julien was right in front of her. It was like a missing piece of her life, her past, her essence just came crashing back into her life. Even without his blonde locks and illumination of the streetlight, he seemed to glow in front of her and a sense of home, a sense of family, came over her. She teared up. Julien reached out and rubbed her arm.

"I'm sorry. This is just so—"

"Yeah, it is." Julien said. Benny stepped forward and stood next to his wife.

"Well, you long lost besties can catch up while we play. Everyone, grab your drink and some snacks and let's get started." Benny commanded. He put his hand on Abilene's lower back as he ushered everyone around the dining room table. Abilene and Julien sat across from each other. Vanessa rattled off question after question from when they last talked, when they met, why they didn't stay in touch, did they ever visit each other after Holden? When she got answers, she rattled off more—did their parents know each other, did Julien's sisters know Abilene, did she like his parents, when exactly did Abilene's mom die, how did he drive her all that way in the middle of the night? Then, the question that was buried underneath it all, the question Benny perked up and stared directly at Abilene as Vanessa asked, the question all other questions were leading up to, "Were you guys in love?" Vanessa's eyebrow spiked up and her lips furled after the questions hit the air.

"No," Abilene said quickly. "He was my best friend." She exhaled deeply and looked at Julien. He tilted his head and smiled at her. "The best friend I ever had when I needed a friend the most." She felt herself tear up again. Abilene swallowed and shuffled the cards.

"Exactly. We were there for each other when shit hit the fan for both of us." Julien said as he ran his hand over his head like he used to do with long hair. "I don't think I could've survived that place if it weren't for Abilene. But as you all can see, we both got out of there. So, it's all good." Vanessa reached over and took his hand.

"Well, I, for one, am glad you left there. I just can't believe all this time I've known Abi, and she knew you first. What a crazy world, huh, Abilene?" Vanessa said as she rearranged her cards and shot a glance at Abilene.

"Yeah, crazy alright. But like Julien said, we helped each other through some shit. If I didn't have Pony—Julien when my mom died, I'm not sure I would've survived it." Abilene said. She swallowed a lump in her throat as their eyes met again. She saw the same 16-year-old she left as she walked to the guard gate in the rain so many nights ago. Years of unanswered questions and worries were laid to rest. He was safe, he was whole, he was out of Holden, and he was right across from her again. Abilene didn't realize just how much she worried about him until she finally realized she didn't have to anymore.

As the night went on, cards were dealt, and drinks got mixed. Abilene and Julien shared stories of that summer. They both broke into laughter talking about seeing Wayne's World together, stealing peach schnapps, and the walks to Mazzy's for hot chicken.

"Man, I thought that hot chicken was the shit until I got stationed in Louisiana." Julien said as he coughed as he swigged too much beer and laughed.

"Right? Remember that night your dad realized you stole his smokes, and he tried to chase us down the street, but he was drunk as hell and barely made it to the corner?" Abilene said as she snorted and laughed.

"He was always drunk as hell," Julien said.

"Still is, at least every time I've met him." Vanessa said. The room grew quiet.

"How's your mom?" Abilene asked.

"No different, I'm sure. I don't go back there. They visit me here and there. Been about two years now, I think? She's still, well, not stable, I guess I should say." Julien said, looking off into the distance.

"Crazy. And your dad makes her that way," Vanessa said.

"Enough." Julien said firmly.

"Alright, enough about childhood and family shit. What's your MOS, Mac?" Benny asked. Abilene was grateful for the change in topic, but felt the urge to hug Julien after his mom was brought up. She saw the same wounds in his eyes she saw when Charlene and her friends made fun of his mom. She looked at Vanessa and for a moment, it seemed Vanessa relished in throwing Julien's parents' struggles in his face for the entire room to see. When he shut her down, she seemed almost satisfied. A smirk on her face made Abilene's stomach drop. The wildness, the provocative instigator that she saw Vanessa morph into at the bars was who she was to Julien too. Abilene could see Julien's mom in Vanessa, the look she'd get when she pushed his dad too far. Abilene thought back to all the times she'd been with Vanessa for girls' nights. The excess of shots, dances, pitting random men against each other, starting fights between couples who got drawn into her web, pushing everything as far as she could go, sometimes to the point where they got kicked out of places or narrowly avoided it. That Vanessa went home all those nights to Julien, where she probably kept up the game, the dance of getting someone incensed enough to yell back, push back, or lose their temper. She wondered why Julien would marry someone so much like his mom. She then entertained the thought that maybe he didn't see it.

As everyone left, Abilene reached out to hug Julien, as everyone else awkwardly stood in the hallway to leave. He squeezed her and drew in a deep breath. She felt the air compress out of her lungs. She felt butterflies, happiness, and a sense of safety she couldn't remember feeling in forever.

"God, I'm so glad we found each other again," he said in almost a whisper.

"Me too." Abilene said as he released her. "We, all four of us, need to get dinner sometime soon. I can't lose track of you again. We have so much to catch up on."

"Yeah, let's do that sometime." Benny said as he opened the door and motioned toward the street. "But for now, we gotta get to bed. Our kid will be up bright and early and I, for one, am beat."

"Yep, we gotta get going. I think we've had enough going down memory lane for tonight. Come on, Mac." Vanessa looped her arm through his. She led him out the door and into the night. He glanced back at Abilene and waved when they got to the streetlight next to their car. For a moment, she felt the same as she did at 16—protected and like nothing in her world could go wrong because Julien was standing there watching over her, making sure she got inside okay. Abilene smiled and held his gaze until Benny closed the door and locked it.

"Well, that was weird, huh?" He quipped as he took his glass from the table to the sink.

"Yeah," Abilene muttered as she gathered up the rest of the glasses. Weird wasn't the word that came to mind for her. It was a miracle. A much-needed miracle that she never expected to walk through her door and back into her life.

That night, Benny pulled Abilene on top of him and made love to her with a passion she hadn't felt from him since they used to sneak moments touching, kissing, and grabbing at each other behind the bowling alley and movie theater. He drew her down close and kissed her frantically. Benny pulled her so tight against him as he came, she thought he'd never let go. He was loud and animalistic from start to finish. She rolled over and reached for her tank top and underwear strewn on the floor. Abilene was exhausted and sweaty. She felt weak in her knees and lightheaded as she reached down. He ran his hand up her spine. She got chills.

"You know I love you, right?" Benny said in the dark. She looked straight ahead as she pulled the tank top over her head.

"I know you do." She whispered as she turned around. Abilene leaned down and kissed him.

"I mean it. What we have, this family. You, me, Bitty. It's everything to me." He said as he stared up at the ceiling. Abilene stood to go to the bathroom. She had wanted to hear those words so many times, after so many nights making love, then silence as he usually kissed her forehead and rolled over, after fights where she felt they had nothing in common other than sex. Now, those words just rolled from his tongue with a sweetness she wasn't sure she ever heard from him. She turned to him.

"I know. It means everything to me, too." She said, then walked away. Tears welled up in her eyes at the undeniable realization that he was only saying any of it because of meeting Julien. That's the only thing that was different from any other night. She closed the bathroom door and looked in the mirror. Her short hair was scrambled. Her life felt scrambled.

One bright light was seared into her head and heart. She smiled, thinking Julien was near again. She always wondered how'd she feel if she ran into him again or even just heard from him. Abilene washed her face and let the cool water sting as she splashed and rubbed away her face scrub. As she washed and dried her face, she couldn't stop smiling. She wanted to run down the street and find his and Vanessa's door and ask Julien to walk with her, listen to her tell him all about Bitty, Sandy and Tom, her sisters, Alyssa, Monique, Roxanne, New York, snow! She wanted to rattle off every detail of having Bitty, being a mom, her panic attacks. He would've been such a help during those. Abilene wanted to loop her arm through his and listen to why he enlisted, what happened to Charlene, how he ended up with Vanessa, what music did he listen to now, where was he when Kurt died? She wanted to walk alone in the night and go for chicken, sip from a bottle of something better than peach schnapps under the stars shining down on a Kentucky summer night. She wanted to be near him again, hear his laugh, let him make her laugh. Abilene blew out a deep breath and looked at herself again. Her smile faded because she knew she couldn't do those things. She wasn't a 16-year-old who could pull on a t-shirt and climb out of the window to meet her best friend. She was a 24-year-old wife and mom—her husband a few feet away, surely snoring already, and a daughter in bed who will want breakfast in the morning. Julien wasn't a 16-year-old grunge-loving kid escaping into the night to get away from home anymore, either. They were different in ways neither of them even realized. Abilene knew that. But, knowing he was near, her best friend, her protector, her guardian, the person she missed the most in all the world, was enough for tonight. She had hugged him, laughed with him, felt his breath in her ear when he said he was so happy to see her again. She knew he was safe, and he knew she was, too. That was the greatest sense of relief and wholeness since that night he drove away from the gates at Fort Patten years ago.

Abilene crawled back into bed and looked up at the ceiling. Benny's bourbon-fueled snore filled the dark room. "Goodnight, Ponyboy." She whispered into the air.

# CHAPTER 24

*July 2001*

In the weeks that followed, Abilene called Vanessa to set up a night for a dinner for the four of them. Vanessa avoided picking a time or day. Julien was going to the field, then Benny would follow for two weeks once Julien was back. Plus, Vanessa declared being swamped at the salon because it was wedding season. Each time, Abilene would hang up and feel deflated as she looked at the floor. She called on a Friday when Benny would have a free weekend before leaving the following Monday. Julien answered. Abilene's heart leapt into her throat.

"Hey! I've been calling Vanessa trying to pin you guys down for dinner. There's so much we gotta catch up on!" She said in a flurry.

"Yeah, she told me. Listen, Abilene, she's not too keen on us hanging out." He said. "You've known her for a while. She's kinda the jealous type. She thinks there's more to me and you than we said that night."

"Oh," Silence flowed through the line for what seemed an eternity.

"But you're right. We need to catch up." He paused. "I've missed you."

"I've missed you, too." Abilene's eyes searched from the ceiling to the floor for what to say next. "I got it. Let me talk to her. I'll convince her we were just friends, and we can all four be great friends if she just let us get together." Julien huffed into the phone.

"You know if she has something in her head, there's no changing it."

"Then what? What do we do? Never see each other again?" Abilene's vision grew blurry as tears welled up. "Julien. I lost you once. You were... you were my best friend. I can't just forget you're right here at Fort Grant, too. So much has—"

"I know. So much has happened to me, too." There was a long pause as they listened to each other breathe. "Listen. She's working all day on Monday. I can meet up during my lunch if you're free?"

"Yes, Benny will be gone for two weeks, and I can leave Bitty with a neighbor. Where?"

"That Chinese place off post? No, wait. Too many guys from my unit go there. Someone will make a big deal out of it and Vanessa will find out. Then shit will really hit the fan." He said. "What about... what about the chicken place in Middleton? About a half hour south."

"Will you have enough time?" Abilene said.

"I'll take care of it. It'll be fine. No one goes there. It's right off Route 30. Middle of nowhere Middleton." He said with a smirk. "Noon Monday, okay?"

"Okay," Abilene said. "Julien? Are we doing something wrong here? Making plans for lunch and not telling either of them?"

"No. We're just old friends catching up, right?"

"Right."

"See you then, bye Abilene." Julien said.

Abilene's exhilaration quickly morphed into nervousness. What if Benny's date to leave changed? What if Vanessa found out? If what they were doing wasn't wrong, then why meet in secret two towns away? Her hands shook and her mind flooded with questions for Julien and things she wanted to tell him. By the time she dropped Benny off with his duffle bag in front of his unit at the parade field Monday morning, her stomach was in knots, and she couldn't drive fast enough to Middleton.

Abilene pulled into the tiny chicken stand in the middle of nowhere. A giant "Moe's Chicken" metal sign spun around on a long rusty pole. When she rolled down the window, she could hear the sign squeak. It was only 11:45, and the place was desolate. It was a Monday, after all, she told herself. Marcy agreed to watch Bitty for the afternoon after Abilene told her she had a dentist appointment. She needed to remember to act in pain when she picked her up. Abilene looked at her watch then glimpsed at her hair in the side-view mirror and realized the shag was growing out again. It was looking more poofy rather than punk the last few weeks. She exhaled, thinking she needed to call Vanessa for an appointment but didn't want it to feel awkward now that she knew Vanessa didn't want Abilene around her husband. Yet here she was waiting in a dirt parking lot on a Monday to meet up with that husband. Just as she felt guilt and a little scared of what she was getting herself into, Julien pulled in. He drove a black Mustang like he always talked about buying. He got out in his uniform and slid his hat on. Abilene hopped out and ran to his arms before she thought not to. He scooped her up and spun her around.

"Wow, you look so different in uniform and you're taller! I just can't get over that you really enlisted." She said as she stepped back from him and held her hand up to block the sun that was shining from behind him.

"Yep, only way out of Holden. And I look different? What about you with this short choppy do? You look, what's the word? Edgy. Not like some wild hippie girl who never had a haircut," He said with a laugh. She tapped his arm.

"What? I loved my wild, long hair. Just figured I'd try something new. Your wife did it." Abilene instantly regretted bringing up Vanessa and wasn't sure why.

"Come on, let's get food and sit and talk."

An hour later, they had both finished lunch, shared fries, and filled each other in on how they got to Fort Grant. Abilene couldn't believe Julien used the mechanic skills from his uncle's shop to fix tanks now. He couldn't believe she got pregnant her senior year and didn't call him right away. She told him he was her first thought when she found out, how scared she had been she would die during childbirth, and how she still had panic attacks on Bitty's birthday. She told Julien how Benny took care of them, took care of her. He told her about meeting Vanessa in a bar and how it's been a messy, wild ride ever since. She kept life exciting.

"Exciting is good, but it sounds a lot like your mom and your dad." Abilene looked down after she spoke. "I'm sorry. I shouldn't have—"

"No, it's okay. You aren't telling me anything I don't already know. She is, like my mom, I mean. But I'm not my dad. That's the difference. Yeah, she loses it, goes ballistic over little things, but I ain't never raised a hand to her. Never will, not any woman."

"Oh, I know. I didn't mean that. I know you wouldn't. I just mean... isn't it... isn't it exhausting? Exciting is fun for a while. But forever?" Abilene said.

Julien stared off past her. "Yeah. It is. But what can I do? It is what it is." He sipped his soda and looked at her, and tilted his head. "And what about you? You say Benny is a good man, takes care of you, but are you happy?"

"Oh, yeah. I fell hard for Benny when I was chasing him all over Fort Patten my senior year. I'm happy even though it was kinda a whirlwind how we ended up. I love him. But whether or not he loved me when I got pregnant and we got married, that's the question. But like Sandy says, sometimes that just isn't the most important thing."

"Love isn't important? That's a shitty outlook."

"No, I mean, love isn't everything. I'd rather live with him not being madly in love with me than end up like my mom, chasing different men until I find the all-elusive one who loves me back. Bitty and I got it good with Benny. I focus on that."

"Well, I guess we both made choices. Compromised, I guess, as they say."

"You'll be happy to know, however, that I never had a friend like you again, though. You were irreplaceable. I didn't even try to compromise on finding a best friend like you again. Even though some girlfriends came close." Abilene said as she took the last sip through her straw.

"Same here, Abilene. That was the best summer I ever had... until I dropped you off. You're right, we were best friends when we needed each other most."

"What now, though? I can't imagine not being friends again. Not talking or seeing each other when we live on the same post."

"We'll find a way. I promise. We will." Julien said. "I'll tell Vanessa we just gotta hang out with you guys and she needs to get over it. I'm sure she'll handle it rationally." He laughed. Abilene laughed too.

"I actually need to get an appointment with her. I'll do my part to put her at ease, too."

Julien looked at his watch and jumped up. He was over an hour late.

"Shit! I gotta get back!" he scrambled for his keys and gathered up his garbage. Abilene jumped up to help. He dashed to his car before turning around. Julien ran back to Abilene as she threw out her soda. He grabbed her by the shoulders and drew her in for a quick hug.

"God, I've missed you. I'll see you soon." He said. Abilene smiled into his chest. He still smelled the same.

"I've missed you, too." She said as he turned to rush away again. He hopped in his car, waved, and disappeared down the road before she could breathe.

Just as he had promised, he got Vanessa to agree to go out to dinner and drinks with Abilene and Benny in a few weeks later. Vanessa called to ask her a time and place.

They all met at the NCO club for appetizers and drinks. Vanessa agreed, since it was close enough that she and Julien could walk home at night if they needed to. By the time Abilene and Benny got from the car to the entrance, they were both drenched. It was steamier than normal for an August in Kentucky night. Even though the temperatures and humidity were unbearable, Abilene loved the birds singing from the woods next to the club. The NCO club was nestled behind a patch of woods that made it easy to miss altogether if you didn't see the sign telling you where to turn. The patch of woods and interconnecting trails that ran throughout the post always reminded her of the trails that connected the neighborhoods to the river in Holden. Vanessa and Julien were already waiting at a table on the back patio. Abilene could tell Benny was already annoyed that they would be sitting outside. He wasn't a born and bred southerner like the rest of them. Denver could get hot, but nothing like Kentucky, Texas, Georgia, South Carolina, and Louisiana where Julien, Vanessa, and Abilene had lived. Julien stood when they walked his way. He shook Benny's hand when they made it to the table.

"Hey man, how was the field?"

"Hot and sweaty. Bullshit as always." Benny said. Julien laughed.

Vanessa smiled and reached over for Julien's arm.

"Your hair looks fabulous, Abilene." She said with a wink and smile.

"Of course it does. Thanks to you, as always." Abilene said as she picked up the menu.

"So, when are we gonna have another girl's night? It's been, what? Months now since Roxanne moved." Vanessa said. She took a long drink of her already half-gone beer.

"I know, right? We need to do it again. I miss Roxanne. I talked to her the other day, by the way."

Vanessa smiled as Abilene relayed details of Roxanne's move and how much she's loving Germany. They exchanged more small talk, then Vanessa turned the topic to Abilene's siblings and the stories Julien told her about their childhood.

"Yep, we were all named for cities even if my mom had never been there, it seems."

"What do you mean by that?" Benny asked. "You said the cities were where you were all conceived."

"Well, yeah, that's what she told me, but when she died, it seems some of the stuff didn't ring true. She had never been to Paris. We... I kinda fought with her about it right before she died." Abilene said.

"Fought with her before she died? That's crazy." Vanessa said as she swigged her beer. Julien shot Abilene a knowing glance. She realized he kept his promise to never tell anyone what unfolded as her mom died.

"You never thought to share those details with me?" Benny said.

"No. I tried to forget some of it. I try to remember the good. Remember, you told me to focus on the good and maybe that would help my panic attacks?" Abilene snapped.

"I think a new topic is in order." Julien said. "Does anyone want me to rehash the details of my shitty childhood, too? I sure got plenty I might not have shared." Abilene smiled at him, relieved he was taking the weight of the conversation off her shoulders. Vanessa rolled her eyes.

They ate and drank into the night. Benny shared endless stories of raising Bitty and almost had Vanessa convinced now is the time to have a kid. Julien talked about music and movies they had seen recently. Abilene found it comforting his taste hadn't seemed to change much. Abilene talked about school and how after each semester she was even more unsure of what she wanted to do because it was all interesting, much more than high school. She added that most of her senior year of high school was spent chasing Benny and sneaking off with him any chance she could find. Benny smirked and laughed when she shared some of the places they'd meet and hide from the prying eyes of Fort Patten.

"Girl, I didn't know you were so bad?" Vanessa said. Vanessa waved to the waitress to bring her another beer.

"I didn't mean to be. I just couldn't stay away from this guy," Abilene said as she nudged Benny's arm. He winked at her. She glanced around and for a second felt lucky. Lucky to have him with her and lucky to have Julien back in her life. What more could a girl want?

As the night went on, Vanessa got louder and louder. She threw a few snarky remarks aimed at Abilene and Julien. Benny kept giving Abilene looks to reaffirm what he always said about Vanessa causing trouble. Abilene could see Julien search for ways to get her to slow down, quiet down, control herself. Abilene felt bad for him, but she also felt bad for Vanessa. Watching her escalate and her voice rise in decibels reminded Abilene of the few times she had seen Julien try to get his mother to calm down, quiet down, or watch Noah try to rein her in. Benny asked for the check.

"We gotta get Bitty from the neighbors. Carry her back to the house. It's way later than we told Marcy we'd be." He said as he fished for his wallet in his pants pocket. Abilene took the last swig of her beer, many behind Vanessa, and grabbed the last fry from her plate.

"Yeah, we gotta head out too." Julien said as he got his wallet as well.

"Speak for yourself. We can stay and have another." Vanessa said. She dotted her mouth with her napkin. "The night is young."

"But it's not really. It's almost midnight, babe." He said as he pulled out a few twenties.

"Oh, come on. Aren't there more stories of you guys sneaking out and being you two against the world of Holden, South Carolina? More laughs to share while Benny and I look on like dumbasses wondering what the hell is so funny?"

"That's enough." Julien said. "I'm sorry." He directed at Benny and Abilene. Abilene mouthed, "It's okay."

"Don't apologize for me." Vanessa said as she stood. She grabbed the edge of the table to keep her balance and tried to jerk her arm away from Julien. Abilene wanted to reach for her arm, but thought better of it. Julien led Vanessa outside into the still humid summer night. Benny and Abilene followed.

"We'll do this again soon, alright, man?" Benny shouted to Julien as he tried to steady Vanessa. "You guys want a ride instead of walking?"

"Yeah, that might be easier." Julien led Vanessa to Benny's car and slid her into the backseat. Besides giving directions to their street and door, silence filled the car. Abilene could almost taste Vanessa's discontent. As they got out, Julien turned back and mouthed "Sorry". Abilene watched them disappear into their house and knew exactly how the scene would play out. She could picture every movement, every venomous word of Vanessa's rant, cries, and dissolving into self-loathing and misplaced anger. There was a pit in her stomach, knowing Julien was in that position.

Once home and with Bitty safely tucked in, Benny came into their bedroom as Abilene changed for bed.

"Why didn't you ever tell me the details of your mom dying? The names were a lie? Your mom just made shit up and you never knew it? You fought with her?" Benny said as she crawled into bed.

"There was no sense in telling that part. I mean, you knew she died right after giving birth. The rest was, well, embarrassing."

"And all these years you had this friend you ran to after finding all of this out and he drove you to Fort Patten in the middle of the night? That seems like kinda important. A big deal."

"I just didn't see the point in telling you." Abilene exhaled.

"Telling me which part? Your mom's lies or about Mac, or Julien, as you call him?"

"Either, Benny. I didn't see the point in telling you about either." Abilene said. She huffed loudly. "You know what? I really didn't think all of that was any of your business. There. That's the truth."

"Not my business? It's all part of your past, part of who you are. It's part of why we haven't had another kid and I've had to walk you through countless panic attacks." Benny crossed his arms. "How can you say it's none of my business?"

"Julien was an important part of my past, of that time. I never thought I'd see him again. There was no point in laying out every detail of the most painful time in my life. You don't need to know everything." She snapped.

"Oh yeah, I don't need to know everything about your past, but you sure throw my past in my face, huh?" His voice rose.

"That's different. You admitted you loved someone else when you married me. I hadn't talked to Julien in about a year when I married you. And we weren't in love. He was my best friend." She sat up on her elbows and gritted her teeth.

"Well, the way you looked at him tonight sure seemed like more than a best friend. It looked like—"

"Like what? The way you'd be looking at Sarah if we ever ran into her back home?" She hissed. "You can say all you want about me and Julien and me not telling you every single detail, but I have never seen you look at me the way you looked at her in those pictures."

"That was a different time. Jesus, we're talking about high school. You're talking about the way I look in pictures from years ago. You're talking about—"

"Love, Benny. I'm talking about looking like you love someone. That's what you looked like in those pictures. You looked at her with love." Abilene collapsed back onto the bed and stared straight up. She clenched her jaw and her heart pounded. She refused to cry.

"Well, if that's the case, I guess that was love in *your* eyes, staring at your best bud tonight."

"No... maybe. Maybe it's love between friends. He just knows me like no one else does. I sure don't know why any of it matters to you. Hell, I don't even know if I matter to you." She said.

"What we have matters. You matter. You know that. We have fun together. You're a great wife, an awesome mom, and my family loves you."

"Do you?"

"What?"

"Love me. Are you in love with me? That isn't a hard question." She said.

"I mean come on, seriously, what the hell is love anyway, Abi." He said into the dark.

"I don't know anymore, Benny. But I can't help thinking this isn't it." Abilene said slowly, wishing for sleep. She suddenly felt alone, even though she knew he was standing over her in their bedroom. She was drifting through their life together, without an anchor. Untethered. Ungrounded, desperate for someone to reach through the night air and hold on to her.

Abilene drifted off as Benny crawled in beside her. He didn't reach for her. She didn't want him to, anyway. She wondered if maybe part of him was right. As much as she lamented Benny never confiding in her, never attempting to connect with her more than on a sexual level, she distanced parts of herself from him too by choice. She hadn't told him the gory details of Ashlynn's death, the things she said, the guilt she carried. She never even told him about Swenson House or running off to find her dad in Julien's mom's minivan. Abilene kept Julien's existence and his place in her past and her heart secret, guarded from her husband for reasons she never admitted to herself. She broke her life into two parts, before her mom's death and life after finding her dad. She never bridged the two worlds. But with Julien back in her life, those worlds had collided. And what surprised Abilene the most was the feeling of relief that Julien was now part of both, and she didn't want that to change.

******

Julien walked in with a stumbling Vanessa ahead of him. She tossed her purse onto the couch and flopped down on the love seat across from it. He slid off his shoes and unbuttoned his sweaty shirt. He walked into the kitchen to get some water.

"You want water?"

"Fuck, no." She yelled. "And what the fuck was all that tonight, huh, Mac?"

Julien rolled his eyes and swigged from the glass.

"What?" He hated asking, knowing he was only opening the door to a drunken rant.

"You and Abi. You know she was my friend, and I really liked her. Then you come along and boom, you two are long-lost friends, leaving me out, of course. You got pet names and stories. You spent a whole summer together. Jesus, she called you Ponyboy." Her eyes were heavy. "Why didn't you ever mention her before?"

"Why would I? I mean really, I told you about Charlene and you still bring that up and that was nothing."

"THAT was nothing? So, what's that mean? That THIS is something? You and Ms. Texas, South Carolina, whatever?"

Julien walked into the living room with his water and one for her.

"Here. Drink some or you'll have one hell of a headache when you get up." He handed her a glass.

"You swear you guys never did it?" She said.

"God, Vanessa. Yes, I swear. I told you we were just friends. I had a pretty shitty home life at that time. You know all about that. She did too. We were all each other had. No one else in that town gave a shit about us except for us." He sipped again. "Look, you've had a lot to drink. Let's just go to bed."

"Did you love her?" She slurred as she finished the water.

"No, like I've said a hundred times."

"I saw the way you two looked at each other and laughed."

"So? We laughed. You gotta quit with this shit. She's my friend and well, we're always going to be—" Bam! He felt a thud on his cheek and the glass bounce off his lap and onto the floor. "Jesus Christ, Vanessa! Are you crazy?" Julien yelled as he put his glass down on the coffee table and stood up. He felt his cheek. "You could've broken my nose!" Vanessa stood and swayed. She reached over to the lamp on the table and threw it at him with a force that caught him off guard. As Julien ducked, the corner of the lamp collided with his forehead. He felt blood run down before it hit the floor. It was stinging. He balled his fist as he lunged at her. She flinched and stumbled backwards into the love seat. Julien stopped and looked down at her. He instantly saw his mom, cowering, crying, mascara running down her cheeks as she drunkenly accused his dad of something, egging him on yet afraid of what he'd unleash. He saw his knuckles turn white just as his dad's would when he'd draw back and hit a wall or Sheila, sending her screaming even louder. Julien took a step back. He unclenched his fist. He shook his head.

"I'm not like him and there's nothing you could do or say to make me be like him." He said.

Vanessa wiped her cheeks with the backs of her hands. She sniffled.

"Go ahead and do it, Mac. I deserve it."

"Shut up, Vanessa. I can't do this anymore." He stepped back further and looked around at their house. The lamp laying on the floor had been thrown before. The glass too. Every glass, lamp, plate, purse, book, anything within reach had been thrown at him at one point or another. "I can't live like this."

Vanessa stood and unleashed more tears.

"Mac, I'm sorry. I love you. Let's go to bed." She reached for his hands. He turned his head away. "You hear me? I love you."

"No, Vanessa. You don't."

"What? Yes, I do. You know I get passionate, temperamental. Jealous. What do you think love is, babe?" She reached for his forehead.

"I don't know for sure, but I know it's not this." Julien backed away from her again and went to the front door. Sweat mixed with blood was pouring down his forehead and cheek as his temples pounded. He grabbed his sneakers and left. The door rattled as he slammed it shut. He heard Vanessa wail for him as he laced his shoes on the front porch. He stood, and in khaki shorts and an undershirt, he ran into the night. Julien knew she'd be passed out when he got back. Before he even reached the corner, he knew it was over between them. It needed to be. He couldn't change her any more than he could have changed his parents. It exhausted him trying. Julien had vowed to never be like his father, and tonight showed him he could end up like his dad if he stayed with a woman like his mom. He left Holden to get away from them, their toxic love/hate. Yet here he was, years later, running from the same thing over and over again. *No more*, he told himself. What his parents had, what he had with Vanessa, wasn't love and he could no longer pretend it was.

# CHAPTER 25

### August 2001

Abilene spent the next few weeks trying to give Bitty all their usual summer experiences before school started. She would be going into second grade and was more excited about it every day. Abilene was grateful she could take off each summer from her own school pursuits to spend her days with Bitty at the park, the pool, lounging around in their tiny backyard, collecting bugs and trimming her flowers. The older Bitty got, the more Abilene saw herself in her. She had wild blonde waves that sprouted from her head and hung down almost to her waist. She had Abilene's easily tanned skinned, Benny's too. Bitty loved being outside as much as Abilene always had when she was little. Sometimes Abilene looked at Bitty swimming and felt pangs of motherly yearnings to give her a brother or sister. As overwhelming as it was for Abilene to take care of her siblings, she knew it would've been a terribly lonely childhood without them. Then, she'd remember Dallas having a meltdown, Austin and Jackson throwing shoes at each other, Savannah and her need to for constant attention, the piles of dishes, changing diapers for years on end, wet sheets in the middle of the night, and she'd be thankful for taking care of one child, one who could make it to the bathroom and tie her own shoes. There were several times in the last two years Abilene almost told Benny she wanted to try for another. However, the last few weeks, she thanked God she hadn't. They had barely spoken after fighting the night they had dinner with Julien and Vanessa.

After a long, sun-soaked pool day, Abilene ran a comb through Bitty's tangled locks and ran her fingers through her own. They needed to stop in the commissary for a few groceries before heading home for the day. She slid a sundress over her bathing suit and dry shorts over Bitty's. They pushed their feet into their flip-flops and walked across the parking lot to the commissary. Having the pool so close to the commissary made life much more convenient for Abilene. As they ducked in and out of parked cars, Abilene thought she heard her name. She slid off her sunglasses and looked around. Julien was standing in the middle of the road in his uniform.

"Abilene! Over here!" He yelled again. She gave him a wave to let him know she had seen him. He ran over to the sidewalk to meet her. "Hey, how are you?"

"I'm okay. We were just at the pool all day," she said as she pulled her sunglasses back down. She took Bitty's hand. "This is Bitty. Bitty, this is my school friend I told you about. The one who lives here too. Sgt. McCulley. Say 'hi'."

"Hi," Bitty said in a quiet voice, using her hand to shield her eyes from the sun behind Julien.

"I was going to call you soon. I'm sorry for how things, well, how Vanessa got that night." He said.

"There's no need to apologize. I get why she was a little, um, upset."

"Yeah, that's an understatement." He said with a smile. "How about Benny? Was he okay with us meeting up?"

"Sort of. Not really. It was weird for him, I guess you could say. We just, well, nevermind. It's a conversation for another day." She said, while glancing down at Bitty. Julien nodded.

"I wanted to let you know I got orders."

"Orders? For where?" Panic bubbled up in Abilene's throat.

"Texas. Just outside of San Antonio. Fort Crockett." He looked everywhere but in her eyes. He told her he got orders a few months ago, but they were put on hold, so he never mentioned it. But now that they were approved and official, he'd be leaving Fort Grant in a few weeks. He was just making his way from the transportation office to line up the movers. Abilene knew she'd cry if she looked him in the eye.

"What does Vanessa think? Is she happy you'll be leaving?"

"Well, that's the other thing I wanted to tell you. She and I had more than a normal fight after our night out. She kinda lost it in a way too outrageous for even her. She threw a bunch a shit, broke a lamp on my face, and, well, I guess you could say it was the last straw." He pointed to the scab above his eye. "I hightailed it out of there that night and decided we were done. She just left to go back to Louisiana a few days ago."

Abilene touched above his eye. "Good God. She did that?" He nodded and stepped back. "Was it because of me?"

"It was because of our friendship, yeah. But listen, it wasn't all that. She has been like this since the week we started dating. I knew what I was getting into. I just thought I could change her, or at the very least, control the worst in her." Julien looked up and drew in a deep breath. "Abilene, you were right. She was more like my mom than even I wanted to admit. And quite honestly, she was pushing me close to ending up like my dad. It was a long time coming and now that she's gone, I know it's for the best."

"I can't say I'm sorry she's gone from your life. And you know I get that whole 'don't want to end up like our parents' thing. The last thing I want to do is end up like my mom." She glanced down at Bitty again as Bitty kicked sand into the cracks of the sidewalk.

"I don't think you're in danger of that. Benny seems like a good guy. You guys have it good, right? He gives you the life you deserve, right?" Julien asked.

"Oh yeah, we've got it good. He is a great dad, for sure."

"And? He's everything you need, right? Everything a husband should be?"

Abilene averted her eyes and looked down at the top of Bitty's head. She fought tears and bit her lip. "Abilene? You're happy, right?"

She nodded. "Yeah. I'm happy with the life I've got. I'd never leave Benny and risk being a single mom destined to have more kids with random guys, making up some crazy myth, handing my kids so many lies none of them know what end is up." Abilene swallowed a lump in her throat and felt heat rise from her chest to her cheeks. "I am good right where I am."

"Hey, if you aren't happy, there's no shame in finding someone who would make you happy or being on your own. You wouldn't instantly turn into your mom and follow her path by leaving. You know that, right? It doesn't have to be one or the other—being with Benny or ending up exactly like your mom. There's a whole world in between the two."

"No, Julien. That's exactly what I'd be doing. She left my dad thinking there was more out there and look how that turned out. I won't do that to myself or to this little one. What I've got is enough. I made a choice. And like you said, we made compromises. We both did."

"Yeah, but I know mine was a mistake. Listen, it wasn't easy telling her it was over. She lost her mind, swore, broke more shit, I mean stuff." He looked at Bitty. "I couldn't live the rest of my life like that. I'd rather be alone."

"You have that luxury. I don't. It's not just about me." Abilene said. "Plus, where the hell would I go, anyway?" She drew in a deep breath. "Listen, I gotta go. You make sure when you get settled in Texas, you call and give me your new number so we can talk still. Okay?"

"I will." Julien said. "Think about what I said. It doesn't have to be one or the other, you know. But listen, I'll call you when I get settled."

"Promise? I just found you again. And I still need you in my life. We're best friends for life, remember?" She said with a forced smile while fighting tears.

"I mean it, Abilene. You deserve everything you ever wanted. We both do." She nodded at him and let one tear run down her cheek. "Don't cry."

"I'm fine. I'm just going to miss you, that's all. I missed you so much all those years. I can't imagine letting you go again."

"You're not. I promise we won't lose touch again. You know how much you mean to me. We promised to always watch out for each other. I'm always here if you need me." He drew her in for a hug. "You know me better than anyone and I missed you too much to let you disappear again, too." She nodded into his chest before pulling away.

"I gotta get in the store." She reached down for Bitty's hand. "Say goodbye to my friend Julien." Bitty said bye and waved. Abilene pulled Bitty behind her as she raced to the door. She could see Julien in the window. His reflection still standing there watching her. She wanted to turn around, run to his arms, and never let him go. She wanted to hop in a car with him and just drive, talk endlessly, and laugh with him. Abilene stopped at the door and watched him for a second. For one last moment, he was right where he said he'd be someday, watching over her. She burst into tears, knowing she might never see him again. Unless Benny got stationed wherever Julien was, there was no way their paths would cross. She took a deep breath and told herself she got this far without him. They'd talk on the phone even if it might annoy Benny. Being a phone call away wasn't the end of the world. Her gut seized. She closed her eyes and stepped on the mat. The door opened. She exhaled and stepped inside. The air conditioning made her tears instantly feel cold on her cheeks. *Keep moving,* Abilene thought. *Forward, not back. He's gone.*

Abilene shopped, made dinner, laughed with Bitty, cleaned her room before bed, and sat with Benny watching tv into the night. She thought about telling him she ran into Julien, and he was getting stationed away and left Vanessa. She mostly wanted to tell him in case Bitty brought up meeting him after the pool. But she kept it to herself, like she had always done with anything about Julien. It was part of her she had no desire to share. As they sat next to each other on the couch sharing a bag of chips, she kept replaying her conversation with Julien in her head. Part of her was happy Julien had found the courage to leave Vanessa and hoped he'd find someone kind and stable. But part of her was jealous he had that ability to leave her and start again. Then Abilene wondered how she got through these last few years without Julien in her life. She remembered all the times she stopped what she was doing and thought about him, where he was, how he was. Her mind tumbled back to that night almost ten years ago when they sat in Julien's minivan plotting out their lives, their hopes, and the promise that they'd find each other if they hadn't married by 30. That kiss, the awkward, silly, sloppy, peach schnapps sticky sweet kiss. Julien under the streetlight, making sure she got inside okay. Then, Julien of today with a high and tight, standing in his uniform on a sidewalk watching her as she went into the commissary. She'd give anything to know he would always be there somewhere in the background of her life, watching over her. She couldn't imagine going forward without him now.

# CHAPTER 26

*September 11, 2001*

Abilene rushed from the kitchen to the living room to help Bitty find her backpack. She crouched down and tied Bitty's shoes for her to get out the door faster.

"Come on, girly, we gotta get going." Abilene snapped. Even though she had been back in school a few weeks, Bitty and Abilene both had gotten too used to sleeping in all summer and weren't used to getting out the door so fast and early.

After she dropped her off and pulled out of the school parking lot, Abilene noticed there wasn't a cloud in the sky. It was the clearest day they'd had in weeks. The last stretch of summer had been drizzly and gray. Abilene walked into the house, clicked on the tv, and went to the kitchen to clear their breakfast mess. She plotted the day ahead—watering flowers, getting vegetables cut up for a salad for dinner, washing Bitty's blankets, maybe walk across the street and meet the family who moved in two days ago, apologize for not making it over sooner, call Marcy and see if she had gone over yet. Abilene took her coffee into the living room to watch a few minutes of news before getting a shower. She stopped dead in her tracks as her eyes caught the images on the screen.

"What the hell?" She said as she made her way to the couch and put her cup down. She watched the burning of the North Tower. A plane crash in the middle of New York City. Her heart sank thinking of the office workers and whoever was on the plane. It was a busy weekday morning. People were probably already at their desk. How could an accident like that happen in the middle of Manhattan? Just as she sipped and listened to the news anchors describe how close the buildings are and the challenge of fighting a fire so high up, the number of police responding and what floors seemed affected, debris falling to the street below, the next plane hit. At 9:03, the second plane hit the South Tower. Abilene felt like she was choking. It all defied logic and reason. In a blink, a plane accident became something else entirely right before her eyes. It had to be a coordinated attack. Terrorism in New York City. She shakily picked up the phone as it rang. It was Sandy. She and Sandy stayed on the phone watching the burning, the smoke, the strained voices of anchors trying to make sense of what happened, how, why, who? Then the Pentagon. 9:37 a.m. As the news scrolled at the bottom confirming it had been hit, Abilene felt she'd throw up right in her living room. Her fear reached an entirely different level. At that moment, she and Sandy both knew what they didn't need to say out loud. An act of terrorism was now an act of war. We were at war even if we didn't know with who or why yet. Sandy sobbed as Abilene felt an unsettling numbness. There was a beep of her call waiting.

"That's Benny. I'll call you back." She said.

"Hey, honey. Yeah, I'm watching. What the hell is happening?" she asked as tears burst from her eyes. "Okay. I'll go grab her. Oh, they're beeping in right now." The school wanted all children picked up as soon as possible. Military bases across the country were instantly on high alert, immediate lock down, the highest alert Abilene had ever seen. Everything was closing. They ordered everyone living on post to stay indoors, lock the doors, and not even think about leaving the post. Abilene couldn't stop shaking as she drove the two miles to the school. She threw it in park and ran to the front of the school where the principal and others stood with clipboards confirming who was grabbing who. Other parents signed out neighbor kids whose parents worked off post and had no way of getting there any time soon. Everyone looked ghostly, horrified, scared. Everyone was scrambling to secure their child, process what was happening, and trying not to scare the little ones. Some were crying, anger emblazoned the faces of some, and sheer shock had overtaken others. Every parent was asking other passing parents if anything else had been hit yet. Everyone was thinking the same thing, fearing the same thing. Abilene glanced around at the moms she saw every day, some from her street, and realized not a single one of them had ever been through anything like this before. Pearl Harbor was the last time there was a direct attack on U. S. soil. She wondered if school had been in session that day, if parents raced to grab their kids and lock their doors. She realized she never paid attention to what day of the week it was when Pearl Harbor was bombed. Abilene paused long enough after signing her name and taking Bitty's hand to realize she'd never forget September 11th was a Tuesday. A beautiful sunny Tuesday.

She called Marcy, Roxanne in Germany, and called Sandy back. It made her feel less alone and powerless to hear others' voices. Benny was on lockdown and wouldn't be back home for a while. He was safe, though. She didn't even eat lunch, unable to peel herself away from the news as Bitty played with Playdough on the dining room table. The clouds of dust rumbling, growing, engulfing city blocks and people covered in ash running, stumbling, hiding, all overwhelmed her senses. Her faith in humanity was shaken as the towers collapsed. It looked like a disaster movie or something that would happen in another part of the world—*not here;* she kept saying to herself. Her stomach was in knots, fearing for every military family she knew, as rumors and insinuations of sleep cells near bases fueled more fear in her heart. What if they started bombing Army posts? What if they rammed more planes into military housing areas? They hit the Pentagon, so to Abilene, nothing was outside the realm of possibility. A plane had nosedived in a field in Pennsylvania and there was nonstop speculation about what its intended target was. Names of passengers on all four planes scrolled across the bottom of the screen. They were all mothers, fathers, sisters, brothers, lovers, sons, daughters, children, grandparents, all loved by someone watching those names across their screens. The military was surely a target, which meant no one she loved was safe. She thought of Julien. He hadn't moved yet. She hung up with Sandy and dialed his house number. It rang and rang. The machine came on.

"Hey. I know you're probably at work. I just wanted to make sure you were okay. I mean, I know you're okay and still here, not in New York or the

Pentagon or anything. I just, I don't know. I guess I needed to just hear your voice. Be safe out there." The machine clicked off. She wasn't even what she had said when she hung up.

Benny made it home a few hours later and became entranced by the footage. Abilene heated leftovers from the weekend and made plates for them to eat in front of the tv while Bitty sat between them. She was begging for cartoons. Abilene felt bad having the news on all day, but this wasn't an ordinary day. When the president came on and delivered an address to the nation, Abilene cried. Benny sat straight and focused on every word. They were both in utter shock and disbelief over what had unfolded. He assured his parents and sister and brother-in-law they were safe at Fort Grant, safer than most communities. Even on lockdown, they'd both rather be on post than off. For the first time in her life, the thought of the civilian world terrified her. She put Bitty to bed and told her there'd be no school the next day because of what the bad men did in the city, but they were safe. The MPs just wanted to be extra safe by asking everyone to stay home. Abilene couldn't even go outside and water her flowers before the sun set. The only signs of life they had seen since she came home with Bitty and Benny came home were Military Police vehicles and four wheelers with additional MPs with automatic weapons draped across their backs. It was such an odd mix of comforting and unsettling.

Benny convinced Abilene to turn off the tv and head to bed. As they lay there, Abilene felt nauseous, replaying the images from the day. Benny looked straight up at the ceiling with a tight jaw and anger.

"You know this means we're at war, right?"

"Yeah. What's that mean for us?" Abilene asked, not really wanting an answer. It was too late at night to process what this meant for her tiny family.

"No idea yet. We'll worry about it when I know something. Okay?"

"Okay."

He said good night and rolled over on his side. She knew his mind was probably racing, just as hers was. Abilene looked at the blank wall. She swallowed a lump when she realized she had been thinking of what this meant for Julien and not Benny, not once until they went to bed. Julien was a tank mechanic, like his uncle was in Vietnam. Her heart pounded at the thought of Julien going off to war, being deployed to God knows where in the middle east. She closed her eyes and vowed to call him again as soon as Benny went to work. Losing Julien to Texas was bad enough. Losing him to whatever was coming next for the country was another matter altogether. She needed to see him and just know he was okay.

The next morning, Benny left for work and Abilene was glued to the news again, waiting to hear if there were any overnight developments. While Bitty ate, she went to the front porch and then out to the street to talk with all the other shaken Army wives. They exchanged scenarios, rumors, fears, conspiracies, tears, and impossible promises that all would be fine for their families, the United States, the world.

As she cleaned up breakfast, she cradled the phone and tried Julien's number again. There was still no answer. The machine beeped.

"Hey, it's just me again. I just want to make sure you're okay and see when you head to Texas, if you still are after yesterday. Bye." She hung up quickly. She couldn't shake wondering where he was, how he was, how he was processing what happened yesterday, and what it meant for him. He weighed on her mind all day as she paced and watched the news. Sleeper cells. New threats. The heroism of flight 93. People wandering Manhattan with printed pictures of loved ones. Lines of people waiting to give blood. Crews digging by hand through rubble. Stranded Americans in airports all over the world. Messages of support from leaders everywhere. Vows to root out evil. And more fear. The world was upended. The safety and stability of being on a military post suddenly seemed fragile, like a fortress that was only protected by a gauzy curtain.

After three days of high alert and nervousness, some places on post opened back up. Abilene took Bitty to school, tried to get back into her normal routine, but she was still within earshot of the news throughout the day. Each time the phone rang, she jumped, hoping it was Julien to tell her he was fine. Benny found out he would stay stateside for the time-being but would work more hours being in cyber security. As Abilene tried to peel herself away from the news to shower, the phone rang again. It was a Colorado number, but not one she recognized.

"Hello?" she asked as she turned the news down and tossed the remote on their blue couch. There was a long pause, then click. Abilene held the phone out and studied the number on the caller ID. It didn't belong to anyone in Benny's family. She dialed the number. It rang three times.

"Hey, you've reached Sarah Hilton. Leave a message and I'll get back to ya!" the machine said, followed by a beep that felt like a knife to Abilene's heart. Sarah had their number. Benny insisted on not having their number or address listed in anything because of his cyber security work. No one had their home phone number unless they gave it to them. Abilene slowly placed the phone on the receiver. She picked it back up and dialed the number again. The machine picked up. Her heart raced, and she thought of a thousand things to scream into the machine and a thousand questions to ask. But she simply sighed and hung up again. She could picture Sarah standing there watching the phone ring and the machine pick up twice. Sarah's cheerful greeting played in her head over again. Sarah wasn't just a picture anymore. She was a voice. She wasn't a distant memory. She was on the other line minutes ago.

Abilene showered and cried for everyone who had been lost, the world that had changed instantly, the lost chances and loves of that day, and for her marriage. She knew in her gut Benny must still talk to Sarah. As the soapy water ran down her body, she realized Sarah was probably desperate to make sure Benny was okay, just as she was desperate to find out if Julien was. Abilene thought about the years with Benny from the ice cream stand, the stolen moments, that first night when he said 'if' instead of 'when'. The confusion and whirlwind of him proposing and wanting to be a family. She thought that was all that mattered, all that would ever matter. They'd be connected forever. But that connection never came. The connection she was always desperate for after losing her mother, she had talked herself into believing she could do without it. Stability was enough. The physical passion in the dark was enough. A good man was enough. A man who wasn't madly in love with her was better than the search for more, a search that could take her down a path she was desperate to avoid—her mother's. It had been enough for years, in some strange way, until Julien walked back into her life and Sarah's voice crashed into her home. Now, she couldn't deny what was right in front of her face as the water started to run cold. She had been clinging to a man who loved another then and now, and as Sarah's voice echoed in her head, Abilene knew Sarah was still clinging to him too.

As the days wore on and more uncertainty filled the air in their house and lives, Abilene felt like the walls and her world were closing in. She hadn't left the post in over a week. She had non-stop phone calls with Sandy and Army wives who lived away, and more conversations with her neighborhood spouses who were just as rattled and off-kilter in this new world. But Abilene told no one about Sarah calling even though the voice on the machine replayed in her head constantly. One night after Benny came home and Abilene cleaned up dinner, she saw him jump when the phone rang. It was his mom. Abilene wished it had been Sarah just to get it out in the open. She wanted to tell him she knew just so they all could stop pretending. Abilene wasn't filled with rage or jealousy like when she found the box of letters. She was almost envious of them. They had something she had chosen to deny herself—real love. He hung up with his mom and stared at the tv. As Abilene sat next to him, trying to get into a movie instead of the news, her hands shook, her heart flip-flopped, and mind raced. Abilene knew there was no stopping the unraveling that had already started days before.

"I gotta get out of this house."

"Okay, maybe this weekend we can leave post and go out for dinner or something." Benny said as he flipped through the channels to find another movie.

"No, right now." She sat up straight and wrung her hands together. "I think I gotta go for a walk."

"It's dark out. Can't you just go burn off some energy after Bitty goes to school tomorrow?" He still stared ahead.

"No."

"Abilene, nothing's open." He shrugged his shoulders. "What are you gonna do? Just wander around housing in the dark?"

"Yeah. I think I am. I'll take the pepper spray with me. I'll be fine. I just need to get out." She stood up. He looked at her confused. She paced. She was afraid she'd burst open. Her heart raced more. A thousand thoughts bounced around her mind, a thousand regrets.

"My heart, Benny. I, just I—"

"Hold on," he said as he stood and took her hands. "Just calm down. You're fine." She drew her hands back.

"No, I'm not. Nothing is fine! None of this is fine!"

"If you're having a panic attack, you need to sit and focus straight ahead. And breathe. Bolting out the door won't help."

"It's not like that. I just need fresh air. It's not a panic attack. I can't sit here. I've been sitting here for days!" Her eyes danced around the room looking at everything they had built together, and she wrung her hands again. Her heart beat hard against her chest as she realized it wasn't built on anything real. The only think that was real in her life was leaving soon and she didn't know if she'd ever see or hear from him again.

"Hey." He said as he reached for her. "I'm fine. You're fine. Bitty's fine. Just relax a second." She stepped back as he tried to draw her into his arms.

"I know you're fine. But I don't know if he's fine!" She shouted at him. He looked as if she had thrown a brick at him. She looked down and shook her hands as if sticky glue were all over them. "I don't mean, I'm sorry. I just—"

"Julien? That's what this is about?" The blood drained from his face and his shoulders slumped.

"No, yes, it's everything. It's, nevermind. I just need to walk. Clear my head." She stepped past him and grabbed her shoes from the mat by the front door. Her hands were shaking so badly, she could hardly tie them. Crouched down, she saw Benny's shadow over her. There was no putting her words back in a box, or her feelings back in her pounding heart. She exhaled and looked up at him. Abilene had never seen Benny appear defeated. What caught her off guard was that she didn't care. She needed to flee and worry about his ego later, if at all. Abilene stood up and grabbed her keys off the hook with the pepper spray dangling from a heart key chain that had Bitty's name and birthday etched on it. She met his downcast eyes.

"I'm sorry. I'll be back. I have to get out of here for a minute." She exhaled. "Besides, you got a phone call the other day. She probably needs to know you're okay." As she turned and pulled the door open, Benny reached for her arm. Abilene turned back and he let go. Their arms fell to their sides and Abilene let out a long exhale. She shrugged, matching his defeated face. Benny looked up at the ceiling then back at her.

"All we've done is talk a few times, late at night. Nothing else."

"Those late night talks, that's everything, not nothing." Abilene reached for the door again. She turned back before stepping through the threshold of their home. "Benny, it's okay, really. I want you to be happy. I see the way you look for her when we're in Denver. Searching. Go call her. I want you to. I was just a girl you got pregnant. You're a great dad, but I know I'm not the one you love and that's, I can't believe I'm saying this, but that's okay. I'll be okay."

Abilene closed the door behind her before he could utter another word. She stood tall on the front porch and drew in the deepest breath she had ever taken. The humidity had broken, and a slight chill was in the air. She pulled up her hood and zipped up her sweatshirt. Abilene stood on the sidewalk and looked both ways. One way led to more streets in housing. The other way was through two stop signs to the track and shoppette which was open 24 hours a day. She walked toward the track. Abilene picked up her pace as if Benny were right behind her. He wasn't, but she still felt she needed to outrun him, outrun her life, her choices, outrun the week, the year, the last seven years. She didn't know what she was running toward, but knew what she was running from. She was running from compromising all these years, punishing herself for her mom's last moments, fearing a fate she convinced herself she deserved. Abilene could make her own path just as Julien said, that there weren't just two choices. There was a whole world in-between. She could have everything she wanted, everything her mom never found. She just had to be brave enough to run toward it. Abilene knew she deserved it all--love, connection, happiness, that feeling of home. She deserved more than just enough.

She was jogging as she crossed the street to the track. Part of it wound through the woods before opening to the streetlights. She thought about turning around and avoiding the woods, but her legs wouldn't consider slowing down. Abilene left the lighted area and started running through the wooded quarter mile. She hadn't run in years. She never liked it. She didn't like it now, but it was relieving her panic. It was stabilizing her heart, her mind. Everything was finally coming into focus. Clarity set it. She took long, hard breaths, and loved the feeling of air leaving her lungs as her feet hit harder. Sweat beaded on her forehead and face. She smiled, thinking she could outrun anything that might jump out at her. Abilene loved the silence, only hearing her breath and footsteps. The dark, the quiet, was like a blanket she needed to cover her, comfort her, guide her on a new path, a new life.

Abilene ran through the last section of woods and found herself back out on the open trail, grass on either side and a streetlight at the end signaling civilization. She slowed for a moment. There was a figure leaning against the light pole alone. She squinted as she got closer. It was a man. Abilene slowed even more to a walk and wondered if she should go through the grass and get to the street to avoid him, but her legs kept moving. She got closer, and he came into full view. It was Julien. Abilene shook her head, assuming she was hallucinating, willing him into existence. She drew in a few quick breaths and pulled her hood off. Abilene put her hands on her hips as it became clear he was real.

"Julien!" she screamed. He turned around, and the light hit his short hair and then his broad smile.

"Abilene?" He yelled back. She started running again, faster, as if she only had seconds to live. She leapt into his arms. He pulled her tight and spun her around. She felt him inhale so close to her neck. "What are you doing here?" He whispered as he stepped back to look at her.

"I don't know. I think I was looking for you. And here you are." She rubbed her forehead. "I'm always looking for you. Under streetlights, in cars, along trails, behind me. All the time, looking for you behind me, hoping you're there watching out for me." She put her hands on her knees and leaned over trying to catch her breath. "Damn it. Why didn't you call me back? I was worried about you. The whole world has gone to shit and we're at war."

"I wanted to call you back, but I'm leaving in a few weeks. My date got pushed back some, and I didn't want to cause any problems. I already ruined my own marriage. I didn't want any part of ruining another." He said as he leaned down to a bag and bottle at his feet.

"You wouldn't ruin anything. I swear. I think I've already done that myself. What's that? At your feet?" She said as she still tried to catch her breath.

"Oh, when I can't sleep, or when I need to think, I run, then I get hot chicken from the shoppette and grab a bottle. I eat chicken, drink, then walk home. It clears my head. Like the old days, I guess. The dark, the quiet." He picked up the bottle and offered it to Abilene. She smiled.

"Peach Schnapps? Are you serious?" She laughed and took it from him.

"I drink the good stuff on a normal day, but when there's big stuff to decide, I go for the sticky schnapps." He took the bottle from her hand after she swigged some. She puckered.

"God, how did we drink this shit? It's like syrup." Abilene wiped her mouth.

Julien picked up the bag of chicken and laughed at her.

"Here, take a piece." She reached in and took a chunk of the red hot chicken. "There you go." He pulled a napkin from his back pocket. "Here, you're gonna need this."

"So, you do this to decide the big stuff? What's the big stuff now? You already decided to divorce. What could be bigger than that?" Abilene said. He handed her the bottle again and nodded for her to walk. They started on the trail back toward the woods.

"You. You're the big stuff." He said. She stared ahead, wiped her mouth, and reached for the bottle again. Abilene took a long drink as they walked.

"Why does this feel like I'm home?" She said looking around.

"Because this, me and you, walking through the night drinking schnapps and eating chicken, is home. It's everything. It's what I've been trying to find again all these years." He stopped and looked at her. He put the bag in one hand and reached for her chin with the other. Julien leaned in and kissed her. The mix of schnapps, hot chicken, and his soft lips took her back to that night. Took her back to who they were then. Abilene felt her hands relax, her heart slow down, her mind still. Nothing was off-kilter, out of sync. Nothing was wrong with her or the world.

"Well now. You said we'd try that again someday and see if it still felt awkward." She said as his lips left hers.

"Did it?" He said.

"No. Definitely not. It felt, I dunno. It felt right. More right than anything else in this world." Abilene released a deep breath. Julien's smile and eyes were the brightest under a full moon and stars. "What now?"

"This. Me and you. We head to Texas. Your girl too. We start a life together like we were always meant to do. You and me against the world." They started walking again. "I've been looking for you all these years too. I felt like I was missing an arm or something until that night I walked into your house and saw you standing there with oven mitts on. From the moment I drove away after dropping you off at that gate, I've been trying to find my way back to you."

"And I've been trying to run back to that moment too, jump in that van and never leave your side. You were, you are, the most real thing in my life. The world only makes sense when I'm with you." She said. He leaned down and kissed her again. She smiled as their lips navigated each other's. Safe. Connected. Home. Love. The only words that swirled in her head. Julien pulled out another piece of chicken then handed her the bottle. He slid his free hand into hers.

"Let's walk, drink, eat, and talk. We'll figure out how to do this by the time the bottle is empty. Now, if we only had some classic grunge to play until we run out of schnapps." He said.

"Nah, maybe some Alicia Keys or Usher." Abilene laughed and sipped again as they walked through the wooded part of the trail together under the stars blanketed by the quiet night.

# CHAPTER 27

*October 2001*

Abilene reached into the back seat and pulled out a bag of chips. She handed it to Bitty. She tore them open.

"You okay, little Bit?" Abilene said as she fished for another bottle of water and handed it to her. "Only a few more hours, well, a bunch of hours, but let me know if you gotta pee."

Bitty nodded. "When do I fly back to see dad?"

"In two weeks after we get you registered for school. Then, for Thanksgiving, he's gonna fly down to our new house and take you to Denver to see Grandma, Grandpa, and Aunt Angelina. Okay? You'll always get to see your dad anytime you want." Bitty nodded and sipped her water.

Abilene turned back to face the road. Dust was on either side of them for what seemed forever. Julien reached over and held her hand. He squeezed it and smiled at her.

"We've got about five hours after we get through greater Dallas. I think we can make by nightfall. Wanna stop for dinner half-way in between?"

"Perfect. I'm sick of snacks. A real meal will feel great."

"Hey, reach in the glove box. There's tapes in there. Stuff you might like now that you're finally cool." Julien said with a laugh. Abilene opened the glove box and pulled out a handful of cassettes. Then she saw one tucked behind the others. It had a hair scrunchy around it. A sticker was across the edge. "Summer of '92" was written in ink. Abilene gasped. She took the scrunchy off and put it around her wrist. It was the one she lost the night he drove her to meet her dad. She put the tape in and smiled at Julien. Her best friend. The one who knew her better than anyone. The man she loved and knew loved her back in every way then and now, and forever.

"Hey look." Julien said as he nodded toward the side of the road. "That sign. 200 miles to Abilene." He looked over at her. "You know, we could take the road to Abilene instead. It'll add a few hours, but you've never been. Maybe we can check it out. Stay the night there. We don't gotta be at the post for two days as it is." He drew her hand up to his lips and kissed her.

"Nah."

"Not even to see Swenson House? We could still burst through the doors and claim it was your family's legacy like we planned to do." He said. "See if some tour guide kicks us out?"

Abilene smiled and looked out the window as the Dallas skyline was coming into view ahead. She looked behind her at her daughter, and then at Julien.

"Nah. You and Bitty. My dad. Sandy. My sisters and brothers are out there raising hell all over the south. That's the legacy I have, all the legacy I need. Swenson House was a myth invented by a heartbroken 10-year-old girl who was searching for something she never found. It's not mine or my story. My story has a happy ending. You, us, real love." She looked over at him. Abilene leaned over and kissed his cheek. She couldn't wait to start their lives together. "Keep driving, Ponyboy. The only road I need to take is the one that leads to the home and life I'm gonna share with you."

# ACKNOWLEDGEMENTS

While Abilene's story, her childhood, her struggle with truths she'd rather not know, and her quest to find love and her place in this world are all fiction, I drew on my childhood experiences as an Army brat and my years as an Army wife for other elements of her journey. The fictional Army posts in the book are based on the military installations I lived at as a kid and as an Army wife years later. I mashed up what I loved about each place and created the world she knew after finding her father—the ice cream stand, housing, parks, the shopette, trails, schools. I also created Holden, South Carolina based on some elements of where I spent the second part of my childhood—Mount Union, Pennsylvania. High school and the summer of '92 in Mount Union were formative times in my life. That town and the people who were part of my life then inspire me in more ways than I can ever express and will always be a part of me.

As much as I drew from real settings, a great deal of inspiration for this book and the motivation to write my stories come from the fellow military spouses in my life. They have given me never-ending characters and stories and, more importantly, amazing support over the years. Through the moves, the struggles, the chaos, the amazing accomplishments, unexpected hard times, and adventures, the military wives I consider family have made life so much sweeter than I can ever give them credit for. I would list names, but I know I'd inadvertently leave someone out. I will never forget the support, laughs, tears, drinks, food, adventures, talks, and encouragement from the ones who helped shape me as a person and as a writer. Thank you, guys. You know who you are.

# ABOUT THE AUTHOR

Karri L. Moser is an Army wife and daughter who has collected character and setting ideas from her travels in a military family. She currently lives in Maine and spends her time writing, gardening, snowshoeing, and bumming around the coastal tourist traps she loves, all with a hot hazelnut coffee in hand.

Karri is the author of four other novels—*The Weathering of Sea Glass*, *Moose Pond Lodge*, *The Thriving of Willows*, and *A Home for the Windswept*. She has also written for newspapers, magazines, marketing firms, and the U.S. Army Medical Recruiting Brigade.

*The Road to Abilene* is her first novel that is based on her life in a military family.

ABOUT THE AUTHOR

# NOTE FROM THE AUTHOR

Word-of-mouth is crucial for any author to succeed. If you enjoyed *The Road to Abilene*, please leave a review online—anywhere you are able. Even if it's just a sentence or two. It would make all the difference and would be very much appreciated.

Thanks!
Karri L. Moser

We hope you enjoyed reading this title from:

# BLACK ROSE
## writing™

www.blackrosewriting.com

Subscribe to our mailing list – *The Rosevine* – and receive **FREE** books, daily deals, and stay current with news about upcoming releases and our hottest authors.
Scan the QR code below to sign up.

Already a subscriber? Please accept a sincere thank you for being a fan of Black Rose Writing authors.

View other Black Rose Writing titles at www.blackrosewriting.com/books and use promo code **PRINT** to receive a **20% discount** when purchasing.

www.ingramcontent.com/pod-product-compliance
Lightning Source LLC
Chambersburg PA
CBHW010734100726
47899CB00009B/3045

* 9 7 8 1 6 8 5 1 3 0 7 9 4 *